Mama's Boy

Mama's Boy

A NOVEL

RICK DEMARINIS

SEVEN STORIES
NEW YORK

Copyright © 2010 by Rick DeMarinis

A Seven Stories Press First Edition

Seven Stories Press
140 Watts Street
New York, NY 10013
www.sevenstories.com

In Canada: Publishers Group Canada, 559 College Street, Suite 402, Toronto, ON M6G 1A9

In the UK: Turnaround Publisher Services Ltd., Unit 3, Olympia Trading Estate, Coburg Road, Wood Green, London N22 6TZ

In Australia: Palgrave Macmillan, 15-19 Claremont Street, South Yarra, VIC 3141

College professors may order examination copies of Seven Stories Press titles for a free six-month trial period. To order, visit www.sevenstories.com/textbook or send a fax on school letterhead to (212) 226-1411.

Book design by Jon Gilbert

Library of Congress Cataloging-in-Publication Data

DeMarinis, Rick, 1934-
  Mama's boy : a novel / Rick DeMarinis. -- A Seven Stories Press 1st ed.
    p. cm.
  ISBN 978-1-58322-911-8 (pbk.)
  1. Young men--Family relationships--Fiction. 2. Parent and adult child--Fiction. 3. United States. Air Force--Fiction. I. Title.
  PS3554.E4554M36 2010
  813'.54--dc22

                                        2010039364

Printed in the United States

9 8 7 6 5 4 3 2 1

... as father had not been rooted in any woman's heart, he could not merge with any reality and was therefore condemned to float eternally on the periphery of life, in half-real regions, on the margins of existence.

from *The Street of Crocodiles*
by Bruno Schulz

My mother was a thinker
who read her way to Zen,
figured everything that happened
would probably happen again.

from *Mineyard Blues*
by Edward Lahey

PART ONE

1

Gus Reppo joined the air force to get away from his doting parents but they followed him to basic training in Texas and then to technical school in Mississippi. They rented hotel rooms and moped outside the gates of Lackland Air Force Base near San Antonio and then Keesler Air Force Base outside of Biloxi. When Gus got a weekend pass they'd pick him up in their new 1957 Buick Roadmaster and take him to dinner in a cloth-napkin restaurant.

"Are they treating you decently, Gussie?" his mother, Flora, said. She was sick with worry and disappointment. Her handsome blue-eyed boy looked thin and wan.

His father, Fillmore Dante Reppo—called FDR by both Gus and Flora—said, "You look like a beached cadaver, Gussie. Don't they give you proper food? Is *starvation* among the disciplines they teach? Mommy, I don't think he's getting the proper nutrients." FDR and Gus had been calling Flora "Mommy" since Gus was a toddler. Flora and Gus had been calling Fillmore "FDR" since the war ended even though Fillmore was a staunch Republican.

FDR and Flora, both heavyweights, dwarfed Gus. His unexceptional body made them uneasy. FDR sometimes wondered how a man of his height and heft could have sired this runtish assemblage of skin on bone. He'd look at Flora with an unaskable question in his eyes and she would laugh and say, "But he's young! He's a pup! He has years to fill out his frame!" They regarded him in silence at these times, each from their own uneasy perspective. Gus was a disappointing five-feet six-inches and 118 pounds. FDR and Flora were twin hills of loving and protective flesh, Gus the thin shadow between.

When he enlisted his muscles were smooth, without definition. But now his once-undetectable biceps were mapped with veins and strung with cords of visible sinew. He was stronger than he'd ever been. He could do seventy-five push-ups, fifty chin-ups, and an indefinite number of sit-ups. He didn't *count* his sit-ups, he *timed* them. A half-hour to forty-five minutes was typical. Once while daydreaming after a barracks inspection he did sit-ups for an hour and a half. He ran faster and longer with backpack and carbine than he once could in sneakers and gym shorts.

In technical school he learned how to climb and then lash himself to the steel framework of hundred-foot radio masts while making practice repairs. He did this once during a tropical storm. He'd pulled himself through and around high voltage cables, avoiding electrocution, tool belt swinging from his hip. A forty-five-knot wind gusting to sixty tried to pull him free of the lanyard that held him to the mast. Bullets of rain stung his face and arms. For this he received a Trainee of the Week award.

On another occasion he ascended through dense fog to find himself isolated in a soundless region above the top surface of the ground-hugging clouds and under the clear blue sky of the Mississippi Gulf Coast. It was as if he had entered another domain, empty and without defect. He lingered in that private space long after he completed his assignment.

He had no fear of heights, no sense of danger. He felt weightless, dangling from a slim lanyard. He felt that if he unhooked the lanyard and let go he'd glide to the ground like a leaf. He knew better, of course. He wasn't crazy. At least he didn't feel crazy. But then, he often wondered, how do the crazy know they're crazy?

Some of his fellow trainees had to overcome vertigo. Gus knew the dictionary meaning of the word but he didn't know it from experience. He was the opposite of an acrophobe. He was an acrophile. On the back of the group photo of his tech school graduation class he signed his name, "Gus Reppo, Acrophile."

Gus learned Newton's law of gravity. The instructors weren't trying to make physicists of the recruits, they were trying to issue a warning. You free-fall at an accelerating rate of thirty-two feet per second per second, they said. At a hundred and twenty feet it takes you a shade under three seconds to hit the ground. A little more Newtonian math and you discover the speed at impact is eighty-eight feet per second, or about sixty miles per hour. *Splat.*

The instructors were fond of the word and the implications of its sound: *Splat.*

"A careless radio tech is a dead radio tech," they said.

FDR had picked out a profession for Gus and the college in which he'd pursue it: The UCLA School of Dentistry. He'd drawn circles on a California map around the best urban centers to establish his practice.

"Orange County," FDR concluded. "Orange County dentists get a lot of respect—well deserved, too!—and their patients can be relied on to pay on time. What a young dentist needs least are financially unreliable patients."

FDR was a retired dentist. His office was in La Jolla, California, a wealthy beach district north of San Diego. "A good dentist can retire at fifty here in La Jolla," he'd said more than once. FDR retired at sixty and had put away a small fortune in thirty-five years of filling cavities, doing root canals, and fitting kids with braces and the elderly with dentures.

But Gus didn't want to become a dentist. He didn't want to muck around in diseased mouths for a living. The prospect of drilling into rot-filled teeth sickened him.

At Gus's thirteenth birthday party, FDR presented a plan for his future. He shoved aside the birthday cake and set up a slide projector on the dining room table. Family practice dentists to oral surgeons at work; how bridgework was made; how the amalgam was mixed and inserted into drilled-out cavities; how Novocain was injected into the gums; how screaming children, having caught sight of the needle and drill, were calmed by the dental assistant's mothering coos and clucks.

"Your life, of course, is your own," FDR said, "to do with what you will, but you must always keep this in mind: Dentistry, my boy, is in your blood."

FDR's grandfather had pulled teeth in the mining camps along the American River in northern California during the gold rush days. His father had been an oral surgeon in San Mateo. Three of his father's brothers held Painless Parker franchises in Los Angeles County. They all retired wealthy men of property, influence, and high standing in their respective communities.

"Point out the flaw in my thinking, Gussie," FDR continued, "if you are not convinced."

Gus, who'd had his first nocturnal emission the night before, was woolgathering. He'd dreamed he was a wirehaired terrier named Skipper lunging at the naked calf of a stout woman. Still vivid in his mind was the pressure and fragrance of the woman's ample flesh, his avid thrusting, the woman calling his name, "Skipper! *No*, Skipper!" Her scolds were harsh but she did not, curiously, push him away. Recalling the dream made him blush.

Flora broke his reverie. "Happy birthday, my darling boy!" she said.

FDR and Flora had raised Gus as if they were grooming the heir to a fiefdom. They spoiled him deliberately, to make him accustomed to—and thus dependent on—the privileged life. But Gus never became a spoiled brat full of demands. Though he had it easy, he never asked FDR or Flora to satisfy his every whim.

Gus didn't have whims. Or the few he occasionally had didn't take much to satisfy. He worked summers with a high school friend in his dad's roofing business for a dollar an hour. He spent summers laying plywood decking and tarpaper. He hauled squares of asphalt shingles and cedar shakes up steep ladders and nailed them down in careful rows. He worked fast and he was good at what he did. Steeply pitched roofs and gables didn't give him second thoughts. His friend's dad called him "Gus, the mountain goat." He lied to FDR and Flora, telling them his work kept him safely on the ground. With the money he made in roofing he bought his own stuff, from comic books to R&B records.

FDR and Flora were distressed by his taste in music and tried to discourage it. They thought rhythm and blues, which they called "jungle" music, was destructive to a young man's moral fiber. They believed there was a contrary element lurking in this music, a toxin that poisoned everything decent and worthwhile. One song in particular disturbed them—"Just Crazy." Gus always played it at full volume. "Just Crazy" threatened to undo gravity as it pried the house off its foundations. It frightened Flora; it angered FDR. "Turn it down!" Flora said. "Turn it off!" said FDR. They made Gus listen to the sane violins of Mantovani to show him what civilized music sounded like, how it uplifted the spirit. They hoped it would imprint itself on him.

Gus asked them what they meant by "moral fiber" but their answer was vague and abstract and seemingly lifted from the pages of *Boys' Life*:

> *Define your ideals and then live up to them. Respect the experience and authority of your elders. When in doubt, seek their advice. Trust your instincts but never act on them without first consulting a trusted adult. Never do in private what would disgrace you in public. Always speak clearly and with measured pace or keep silent: A quick tongue coupled to a slow wit reveals a blockhead. The silent, thoughtful boy eventually wins the prize. Above all, never disappoint your*

parents. They brought you into the world and nur-
tured you. What you are you owe entirely to them.

Listening to Mantovani on FDR's coffin-sized Stromberg-Carlson High-Fidelity Radio/Phonograph, Gus felt as if he had a front row seat at his own funeral.

Gus loved FDR and Flora even though he and they were on different wavelengths. He was their only child, a "miracle" baby, born in their middle age. FDR, born in 1891, was a few years past middle age when Flora became pregnant with Gus, an event that shocked them both. They were elated but also anxious, believing the powers that dealt out miracles might see the gift as a mistake and take remedial action. Throughout his childhood, FDR and Flora acted as if there was something temporary about Gus: Maybe he would vanish out of their life as miraculously as he came into it.

Gus came to feel that way about himself. He *felt* temporary. It wasn't a bad feeling. In fact it was a liberating notion. Being a visitor with limited staying rights was ideal. A visitor did not have to shoulder the responsibilities rightfully belonging to the host. The routines of ownership were the source of boredom—like a record needle stuck in a groove, playing the same broken lyric over and over until it became as meaningless as a hiccup. Life had more to offer the visitor.

The world was kinetic. It was happening with every breath, and it was happening fast. Time was like gravity. You fell through it, at a rate of acceleration similar to Newton's thirty-two feet per second per second. At eighteen you are just beginning to see the fabric of the world pass by, but an old man can see the moon turning in its orbit, the stars inching up the sky, a rosebud opening. Your rate of time travel in old age becomes so great you hardly notice the passing days and weeks as you accelerate through them toward the inevitable stop.

Splat, said the instructor.

2

Gus got on a plane in Gulfport, Mississippi. Tropical storm clouds out in the Gulf fluoresced with internal lightning. To Gus, they looked like gigantic Japanese lanterns, the windblown wicks flickering, flaring, dying, and flaring again. The usually flat water was showing confused crosscurrents, producing a potato-patch surf. Waves collided with waves and broke in conflicted patterns. Shore birds, outmuscled by the wind, flew backwards. The green sky was unnaturally green as if the physical properties of the spectrum had shifted. Seen in this light, the world became unreliable, even arbitrary. It made Gus uneasy. If the plane didn't take off soon the storm would ground it. In the terminal an authoritative voice had said, "Bad one out yonder."

From his cabin the handsome pilot looked back at the passengers and winked. His dashing smile seemed deceptively reassuring, as if the approaching bad weather posed no threat to modern air travel. Gus didn't trust the winking pilot or his reassuring smile.

It was a small plane, a Dixie Airlines Lockheed Lodestar. Gus buckled his seat belt and waved goodbye to FDR and Flora who were standing forlorn out on the gusty tarmac as the engines turned over, spit flame, and roared.

Storm-generated air currents mauled the plane, making it yaw and pitch once it became airborne. Earlier, Flora and FDR had taken Gus to lunch: shrimp scampi and clams casino followed by a strawberry milkshake. The undigested feast argued up his esophagus in the wallowing Lodestar. Gus kept a barf bag handy.

During lunch, FDR had asked him where he was going to be stationed. "Montana, near the Arctic Circle," Gus said.

"Montana," FDR mused. "Are you sure there are military installations there, Gussie?"

"Several," Gus said.

"But you don't know which one you'll be going to?"

Gus squirmed evasively in his chair. He speared a clam and chewed it with vigor. "Radar squadron," he mumbled. "Doesn't have a name. No-name radar squadron. Dogsleds in winter. Rations dropped by parachute. Very remote, very cold, no roads. No visitors. My instructor called it the American Gulag."

"Don't talk with your mouth full, Gussie," Flora said.

The Milk River Air Force Base was part of a string of early warning radar installations on the Canadian border from Maine to the state of Washington. A sneak attack by the Russians was anticipated. Early detection would give the Air Defense Command time to alert squadrons of interceptors. The interceptors, F-89 "Scorpions," scrambled from air force bases such as Malmstrom in Great Falls, would meet the Russian bombers—Tupolev "Bears"—and shoot them down before they could carry out their mission which was to transform America, city by city, into radioactive rubble. Gus's job would be to maintain the radios that kept the controllers at the radar squadron in touch with the Scorpions.

The town of Milk River had ten thousand inhabitants. It had two movie theaters, seven churches, and two dozen bars. Grain elevators the size of ten-story buildings loomed over the railroad tracks on the east end. It was a morally self-satisfied town even though it had three brothels and a police force known for its corruption and brutality. It had been a frontier settlement with a violent and carnal history. Gun-wielding men had died in its streets. Some of the swagger of that era still smoldered in its barrooms. An impudent glance or triggering word could lead to bloodshed. Gus learned all this from the driver of the air force van that carried new personnel from Malmstrom to the Milk River radar base, forty miles north of the town. The driver was a graying sergeant who spoke in a slow whimsical drawl. He steered with the two fingers of his left hand, his right arm thrown over the back of the empty front passenger seat.

"Tell you somethin else, youngbloods," he said. "You got to mind these Milk River womens. They be hungry—you know what I'm sayin?"

Gus didn't. He looked at the other newcomers, seven in all, in the back seats of the van. They didn't either.

The driver explained: "None of them, see, want to *stay* in Milk River. Uh-uh. They figure they hook up with some dumb-ass flyboy, they can move the fuck out when the dumb-ass flyboy move the fuck out." The driver adjusted the rearview mirror so that he could see his passengers. "Knock one up, you buyin her ticket out. She *own* your lame ass. You do her, you best keep your unit tarped."

The airmen looked at each other. Gus said, "Huh?"

The driver shook his head and laughed.

They crossed a viaduct that passed over the railroad tracks and river, then headed north on graveled washboard.

"Welcome to the Big Muthafucken Empty," the driver said. "Bible say God made the world outa nothin. Up here the nothin still show through." Gus looked out at the vast prairie. "Maybe you be from a actual city. Chicago? New York? Frisco? You got to go apeshit after a time. Oh yeah! The Big Empty turn loose snakes in your head you didn't know you had!"

"How so?" Gus ventured.

The driver's generous laugh rumbled in his chest. He adjusted the rearview mirror, aiming it at Gus. "How so?" he said. "When it happen, airman, you fucken *know* how so. Listen up, Milk River be honeycombed underneath the sidewalks with opium dens and bordellos from the Wild West days. Your *head* be like that—*honeycombed,* but since you be youngbloods, you don't know it yet. You see what I'm sayin?"

"No," the new airmen said in unison.

"The Chinamens what laid the railroad? They had to take they poontang and opium underground cuz of snakes the Big Empty turn loose in they heads. You can't be havin Chinamens go apeshit in the streets of the wild muthafucken west. Uh-uh. This road we on? Called Crazy Horse Highway. You ever get on a crazy horse? You don't take it for a ride. It take *you.*"

The van skated on loose gravel. Gus felt the yaw and pitch as the tires sprayed the small stones into the undercarriage. The driver, still using only two fingers to steer the van, kept the speed below fifty. The trip seemed to have no end. Then, in the distance, Gus saw the white spheres of the radar domes.

"That be your home for the next few years," the driver said. "Only one airman hung himself since I been here. Hung his sorry ass from a showerhead. Used a ten-amp jump cable."

"How long have you been here, Sarge?" Gus asked.

"Seven months, goin on seven years."

The newcomers sat upright in their seats. They stared at the mushroom-like domes on the horizon.

"It still twenty miles away," the driver said. "What looks close, aint. You think you almost there but you got a long stretch to go. That's how it be in the Big Empty."

The driver was quiet for a while, then started singing the R&B hit "My Baby Loves Western Movies" in a wheezing mirthful baritone.

3

It took a while for Flora and FDR to find Gus's duty station. They were disappointed and hurt that Gus had not been forthcoming. They hired a Biloxi private detective to find out exactly where he'd been sent. They could have asked the air force directly but they didn't know where to begin such an inquiry. Easier to hire someone who did.

In two hours of phone calls the detective found out where Gus was stationed. He'd called every air force installation in Montana, talked to the personnel officers, told them that he was a credit manager from a Biloxi auto dealership and that Airman Gus Reppo had run out on his car payments. The air force didn't like to harbor deadbeats. A personnel officer at Malmstrom gave up Gus's duty assignment to the detective: The 999th Aircraft Control and Warning Squadron, on the Canadian border, north of Milk River, Montana.

FDR rented a house in Milk River. It was a two-story turn-of-the-century "Plains Cottage" with ornamented gables. It had a wide bay window on the lower level that looked out on the Milk, the grazing fields north of the river, and the limitless horizon beyond. FDR had rented a similar house in Biloxi. In Biloxi it was called a "Bayed Cottage."

They furnished the house so that it would remind Gus of home. Photos of Gus at varying ages, including his high school graduation picture, hung on the walls. His bedroom was made to look like his bedroom back in La Jolla. They'd brought his childhood toys and comic books and strewed them about the room, as if by a careless boy.

The barracks Gus was assigned to was partitioned into small rooms. Gus shared one of these with a senior radar operator and a mess hall cook. The cook was a tall country boy with enormous feet named Lamar Harkey. Gus got the bunk above Harkey.

The senior radar operator, Staff Sergeant Ray Springer, had his own bunk. Springer was a lifer on his fourth enlistment. He was thirty-five years old and had joined the Army in 1942, a month after Pearl Harbor. He'd been assigned to the 8th Air Force in England. Springer had flown thirty-six missions as a B-17 ball turret gunner before he was wounded during the punitive fire-bomb raid on Dresden. The incendiary bombs created a firestorm five miles across. The red tornado at the center of the firestorm fed itself on, among other things, the bodies of forty thousand German civilians. They were sucked into the whirling fire by hundred mile an hour heat-generated winds. Shrapnel from an antiaircraft shell had sliced into Springer's abdomen on that mission. He kept the piece of steel and had it fashioned into a pinky ring by a metalsmith in Canterbury.

Gus learned all this during his first week in the barracks. Springer showed the pinky ring to Gus. He said it served as a reminder.

"Reminder of what?" Gus asked.

"To not take anything too seriously, Gate. Especially yourself."

Gus liked being called "Gate." Gus, in Springer's presence, thought of himself as Gate.

"I was always afraid of taking a bullet up my ass," Springer said. "You lay back in that turret, legs up and wide, like a woman taking on all comers. You had good armor but you still offered your puckered asshole to the world like a little bull's-eye. We called it the Fuck Me Adolf position."

Springer, like Gus, was a small man. He was good looking in a diminutive way, with hair as carefully combed as a gigolo's. His nickname back when he was a gunner with the 8th Air Force was "Little Slick." No one at the 999th called him that.

Springer had been stationed in Japan before he changed his MOS to "Scope Dope" and reassigned to the Milk River radar squadron. He'd found a home in the air force. He had no higher ambition other than to keep reenlisting until he got his thirty years in.

He loved Montana. "I've seen just about every type of geography the world's got to offer," he said. "But if you're looking for country that hasn't been stepped on a whole lot, then Montana's the place. You'll never want to go back to whatever you came from. I shit you not, Gate."

Springer had a collection of old jazz and blues records and played them late into the night. Lamar Harkey complained but had no rank and would not, in any case, take his complaint to the first sergeant. The first sergeant, like Springer, had been in the big war. Gus listened respectfully to Springer's music but admitted he didn't know much about it.

"You don't need to know anything about it," Springer said. "If it makes you tap your toe, you already know enough. If it makes you get up and stomp—amen, brother."

Springer drove a customized 1951 Olds 88 sedan. Its horsepower had been increased by dual carburetors, dual ignition, headers, and dual glasspack mufflers. The modified Olds could lay rubber in all three gears and top out at one-hundred twenty miles an hour.

"Why all that power?" Gus asked, even though having grown up in an automobile culture he understood horsepower for its own sake was the only justification needed.

"Why anything?" Springer said. He looked at Gus. Gus shrugged. "Let me put it this way. My daddy ran moon in the Cumberlands driving a full-race flathead Deuce."

"He trucked homemade booze in a souped-up '32 Ford?"

"I believe I just said that. Whiskey and fast cars are in the bloodline, Gate."

Gus and Springer were on the same nine-days-on and four-days-off work schedule. He offered Gus a ride into town after they'd both finished a day shift and had changed into civvies. Gus jumped at the chance, even though he'd told FDR and Flora that he couldn't come into town during his workweek.

Springer talked him out of staying on base. "There's nothing to do here except watch old cowboy movies, flog your mule, or play penny-a-point pinochle or nickel-dime poker with the lifers. You could play flag football or half-court basketball with the jocks, but those hardlegs like to pound the shit out of little guys like us. Come to town with me, Gate. We'll eat a steak, get drunk, and get our ashes hauled—more or less in that order. It won't cost you more than seven or eight bucks."

"Get our ashes hauled?" Gus said.

"Oh man, a virgin," Springer said. "All the more reason for you to go. You got to give up that cherry, Gate, before it turns into an embarrassing curiosity. You got to get something on you besides palm grease."

"I don't know, Ray. I mean, who . . . ?"

"*Who* is not the problem," Springer said.

"Geez, Ray." Gus hated the sound of his voice, which had risen with the tide of panic.

"What are you—nineteen, twenty?"

"Eighteen," Gus said.

"Still too old to be sporting a cherry. We got to do something about that. Let's get this out of the way, Gate."

Springer kept the speedometer at seventy on Crazy Horse Highway. The car seemed to float above the washboard-rippled road. Gus felt the car fishtail. Springer seemed unconcerned.

A herd of fifty or more pronghorns running parallel to the road raised a cloud of dust before they veered away. Straight ahead and high above, a pair of red-tail hawks rode a thermal in wide circles. The sky's blue arch seemed too deep and too wide, the dimensions too generous. Gus was getting used to Montana's enormous horizon-to-horizon sky but now and then it took him by surprise. He'd never taken in so much of the planet in one glance. It took some adjusting to. Springer punched Gus's shoulder.

"You see it?" Springer said.

"See what?"

"It. Out there. The works. *It*."

Gus looked out his window. "Nice country," he said.

Springer laughed. "Wake up or close your eyes, Gate."

The grain elevators of Milk River came into view. Their massive, shoulder-to-shoulder shapes made them seem like gray sentinels guarding access to the city.

"The metropolis and all its pleasures," Springer said as they crossed the viaduct into downtown Milk River.

They ate steaks at the Townhouse Café then cruised the streets of Milk River until dusk. The dirty trombone tones of the Oldsmobile's twin glasspack mufflers turned heads wherever they went. They idled past an ice cream parlor called the Athenian.

"That's where the local kids hang out," Springer said. "The girls, some of them anyway, think airmen are cool."

"I've heard," Gus said.

"You'll want to steer clear of the town boys. They catch you alone, they'll stomp your ass. They don't care for airmen. Young bucks in blue represent unfair competition."

Springer pulled into an alley and pointed to a clapboard addition to a concrete block building. The building the addition was attached to was the Moomaw Dairy.

"This is the airmen's poontang parlor, Gate. There's a house down the street with Indian girls, the prettiest girls this side of Reno, but they don't let flyboys in. Screwing flyboys for them would be like screwing Custer's pony soldiers. The Indians up here have long memories. You got five dollars on you?"

Gus's pocket was heavy with silver dollars. The old cart-wheels, most of them minted in the 1880s, were the only dollars in circulation. They were standard for Montanans who still didn't fully trust paper money.

The whores—three of them in black underwear and garter belts under their filmy kimonos—were middle-aged heavy-weights. They lounged on a sofa in the small foyer. A ceiling lamp infused the room with purple light, making the women seem randomly bruised. One of them pushed herself out of the sofa and took Gus by the arm.

"Got me a young'n," she said to the others.

"Eat him up, Norrie, he looks sweet as candy," one of the women said.

"Give Tiny Tim a good roll, girl," the other one said.

Gus said, "I've got to . . ."

"You got to pee, Little Britches?" Norrie said.

". . . think about this."

"Too late for thinkin. Thinkin won't do it no good."

Her stiff orange hair was held down, front and back, by steel barrettes. Her nose was off-center, broken at least once, and her upper left bicuspid had a silver crown. Even so, she reminded Gus of Flora. She could have been Flora's loose-living sister gone to low-rent whoring.

Gus said, "Whoa, ma'am . . ." but she pulled him into her crib before he could complete the thought, which, at any rate, he hadn't been able to find words for. The reek of dimestore cologne and the musky residues of sex made him queasy. Something—a white toad—floated in a jam jar on the shelf above her cot. Gus couldn't take his eyes from it.

"Take no notice of that, Little Britches," she said. "Strip down but leave your socks on." She rolled onto her back. Her kimono slipped open. "Come on now, get with it, son. Five cartwheels don't buy you half the goldurn night."

Gus tried to kiss her lips (wasn't that how you made love?) but she averted her face. He stroked her breasts (she allowed this but grimaced and rolled her eyes.) The tips of her nipples became hard (in spite of her impatient get-on-with-it sighs.) They were fissured, as though teams of babies had pulled at them over hungry decades. (Gus lingered too long on this sobering possibility.)

"Quit *think*in, boy," she said. "I can hear the wheels in your head turnin." She pulled him down into the unfamiliar terrain of her body. Gus felt helpless as an infant sprawled on its mother's belly. A pang of guilt assaulted him. His only desire was the desire to run.

"I never made love before, ma'am," he confessed.

"This aint love, Sunshine. It's just fuckin."

She took him in hand, got him ready. "This here's where you normally put it," she said, guiding him in.

Gus, hesitation gone, gave way to the kinetic impulses of his body.

"Whoa pup!" she said. "Don't be a-*lungin* like that, gol-durnit! Slow 'er down! What are you, a jackrabbit? I'm feelin sorely put-upon tonight. Some rank sodbuster done me like he was diggin post-holes in hardpan. Said the missus couldn't take him no more. Can't says I blame her. These tractor jockeys come in firedup and fulla grit, specially they got a tight old lady at home parcels it out real stingy-like, or not at all if she smells drink."

Gus got dressed while she douched. When she finished she bit a piece off a twist of chewing tobacco. She studied Gus as she worked it down to cud. "Tell you true, Sunshine," she said, "you aint much in the saddle." She offered this as disinterested analysis, her jaw muscles bulging. "You got another five cartwheels, I'll take you to school. You the type could benefit from instruction." She spit a brown stream into an empty soup can. "You come back, Norrie'll show you how to mount and ride and how to rein in so's you won't disappoint the ladies more'n you need to. I was you, gunfighter, I wouldn't apply for stud work just yet."

"Gunfighter?" Gus said.

"You got a hair trigger, Little Britches," she said. "Ladies who know better won't crib-up with Quick Draw McGraw more than once, less'n they're desperate."

Gus tied his shoes, aware she was still studying him.

"You a mama's boy, aintcha?" she said. She was sitting on her cot in her unbelted see-through kimono. Cross-wired emotions confused him: Pity and shame. Anger and remorse. Resurrected lust. He wished he had five more dollars, glad he didn't.

"No way," Gus said.

"I'd put a dollar on it," she said.

"You'd lose," Gus said.

She looked at Gus sidelong. "Naw, I can always tell a mama's boy. Aint nothin particular *wrong* with it. It just takes them a stretch longer to cut the cord. Until then they can't figure out what the ladies look for in a man. They think it's loyalty, respect, and keeping the cupboards stocked. The ladies want that, all right, but these days they want a sight more than that."

"You're wrong about me, ma'am," Gus said.

"I'm hardly ever wrong about you young'ns. But somethin else aint right about you. Probably gonna cause you some trouble down the line. It's writ all over you. You a touch crazy, maybe?"

The question annoyed Gus. The jam jar on the shelf above her bed caught his attention again. "What is that, a toad?" he said. Gus stood, stepped close to the shelf. The white thing was not a toad. "Jesus, it's a baby," he said.

"Fetus," she corrected. "Can't be havin babies in this line of work. Wayne's pickled in brine. He wanted out five months early. Couldn't wait to see the big ole messed-up world. Lucky for him he come out with undeveloped lungs. Stillborn. I call the trick-baby Wayne, after the cowboy actor. Wayne'd be about your age by now."

Gus stumbled over the feet of a long-legged whore on his way out, the one who called him "candy." She was playing solitaire in the foyer and smoking a cigarette. "Watch it, Tiny Tim," she said. Out in the alley he emptied his bladder. Then he got into Springer's car.

Ray Springer came out ten minutes later. "So it's not the Tokyo Ginza," he said. "The ladies here get shipped up from Kansas City by the syndicate that runs them. The local cops are on the their payroll. They protect the girls and get free tail when they want it. You want to find out what the local cops are like, shortchange a whore. The ladies are mostly over-the-hill types, like old ballplayers getting sent down to the bush leagues. It's one of the drawbacks of getting your ass stationed in the boonies. The town girls take up the slack. For an old man like me the boonies are their own reward. This is God's own country."

Springer's pinky ring gleamed in the dim light of the alley. The heated piece of shrapnel had been pulled into the shape of a snake, the head swallowing the tail. Springer saw Gus looking at it.

"It's a one-shot deal, Gate," he said.

"What is?" Gus said.

"It."

"It? What's that supposed to mean?"

"It is what it is," Springer said.

"Is it?" Gus said.

"It is."

Ray Springer laughed. Gus decided it was funny, whatever it was.

4

"What's *happened* to you?" Flora said. She looked at Gus across the dinner table. He'd changed, but she couldn't sort out and identify the details of the change. He looked the same. He sounded the same. Was it his eyes, a new darkness in them? They were blue, but not the same blue. A darker blue, a blue with shadings. Untrustworthy blue. Or the way he smiled when there was nothing to smile about, as if he had thoughts he couldn't— or wouldn't—share? Or was she imagining these things? All she knew was that Gussie was not the same. "You don't seem yourself, Gussie," she said, and immediately felt the inadequacy of her words.

FDR said, "Mommy's got the fantods, Gus."

"I have no such thing!" Flora said. "I'm simply worried about Gussie's well-being!"

"Our young man's just tuckered out, Mommy," FDR said. "They've been working him hard. That's all it amounts to. Isn't that right, son?"

Gus looked at FDR and Flora. He looked at the gravy on his plate. A membrane had formed on its cooling surface. He'd run out of excuses to stay on the base, and now was staying with FDR and Flora on his four-day break in their Plains Cottage overlooking the Milk River. From the dining room window, Gus could see the river, the grazing land beyond, the impossibly wide horizon.

A few mergansers drifted idly in the river's slow summer current. A dozen Black Angus, jaws rotating with cud, were staring at the river from behind a barbwire fence. The sun was still high and hot even though it was seven p.m. There were almost eighteen hours of midsummer daylight at this latitude. In the distance, fifty miles away, broad anvil-shaped thunderheads squatted on the horizon.

After dessert, Flora said, "Are you having trouble at the base, Gussie?" She poured herself a tumbler of Rhine wine. Which surprised Gus. He'd never seen her drink alcohol of any kind.

"I'm fine, Mommy," he said.

Gus thought: I'm getting laid at five cartwheels a pop. The old whore, Norrie, is teaching me how to mount and ride and how to hold back and not be selfish. Be a gent, Little Britches, she said, never spend your load before the lady spends hers.

As if he'd read Gus's mind, FDR said, "Set your sights higher, Gussie. Otherwise you will sink into the mire."

Gus wondered if they had detected stray molecules of sweet whorehouse disinfectant on him. Was that why Flora was wrinkling her nose as she searched his face for newly acquired flaws?

"Is it the work they have you do, Gussie?" Flora said. "Are you being treated humanely?" She refilled her glass, raised it carefully. Her puckered lips anticipated the rim.

"No, nothing like that, Mommy," Gus said.

"I don't want you to work those late hours, Gussie," she continued. "Graveyards—is that what they call them? All night alone in the dark? How dreadful. I don't like to think of you climbing those awful towers in the dark, suspended hundreds of feet above the ground. I've heard there are owls out there as big as eagles. What if an owl attacked you and made you fall? How can you defend yourself against an angry owl? I'm going to call your commanding officer. I think of you up on one of those towers during a lightning storm and I get frantic! Those others— the ones from poor families with no real future to look forward to beyond military service—let them do those dangerous jobs. You should do all your work inside, in safety. I'm going to ask your commanding officer if he can arrange it. I'm sure he'll understand, since you are our only son."

"I hardly ever climb a mast," Gus said. "I like my work. I like the way I'm treated. Jesus, Mommy, do *not* call Major Feely."

Major Frank Feely was a legendary hothead. He'd been a fighter pilot in the war. He was an ace with six confirmed kills and three probables while flying cover for the B-24s of the 15th Air Force over the Ploesti oil fields. He also became an ace in Korea, flying Sabre Jets. He hated the dull work of commanding a radar squadron. He felt betrayed by the air force for not giving him command of an F-89 squadron. The F-89 Scorpion was the primary all-weather interceptor of the Air Defense Command. Feely, a forty-year-old drunk, felt he'd been sent to the hinterlands as punishment for some trumped-up offense. He loved the air force, had been a good soldier from day one, and the injustice of his exile, fueled by alcohol, eroded his stability.

He did his drinking in the NCO club. During his monumental hangovers he was not to be trifled with. He killed the club's pinball machine with his .45 after a dozen poor scores, then took the fire axe off the wall to finish the job. He chopped the machine into colorful fragments. Major Feely had movie-star good looks, but his haunted gray eyes were inconsolable.

Gus kept his distance from him. Gus thought: All I need is Flora calling him with a list of ground rules covering the care and feeding of her precious son. I'd probably wind up cleaning toilets in the Great Falls stockade for the rest of my enlistment.

Flora reached across the table and dug her fingernails into Gus's hand. "You're all I have in this world," she said. Her drunk face relaxed into a maudlin facsimile of her sober face.

Gus glanced at FDR. FDR looked at Flora, hurt and perplexed. "You have *me*, Mommy," he reminded her.

Flora broke down. Racking sobs made her soft flesh quiver. FDR helped her up and led her into the living room.

Gus went into the kitchen and took a beer from the refrigerator. He returned to the dining room and gazed out the picture window.

Flora's diminishing sobs mixed with static from the TV. The low-power relay station in Milk River that brought a lined and snowy picture in from Great Falls was out of commission.

Gus sipped his beer and watched the coming storm. Fifty miles away, soundless lightning forked from the rippled underside of a thunderhead.

5

The Air Defense Command called a nationwide practice alert. B-52 Stratofortresses playing the part of the Russian Tupolev Bears would attack the United States from SAC bases in Alaska. Radar warning systems were going to be put to the ultimate test. From Canada to Mexico, the country would defend itself or perish. There would be no second chances.

The alert would be in effect for three days, days that Gus would normally be on break. He phoned FDR and Flora to tell them he wouldn't be coming to town for a while. Flora demanded to know why. Gus told her he couldn't discuss it with civilians.

"I'm not a civilian, I'm your mother!" Flora said.

"I'll be on guard duty," Gus told her. "The swing shift people will maintain the radios."

"I'm sorry? You'll be on *what*?"

"It's a military exercise, Mommy. I can't tell you anything more about it. I'm in the military, you see. It's called the air force. Our job is to protect the nation against sneak attack. Maybe you don't understand the concept. Let me explain. You see, we have these enemies overseas. They're known as the Russians, or the Godless Commie Horde. They want to kill the men and make sex slaves of the women. Our job is to stop them."

"Don't speak that way to me, Gussie!" she said. "My God what's become of you? I worry about you day and night. I can't sleep. Oh dear God how I worry!"

Her voice cracked; she began to sob. Gus was sorry he'd been such an ass.

"I'm sorry, Mommy. I really can't talk about it. It's my job, I've got to do it."

She hung up.

Gus sat on his helmet, his carbine across his knees. The sky was crawling with Scorpions as they attacked the bombers at right angles. Their contrails and those of the bombers made a chalkboard grid of the sky. It was impossible to tell if the Scorpions were scoring hits. Gus assumed someone was keeping score.

A bigger concern was the mosquitoes. He was fighting a losing battle with them. Hundreds floated around his head, heavy with blood. He'd pulled his collar up to shield his neck but they went past his collar, finding their way to the vulnerable pink flesh behind his ears. He'd stuffed his pant legs into the tops of his brogans. But mere cloth didn't stop them.

A few hours into the alert, the airman on guard duty a hundred yards from Gus, yelled something. He was a skinny kid from Texas named Jack Perez. Perez was on his feet, waving wildly. When he got Gus's attention he pointed to a billowing dust cloud on Crazy Horse Highway. Gus grabbed his carbine and stood up.

A pale gray sedan made its way out of the cloud. It crawled ahead in low gear. It stopped a quarter mile short of the radar base. Two people got out, a man and a woman. The man raised a pair of binoculars and scanned the perimeter of the radar base, sweeping left to right and back again. He stopped scanning when he saw Gus and Perez, who were now standing together, rifles up. The man shouted something neither Jack nor Gus could make out. The woman waved a white hanky. She had trouble standing against the wind. The man opened the trunk of the car and took out a large wicker basket.

"They're coming straight for us," Jack Perez said, raising his carbine. "Hey you people! Stop! I'll drop your asses!"

They kept working their way through rabbit brush and sage. A dust devil screened them in a whirling brown haze. Jack and Gus took kneeling positions and aimed their carbines at the hazy silhouettes and yelled again for them to stop. Perez worked the slide of his carbine, chambering a round.

Gus had a familiar sinking feeling. "Don't shoot them, Perez."

The woman stepped out of the brown haze. "Gussie! We brought you a picnic lunch!"

"This isn't happening," Gus said.

"What are you doing with that gun, Gussie?" Flora said. "You look ridiculous! Put it down this instant! You know how I feel about guns! You might hurt yourself!"

"*Que la chingada*," Perez said.

"Damn it, Mommy!" Gus said. "You can't be here! You almost got yourself shot!" He pointed his carbine skyward. Fifty thousand feet overhead the multiple contrails of the B-52s streaked southward while the Scorpions fell back. The distance between bombers and interceptors increased every second.

"We're on simulated red alert," Gus said. "Our F-89s are shooting down Russian bombers."

Flora and FDR, shading their eyes, watched the remains of the mock battle.

"What's that stink?" FDR said. Flora wrinkled her nose. She gagged.

"It's the squadron sewage lagoon, mister," Perez said. He pointed to the dark pond below the north side of the perimeter. "That's where all the *mierda* from the squadron toilets go. These *pendejo* mosquitos come from there. Excuse my language."

"You're out here guarding *sewage*?" FDR said.

"Who are these people, Reppo?" Jack Perez said.

"My parents," Gus said.

"I'm going to be ill," Flora said. A bloated sewage lagoon mosquito, fat as a housefly with blood, lit on her cheek. She slapped it, streaking her face red.

FDR put down the picnic basket. He spread a blanket and opened the lid of the basket. "Roast beef sandwiches, Gussie," he said. "Potato salad, pickles, coffee, a nice white wine—that's for Mommy—and a three-layer chocolate cake."

"Close the basket!" Flora said. "We can't eat it here, next to a sewer, with all these mosquitoes! Come, Gussie. We'll sit in the car and listen to the radio. They're actually playing Mantovani! Your Spanish friend can join us, if he wishes."

A jeep came bouncing over the tundra. Two Air Policemen, Loftus Runkle and Jeff Sparks, got out of the jeep. Runkle was a stocky no-neck; Sparks, tall and narrow-shouldered. Both APs were wearing .45s and nightsticks. They were known in the squadron as Mutt and Jeff, but there was nothing amusing about them. They looked for excuses to hassle airmen. Most steered clear of them.

"Anybody ID these people?" Runkle said.

"We have every right to be here," FDR said.

"You from division?" Runkle said. "Mock saboteurs?" He searched the picnic basket for weapons.

"We are from La Jolla, sir!" FDR said. "We're not mock anything! We are our*selves*, and have every right . . ."

"They're lost," Gus said, hoping to defuse the situation.

"Two mock infiltrators, north sector," Runkle said into his walkie-talkie. "Probably sent by division."

Flora sagged into FDR. The wind took her hat and carried it away with the tumbleweed.

"Infiltrators? This is absurd!" FDR roared.

"They're my folks," Gus admitted sheepishly.

"*You're* in on it, too?" Sparks said.

"Let them go," Gus said. "They made a mistake."

"It don't work that way, Reppo," Runkle said. "If this was for real, they could have lobbed mortars at the domes. I let them go, I could lose a stripe."

"Division didn't send them," Gus said.

"Says you," Runkle said.

The APs handcuffed FDR and Flora and put them in the jeep. They drove away.

Gus picked up the picnic basket that had been left behind. "You want something to eat, Perez?" he said.

They ate the sandwiches, pickles, potato salad, and cake. They drank the quart of Rhine wine as the contrails faded and World War Three drifted south.

The first sergeant gave Gus a month of KP duty and restricted him to the base during that time because of FDR and Flora's unauthorized visit. Flora didn't call Major Feely to make her displeasure known. She was unwilling to cross swords with the air force again after having been detained and interrogated for three hours in the Air Police shack as a possible saboteur.

Major Feely was taking heat from Division Headquarters in Great Falls. The interceptor squadrons of the 29th Division of the Air Defense Command hadn't "splashed" a single B-52. The big bombers slipped through the net. It was a total victory for the Strategic Air Command over the Air Defense Command. Air Defense generals were humiliated and looking for scapegoats. It wasn't just Major Feely who got dressed down—the commanders of every radar station on the Hi-Line of the Montana/Canadian border were singled out by Headquarters for substandard performance.

"We lost Cheyenne, Omaha, St. Louis, Kansas City, Dallas, Fort Worth, Houston, and maybe the planet Mars," Ray Springer said. "Five to ten million killed outright, another thirty to forty million will die of radiation burns and fallout. In short, the kingdom is not well defended."

It wasn't anyone's fault. The B-52 was a superior airplane to the F-89 Scorpions. It had a higher top speed and service ceiling as well as superior firepower.

The B-52s also dropped tons of chaff, aluminum strips that

presented thousands of false radar images, confusing the ground controllers and causing them to give wrong headings to the fighter pilots. The subsonic Scorpions were capable of making one pass and one pass only at the bombers. If they didn't score a major hit with guns and rockets on that single pass, the B-52s were home free.

Major Feely took the whole fiasco personally, especially since the reprimands were not justified. The fault lay with the F-89, which was designed toward the end of World War II. A new supersonic interceptor, the F-102, was on the way, but would not be delivered to the Air Defense Command for a year or more. As a stopgap measure the air force considered attaching unguided atomic missiles, called Ding Dongs, to the underbellies of the Scorpions. The Ding Dongs had a one-and-a-half kiloton warhead and would be fired into a formation of attacking bombers. The interceptors would approach the bombers head-on and a thousand feet low, then pull up sharply and release the rocket-powered nuke into the formation of intruders where it would be detonated, wiping out the formation—and most likely the interceptor as well. This kamikaze notion was dropped after a few hundred million were spent developing it.

When the mission was over and the dismal battle reports were in, Major Feely got drunk in the NCO club, the only bar on the base. "The sons of bitches passed the buck to us," he said to the off-duty enlisted men. "They give us straight-wing fighters that can't out-fly a castrated woodpecker, and radar that can't see through chaff, then put the blame on us. Why? I'm glad you asked." (No one had dared to ask.) "Because the generals, no matter how idiotic or self-serving, are *never wrong*. Blame falls to the lower ranks. Remember that and you'll go far in this man's army."

After half a dozen boilermakers, Major Feely went down to the small airstrip that doubled as a softball field, outside the fenced perimeter of the base. He cranked up the L-20 "Beaver," the only aircraft assigned to the 999th. The L-20 was an unarmed, high-winged reconnaissance-type aircraft with a big 450 horsepower radial engine.

Major Feely took off in a cloud of dust and climbed quickly to a thousand feet. He did risky low-level aerobatics over the base, swooping down between the radar domes and barracks, then headed south doing loops and rolls and wingovers.

He made full-throttle strafing runs on the citizens of Milk River, dropping lower than the city's water towers. In one spectacular demonstration of low-level strafing, he snagged a backyard clothesline with the Beaver's landing gear. A woman, who had just come out of her house carrying a clothes basket, fainted as the L-20 roared away with laundry streaming from its wheels. The woman had been a few weeks pregnant and she miscarried minutes after Feely strafed her backyard.

After his strafing run, Major Feely climbed high above the city and performed a one-quarter loop to vertical at which point he applied full left rudder as his airspeed dropped. The L-20 rotated around its yaw axis until its nose fell through the horizon. The subsequent vertical dive took the plane and Major Feely directly into the shipping docks of the town's lone slaughterhouse. The explosion killed two polled Herefords. Dinnerware throughout Milk River rattled on its shelves.

Some witnesses in the streets of Milk River said:

> *That boy could flat fly a dang airplane couldn't he?*
>
> *It was like he was performing for the town folk!*
>
> *A one-man air circus! Wonder why he didn't pull up?*
>
> *We'll never know. Sometimes you get a dark notion.*
>
> *I wanted to jump off the top roof of my granary once.*
>
> *What do you mean by that, Mr. Frimler? I don't follow.*

Sometimes you figure it's just not worth the trouble.

One day folds into the next and they're all the same.

A switch is flipped letting the blackness flood in.

I know what you mean. Easy to feel that way sometimes.

You boys take it too far. He just lost control.

A man who can fly like THAT? Not very dang likely.

But I ask you, what exactly does this portend?

Portend? Who said that? Who the HELL said that?

No one. Person or persons unknown. Face in the crowd.

*You're quite the joker, Mr. Howling, but a very fine pilot,
a real hero in my book, happens to be dead.*

Major Feely's replacement, Clive Darling, was another burned-out major who'd been transferred to the 999th, also against his will. He'd been with a transport wing stationed in West Germany. At forty-eight, Darling was an "old" major. He was ready to retire but he wanted to achieve a goal before then. Major Darling wanted to retire as a lieutenant colonel.

Darling believed a radar squadron assignment was a graveyard—sometimes literally—for majors. No one ever got promoted to lieutenant colonel while commanding a radar squadron. It just didn't happen. He hoped to establish a new precedent, not by performing well (performing well was not an option since no SAC bomber was ever going to be shot down by the current inventory of Air Defense Command interceptors), but by kissing the right asses at division Headquarters and beyond. It was not a great strategy, but it was the only strategy Major Darling believed he had at his disposal.

If the general in charge of the 29th visited the radar base

Major Darling would whip the place into class-A shape. Barring that remote possibility, he didn't care what the place looked like. He came to work late and left early. Like Major Feely, he was a heavy drinker. When he came into the dark radar ops blockhouse, he found a comfortable chair on the command dais and napped.

He installed his mistress, Heidi Zechbruder, an East German woman, in an apartment in Milk River and spent all of his downtime with her. He sometimes came to work in civvies, drunk or hung over. Occasionally he wore a mix of mufti and regulation: Hawaiian shirt and uniform pants; full-dress blues with tennis shoes and baseball cap; cowboy shirt with pearl snap-buttons; khaki shorts. You had the impression that Major Darling grabbed whatever clothes were within reach when he got out of bed in the morning. If he suspected a visit from an inspection team from division, he wore his best gabardine blues and carried a handsome swagger stick he'd won in a poker game from a Brit who'd served with the Somerset Light Infantry in India. The stick was a symbol of discipline and control. It would not go unnoticed, Darling believed, by the inspectors. He wore tinted aviator glasses even at night to hide his jittery insecure eyes.

He didn't hold inspections, didn't care if the airmen grew beards or came to work in civvies. He'd flown medium bombers in Italy during the war and C-47 transports during the Berlin Airlift. Commanding an obscure radar squadron did not live up to those glory days. Apart from his desire to be promoted to lieutenant colonel, Major Darling had washed his hands of the air force and its many rituals.

In his first week as base commander, he called the off-duty enlisted men and junior officers together and told them he was not going to aggravate anyone by imposing strict military discipline on a routine that never varied. He told them to pass the word to those not present.

He also issued a warning. "Just do your goddamn jobs and don't fuck up, and we'll get along fine," he said. "You've got problems, take them to First Sergeant Burnside or to the chaplain. Does this shithole even have a chaplain? In any case, *I* don't want to hear about your goddamn problems. I've got my own goddamn problems. In short, go your own way but do your job and leave me the hell alone. You want to be promoted? Stay invisible.

"One thing, though, is of paramount importance: You make me look bad to division and I consequently get passed over for light colonel *again,* I will personally see that the no good rotten bastards who fucked me spend the rest of their enlistment disinfecting commodes in the Malmstrom stockade. Am I clear on this point? Am I being too arcane?" He took off his sunglasses for emphasis. His red eyes danced before the men.

Later, in the barracks, Ray Springer said, "Watch out for him. He's a crafty old fuck, a hair short of losing it."

"Major Darling seems okay to me," Gus said.

"He's not anywhere near okay, Gate. I've seen humps like him before. When they crash they take people with them."

"Crash?"

"He's crazy. Out of his mind crazy."

"How do you know?"

"He's got worms in his head. Maybe syphilis worms—spirochetes. Screwworms. You saw how his hand was shaking? His eyes? And that crap about not taking military discipline too seriously? Forget it. That's how these pricks set their traps. They want to fuck you, they first tell you how easygoing they are."

"What're you fellers talking about?" Lamar Harkey said. "Somebody go crazy again?"

"No one you'd know, Harkey," Springer said.

"And I don't *want* to know neither," Harkey said. "I'm the one found that feller who hung hisself from a showerhead with them extry long jumper cables. Like to make me lose my dang breakfast. Had bad nightmares about that feller for a week.

Woke up wanting to puke. Don't ever want to see nothing like *that* again. No sir."

"You're a smart man, Lamar," Ray said.

Harkey smiled shyly. "Thank you, Sergeant Springer. My ma said I could go far if'n I put my mind to it."

"And here you are," Ray said.

"Yes sir, here I am."

6

Gus met Beryl Lenahan in the Athenian ice cream parlor. She was a senior in high school but could have passed for a twenty-five-year-old woman with a brood of children. Her hair was a loose tangle of black ringlets. She seemed to radiate measurable heat. Her sea green eyes were large and direct and when she looked at him Gus felt his stomach muscles tighten and quiver. He was the latest in a series of airmen she had dated. Even so, Gus, like others before him, was smitten.

"Do you know Tommy Jenkins?" she said. "He's a nice boy, but he falls asleep in the movies. Even in *Quo Vadis*, starring Robert *Tay*lor! Can you believe it?"

Gus didn't know Tommy Jenkins.

"Mitchell Donelli?" she said.

"I think I heard of him," Gus said. "Motor pool guy. Drives the deuce and a half to town to dump garbage and pick up supplies."

"Billy Joe Watson?" she continued.

Gus didn't think much of Watson, a loud muscleman who liked to turn smaller airmen upside down and shake them until coins and personal items fell out of their pockets. Watson was a red-faced lunatic from Georgia and if he wanted to turn you upside down you had to let him. If you protested, he had other gymnastic feats to entertain you with. Gus avoided Billy Joe Watson.

"Don't know him," he said.

"Phil Ecks?"

Gus thought for a minute. "The medic," he said.

"He's sooo good looking," she said, "but he's obviously stuck on himself, don't you think?"

"Never thought about it," Gus said.

"Greggie Fontana?"

"No."

"Loftus Runkle?" she said.

Gus thought: Jesus, would her god-awful list never stop? Loftus Runkle was one of the AP thugs, Mutt Runkle. She'd dated him, too!—the jackass who'd arrested and handcuffed FDR and Flora!

"Seen him around but I don't know him," Gus said.

"Candidly speaking, Gus, Loftus is *quite* the weirdo."

Beryl found certain words appealing, especially those ending in "ly." "Candidly," "incredibly," and "frankly" were some of her favorites. She sprinkled them through her conversation even if they didn't quite fit.

"I hope to live in a real city someday," she said. "Like New York or Minneapolis, where people communicate intelligently."

"I think Runkle is from Pittsburgh," Gus said.

"I'm not sure where that is," she said, frowning. "In any case, Loftus and I, specifically or otherwise, did not have much in common."

"I hope not," Gus said.

"Then you do know him," she said.

"Not really," Gus said.

"All Loftus talked about was his Doberman back home. He spoke lovingly of Rascal but the dog was obviously a sicko. Rascal killed neighborhood cats and brought them home incredibly ripped up with their innards dangling from his jaws. I didn't care for his Rascal stories. Loftus also liked to show off his biceps. Candidly speaking Gus, I am bored by Tarzan muscles."

Beryl drove Gus to Tiber Dam above the Marias River in her mother's copper-colored prewar Hudson Terraplane. Gus had checked out fishing gear from Special Services. Beryl had her own gear, including a pup tent.

The reservoir behind Tiber Dam was a brown, unrippled expanse sixty miles west of Milk River. Beryl fished with hook, lead sinkers, and bobber. She used night crawlers and luminescent pink mini-marshmallows for bait.

She had the broad-shouldered, narrow-hipped body of a competitive swimmer, and when she cast her line and bobber out, black ringlets flying, she looked to Gus like a goddess in motion.

Beryl was serious about fishing. She caught a three-pound Dolly Varden, a midsized rainbow, and a Fish-and-Game "planter" trout that was packed with orange beads of roe. Gus caught a long, skinny northern pike on a red-and-white Dardevle with a treble hook. The pike looked like a legless alligator. Its wide sinister mouth was dangerous with rows of fine, razor-sharp teeth, capable of taking a fingertip off. He changed lures, a Super Duper this time, but caught another pike. Gus wanted to throw both pike back but Beryl said pike meat was tasty if a bit bony. You had to fillet them carefully.

At one point, Beryl reeled in her bobber and hook and laid her rod on the sandy beach. She walked into the brushy area behind the beach and came back holding a fat grasshopper cupped in her hand. She slid her hook with its remnant of worms into the big green insect, making sure it couldn't escape, then tossed her line out again. A large rainbow struck the grasshopper before it had time to sink. Beryl reeled in. The fish fought hard all the way, breaking the surface several times. The huge trout weighed at least six pounds.

Beryl cleaned the fish on the muddy beach with a pocketknife after first digging their eyes out. She slit the pale bellies from rectum to gills and pulled the string of intestines out and tossed them into the lake. She cut the eyeless heads off and tossed them into the lake, too. Then she filleted the fish on a flat board she kept in the Hudson's trunk along with the filleting knife. Beryl handled the knife with the skill of a butcher. She separated bone from flesh, lifting the white spine and threadlike ribs out of the meat, her hands slimy with gore. When she finished she washed her hands in the lake.

"Why did you cut their eyes out?" Gus said.

"I don't want the fish to see what's happening to them."

"They're dead, Beryl," Gus said. "They can't see anything."

"My Uncle Willard took me fishing a lot when I was little. I always believed that the fish could see me even after they were gutted because their eyes stayed terribly bright and alive-looking, unlike other animals. When you kill a deer or a squirrel, you can actually see the light go out of their eyes. Fish are different. A fish will sometimes flop around even after you've pulled its guts out, and its eyes do not fog."

"You've hunted deer?" Gus said.

"I've got my own rifles, a .22 for gophers and prairie dogs, and a .30-.30 for deer and pronghorns. My twenty-gauge shotgun is for prairie chickens, wild turkey, and pheasant. I shot my first antelope with Uncle Willard's .32 caliber pistol from forty yards when I was thirteen. Hit it in the neck and broke the spine. Uncle Willard said 'You've got some kinda eye, girlie.' I've got the head mounted on my bedroom wall."

Gus was impressed. He thought of the girls he knew in La Jolla. He couldn't picture any of them skinning a deer or gutting a trout. He couldn't picture their hands slick with fish blood.

"Don't laugh, Gus, but I don't want the fish to see me toss their guts into the lake. My face would be the last thing they saw. The idea kind of bothers me. Now see? You're laughing."

"I'm not laughing," Gus said. He stiffened his face against something but it wasn't exactly laughter.

"I'll be candid with you, Gus," she said. "I'm deeply sensitive."

Gus heard overtones in this but didn't try to decipher them.

Beryl fried strips of bacon in a cast-iron skillet, then cooked the fish in the fragrant grease. The skillet sat on a wire frame over a Sterno can. The Fish and Game Department's planter trout was inedible. The flesh was mealy and it tasted muddy, like lakebottom silt. The flaky white meat of the Dolly Varden, pike, and rainbow, when salted and sprinkled with lemonpepper, was delicious. They ate out of the frying pan with their fingers. Beryl had packed apples and gingersnaps in a paper bag. By the time they finished the sun was low. Beryl set up her pup tent in a flat patch of dry sand away from the beach. Other people had used this patch of dry sand to set up their camps. A litter of beer cans, cigarette butts, and potato chip bags, were scattered along its edges.

Gus and Beryl drank warm cream soda inside the tent. The wind had come up strong and the panels of the tent flapped like the spankers of a sailing ship. It was their third date and Gus had yet to kiss Beryl.

Beryl had a portable radio but all it picked up were voices buried in static. The voices described the battle of the Little Big Horn as if it were happening now. Gunshots and the sound of galloping horses. Blood curdling screams in the windy sage. Bugles and fifes. War drums. Gus reached across Beryl and turned the radio off. Their knees touched, then their shoulders. Gus felt Beryl's humid warmth.

Thunder roared in the distance. "Think it'll rain?" Gus said.

"So what?" she said.

She took off her pullover and brassiere. She unbuttoned her jeans and slid them off. She wriggled out of her panties.

"Are you just going to sit there staring at me?" she said.

Gus took off his clothes. He folded and stacked them.

"I want to get married," she said. "I expect to have lots of fat pink babies. Six or seven, maybe eight."

"Really?" Gus said.

"That's the point of everything, isn't it?"

Gus wasn't sure about that.

"But not here," she said. "I want my babies to grow up in New York, or even Salt Lake. This is no place to raise babies."

Gus offered no opinion on the subject. He had other pressing needs.

"Wait," she said. "Do kitty first."

"Do what?" Gus said.

"I prefer you do kitty *first*."

"Huh?" Gus said.

"Don't you know *anything*?" she said.

She indicated what she meant by applying both hands to his shoulders and pushing him down. She was so insistent that Gus thought it was another one of her superstitious rituals, like carving the eyes out of dead fish. Gus went along with it, not that he had a choice. Doing kitty was a new experience for him. Beryl gave him detailed instructions. Gus, always a quick study, applied himself.

"Keep your eyes closed," she said.

"Why?"

"You don't need to see anything."

Gus did kitty in the dark until his face ached.

"Oooh oooh," she said.

Gus felt trapped in a tropical bog. His jaw felt dislocated. An evil thought occurred to him. He raised up.

"Did Uncle Willard do kitty?" he said.

"Don't talk dirty," she said.

"Did he?"

"Just the once," she said, pushing him down. Gus fell to work again as Beryl called out instructions.

After a few minutes she let him up. Gus, overeager, entered her. He found generous passage.

"I love you, Beryl," he said, thinking it had to be true. If this wasn't love, what was?

"Gee willikers, slow *down*," she said. "Don't be in such an all-fired hurry."

Gus did as he was told.

"Oooh oooh," she said.

When he finished she said, "To be candid with you Gus, I find your ornament only marginally adequate."

"My *ornament*?" he said.

"I don't care for the common terms for it. They're utterly demeaning."

"My ornament," Gus said, thinking that the common terms for it were less demeaning. He imagined his marginally adequate ornament sparkly with glitter hanging on a Christmas tree among the angels, candy canes, and silver balls.

"Your ornament is also selfishly impatient," she said. "Luckily I'm overly sensitive, so it was passably useful."

Now that Gus understood her sensitivities, he wondered about his.

"Thanks loads," he said.

She patted his head. "It was actually better than merely useful. I experienced fulfillment twice. Almost a third time—if you had been less selfish, Gussie."

"It's Gus, not Gussie," he said.

"We're going to be extremely happy, Gus."

"With seven or eight babies," he said.

"None of whom will grow up in Milk River."

She crawled out of the tent and washed herself in the lake. She emerged from the water like a goddess rising from the sea glistening with beads of liquid light. Gus could not believe his good luck.

7

Mutt Runkle said, "Word's out your knockin boots with the town punchboard, Reppo."

Gus was the charge-of-quarters that morning. Runkle had stepped out of the AP shack to watch him raise the flag as reveille was bugled at earsplitting volume over the squadron PA system.

"Give her some tongue, she drops her oyster," Runkle said. He intoned the words musically, like song lyrics.

"Oooh, oooh," Runkle said, musically.

Gus restrained himself. He concentrated on getting the flag up without tangling it in the ropes.

"She mention how she wants a busload of rug rats?"

The flag reached the top of the pole in good condition. The wind took it and it flapped hard, straining at the ropes. Gus tied the ropes to the bracket on the flagpole. The flapping flag reminded Gus of Beryl's windblown pup tent.

"I don't know what you're talking about, Runkle," he said.

"You're the type of dipshit who'd actually marry the town nymph," Runkle said. "Let me give you a thumbnail sketch of life with Beryl: You marry her, make a nice little love nest for her. Then when you're out peddling vacuum cleaners door to door, she's banging the milkman in the morning and the meter reader in the afternoon. You'd better talk to a chaplain, kid. Get some serious counseling before you deep-six your life."

"You've got a rotten mouth," Gus said. He threw a wild

looping punch. The punch bounced off Runkle's thick nose. Gus threw another wild punch that Runkle slapped away.

Runkle smiled as if Gus had done him a favor. He touched the trickle of blood on his upper lip. His smile widened.

"The Board of Inquiry is going to call it self-defense," he said. "When you get out of sick bay, kid, I'll teach you how to punch."

The last thing Gus remembered was Runkle unseating his nightstick.

Gus got an in-squadron Article 15 court martial after he got out of sick bay. He had an egg-sized lump on the side of his head, two black eyes, a swollen nose, and a loose tooth. He lost his single stripe and First Sergeant Burnside restricted him to the base for two months. He pulled KP duty every day of those two months and worked swings and graveyards at the radio shack.

Gus was afraid to call Beryl. Afraid to find out what Runkle said was true, and that she had been intimate with him. But how else could Runkle have known about her desire to be married and have babies?

Gus felt sick and vengeful and helplessly in love. These cross-wired emotions called for some kind of action. He couldn't just let them stew while he did nothing. He wanted to forgive her; he wanted to slap her. He wanted to hug her; he wanted to strangle her. He wanted to buy a ring; he wanted to buy a gun.

He imagined being married to her. Imagined her telling the mailman to close his eyes and do kitty while neglected babies—possibly his, possibly not his—cried in their cribs. Imagined coming home early from work and catching her in bed with the milkman. Imagined her telling the meter reader and milkman and a dozen others that her husband's ornament wasn't, candidly speaking, *adequate*.

He imagined taking the deer rifle out of the closet and killing the milkman, the meter reader, and Beryl, repeating with each discharge of the rifle, "Is *this* adequate? Do you find *this* adequate?" He imagined their heads mounted on a wall, the dead glass eyes staring. These awful scenes gave him a throbbing headache. Crazed and sick at heart, he punched the wall next to his bunk, breaking the skin on his knuckles.

Ray Springer, who'd been reading a book, looked at him. "Work it out, Gate," he said. "Whatever it is." He put a blues record on his turntable. Lightnin' Hopkins told a story in a slow striding rhythm that seemed to be Gus's story. Hopkins' guitar and voice spoke directly to Gus. Jim Jackson's "St. Louis Blues," with the original uncensored lyrics, did the same. The stories weren't his stories—they were beyond his experience, the lyrics difficult to understand—but the sound and rhythm that drove them moved something in his chest that needed moving before he could take an easy breath. Jelly Jaw Short's "Barefoot Blues," Henry Townsend's "Long Ago," Charlie Jordan's "Keep it Clean" untangled gridlocks in his head.

"I'm stupid, Ray," he said.

"You're not stupid, Gate, you're ignorant. You got some catching up to do. Unless you get seriously sidetracked, you'll do it. Keep it clean, like Charlie Jordan says. What he means is don't sell yourself a line of crap. Listen kid, half the people in the world are walking around up to their eyebrows in their own bullflop and feeling righteous about it."

"Half?"

"Considering the shape the world's in, make that ninety percent."

8

By the time Gus was allowed to go into town again the weather had changed. Winter was in the air though it was only late September. Days were warm, nights were cold. Canada geese flew south to their winter refuge in vast imperfect vees.

Gus decided to confront Beryl. He went to her house. Beryl's mother, a narrow woman in housecoat and carpet slippers, answered the door. A bent cigarette dangled from her lipless mouth. She squinted at Gus through blue smoke, sizing him up.

"Is Beryl home?" he said.

"Take a number," she said.

"Ma'am?"

"She's got company."

"I'm Gus Reppo, her fiancé," he said. "From the radar base."

"A flyboy? How unusual," she said. "My daughter usually dates divinity students." A flicker of amusement livened her eyes. "You might as well join the party." The corners of her thin mouth twitched, as if her lips were trying to remember how to grin.

The shotgun house was small and shabby. The floorboards groaned under Gus's feet. The threadbare furniture was ancient and the faded flower-printed carpet showed the cords of its sisal weave. The walls were dark with years of cigarette smoke and airborne fry grease from the kitchen. A fat mongrel slept in the middle of the living room floor, its paws twitching with dreams of the chase. Two antelope heads above an iron stove stared down at Gus. There appeared to be no Mr. Lenahan.

Beryl was sitting on the sofa with Dwight Hammond, a motor pool mechanic from Detroit. Gus knew Hammond. He was one of those guys who looks athletic but trips on sidewalk cracks.

Beryl looked at Gus without reaction. Gus had expected her to jump up, excited that her one and only had returned at last, but she remained seated, looking at him with blank indifference. She seemed to not recognize him.

Gus had changed somewhat. He knew that. But had he changed so much that Beryl couldn't place him? He found this hard to believe. He'd lost some weight—he was down to 112. His clothes were loose, his hair was longer, his nose had a blue-tinged knot at the bridge and it was bent slightly to the left, but he was still the essential Gus Reppo.

"It's *me*," he said. "Gus Reppo."

After a moment, she said, "Oh. Hi. What are you doing here?"

"What am I doing here?"

"Surely you're acquainted with Dwight?" she said.

Gus and Dwight Hammond nodded at each other.

"Dwight and I are engaged," she said. She held out her left hand. She was wearing a thin gold band that supported a solitaire almost big enough to fill a pinhole.

Dwight Hammond grinned at Gus. It was an innocent grin, no brag or challenge in it. Gus saw it as the grin of a simpleton who had no grasp of what he was getting into. He allowed himself the small pleasure of feeling sorry for Hammond.

"How have you been, Gussie?" Beryl said. "Did you get your car fixed?"

"I don't have a car," Gus said.

"Oh. Maybe that was Terry Wankel," she said.

"Wankel totaled his Impala," Dwight Hammond said. "Went into a barrow pit and rolled. Luckily he has comprehensive insurance."

"I'm the one who went fishing with you, Beryl," Gus said.

"Oh, of course. The pike catcher," Beryl said. She exchanged grins with Hammond, as if 'pike-catcher' was their code word for an incompetent angler.

"Beryl and I caught six native brookies on Beaver Creek just yesterday!" Hammond said. "Beryl fried them up, right there at our campsite. Yum."

"Jesus H. Christ," Gus said. Another meaning of Hammond's "yum" occurred to him.

"We've got a little basement apartment picked out over on Twelfth Street," Hammond said. "Beryl will get a dependent's allotment every month. I'll get supplemental pay for moving off-base. I think we'll have enough left over for a nice car. I'm looking at a used '57 Fairlane six with only seventeen thousand miles on it. They want twelve hundred for it—too much for a six? But I think I can get it for ten, eleven tops. What do you think, Reppo? Ten about right for a six? Maybe ten-fifty?" Hammond squeezed Beryl's knee. Beryl sagged against Hammond. Hammond's visible boner strained against his chinos. The room temperature went up. Gus felt sick.

Beryl said, "Frankly, I'm just *dying* to have my own place."

Beryl's mother followed Gus to the door. "Come around tomorrow, flyboy. Maybe your luck will change," she said.

Gus walked to the Cabin, a long narrow bar on the east end of town. The Cabin's walls were varnished ponderosa logs, the low ceiling covered with hammered tin. Deer and pronghorn heads were mounted on the walls at three-foot intervals. Gus ordered a double shot of Lemon Hart rum. The bartender didn't ask him for ID. Gus downed the Lemon Hart, a 150 proof rum that didn't taste like rum. It tasted like napalm. He ordered another.

An Indian old enough to have been at the Battle of the Little Bighorn saw Gus looking at him in the mirror behind the liquor bottles. He was sitting two stools away. He wore a broad-brimmed Stetson with a faded snakeskin band at the base of the tall crown. Silver braids hung out of the old man's oversized hat.

He might have been a boy warrior eighty years ago, taking the hair of Custer's wounded soldiers then caving in their naked skulls with a river rock.

"What do you think you're looking at?" the old man said.

"Sorry. Didn't mean to stare," Gus said.

"What did you mean to do?"

"I don't know."

"That about sums it up," the old man said, lifting his beer.

The bartender refilled Gus's shot glass. Gus slid a silver dollar toward him. The bartender gave him fifty cents change.

"She should have cut my eyes out instead of the fish's," Gus said.

"Then you wouldn't be bothering people by staring at them," the old man said.

"She didn't want the fish to see her gut them," Gus said.

This amused the old man. "Oh ho," he said.

"But she didn't mind gutting me."

"She figured you out," the old man said. "She gutted you then cooked you on a stick." The old warrior, remembering earlier times, drained his mug. Gus downed his Lemon Hart. Gus ordered another beer for the old man and another double Lemon Hart for himself.

"I can see that you are a young fool from what you choose to drink," the old man said. "You are going to have to lean just to stand straight."

"I'll try to do better," Gus said.

The old man sipped his beer, Gus sipped his rum.

After a while, the old man said, "What will you give me for this timepiece?" He showed Gus a Timex that hung loosely on his thin wrist from a broken expansion band.

"Ten cents," Gus said.

"What will you give me for Antelope County?" the old man said.

Gus didn't know what the old man meant. Milk River was the seat of Antelope County, so he figured it was some kind of joke. He went along with it. "I'll have to contact my banker," he said.

The old man spit on the floor next to Gus's stool. He looked all of ninety, but he wanted to settle an old score. He wanted to cave in Gus's head with a river rock. But first the old man wanted to carve Gus's eyes out so that Gus wouldn't take his image to the grave. Gus could see these mad schemes glittering in the old warrior's eyes.

"You are about as dumb as you look," the old warrior said.

The Silver Dollar on the west side of town was the last bar in Milk River before Main Street became US Route 2. Gus went in. There was a narrow staircase recessed in shadow at the far end of the barroom. Gus climbed the stairs to a foyer furnished with sofas and armchairs. There was a red door in the back wall of the foyer. Gus knocked.

After a few seconds a peephole opened and closed. A woman's voice said, "No, Fremont. Not one of those sons a bitches." Gus knocked again. Gus was dressed in civvies but he wasn't fooling anyone behind the door.

The door opened. An Indian—Fremont, Gus assumed—filled the doorway, side to side. His head grazed the top of the frame. Fremont said, "You go on up the street to that house behind the Moomaw Dairy. You got no business here, flyboy."

Fremont had a scar running down his cheek to his lower lip. The left side of his mouth drooped. Severed facial nerves had given his mouth a dubious sneer. He was a man who could look Jesus in the eye and not lose composure. There was a leather sap hanging from his belt.

"I'm not a flyboy," Gus said. "I'm a dental student."

"And I'm Rock Hudson," Fremont said. "I sell pussy when I'm not making movies, but not to drunk dental students."

In the room behind him a woman giggled.

Gus left the Silver Dollar and went to the flyboy's whorehouse behind the Moomaw Dairy.

"Long time no see," Norrie, the tobacco-chewing whore, said. "You getting all you need from the local beaver pond?"

"Not exactly," Gus said.

Norrie spit a brown stream into the soup can next to her foot. Her accuracy impressed Gus once again. "Guess I'm the only girl a fella like you can count on," she said.

"I'm pretty damn drunk," Gus said.

"I got a remedy for that," she said.

Gus woke up the next morning under a car in the alley behind the Milk River Hotel. He'd been rolled. His shoes and belt were gone, along with his wallet. He couldn't remember how he got under the car, or who rolled him. Town boys, probably. He crawled out into the cold morning light and walked to the viaduct avoiding broken beer bottles. He hitched a ride to the base with some hung-over radar operators.

"You look like Death-Eating-a-Cracker, Gate," Ray Springer said when Gus dragged himself in. "Need some hair of the dog?"

Springer kept a pint of bourbon in his footlocker and offered it to Gus. Gus shook his head no. The sight of the bourbon made his stomach lurch. He was dry-heave sick and still a little drunk and had to get ready to relieve the day shift. Gus and Ray Springer went to the chow hall. Gus didn't want food. He wanted something for his raging thirst.

The chow hall wasn't crowded. Mutt Runkle was at a corner table sitting by himself and reading a newspaper. The bold headlines said: Red China Shells Quemoy. All the tables around Runkle, in a radius of fear, were empty. No one socialized with him, except for his partner, Jeff, who was on duty.

Runkle's square head looked too big for his body. His slow, ruminating jaws flexed and unflexed as he methodically ate his way through a heaping plate of sausages, eggs, hash-brown potatoes, and biscuits. He allowed himself an amused, self-satisfied grin as he studied his paper.

Ray Springer said, "See that grinning AP?" he said to Gus. "He keeps notes on everyone in the squadron."

"Notes?"

"He keeps a private notebook. He's probably writing in it right now, about me and you talking about him. Figures to cover his ass if and when the shit hits the fan."

"What shit?"

"Any shit. He keeps track of the details most people forget, just in case."

Gus looked over at Runkle. He couldn't see what Runkle was doing behind his newspaper.

"Everybody knows about his notebook, so when Runkle comes into a room, ordinary human beings act like zombies. He loves having the power to turn people into zombies. Even the junior officers are scared of him."

"I didn't know about his notebook," Gus said.

"Now you do, Gate," Springer said. "There's only one person he doesn't have in his notebook."

"Who?"

"Himself. He'll never figure out Mutt Runkle."

"If he does, he'll have to shoot himself," Gus said.

"Don't be too sure of yourself, Gate," Springer said. "Lots of folks, some smarter than you, don't know what they got locked up inside their heads."

"Heard something like that my first day on base," Gus said.

"You'll probably hear it again, Gate."

Gus put on his field jacket. He walked to the radio shack and picked up his climbing gear. An insulator had to be replaced. The LF mast was cold as ice. Winter was a promise in the air. For the first time ever Gus was reluctant to climb. Wind from Canada sang like a band of wolves in the latticed framework of the mast.

9

"Where's Mommy?" Gus asked.

"Mommy's lying down," FDR said.

"You've already had dinner?" Gus said.

"We were waiting for you, Gussie."

Something was wrong. The kitchen was cold. Nothing was on the stovetop or in the oven.

"Is she sick?" Gus asked.

"Not exactly," FDR said.

Gus went into the bedroom. It was after six o'clock and Flora was lying on the bed in her nightgown. The nightgown had gathered on her thighs. She was wearing stockings but they were rolled down below her knees. Her hair was lumpy with pink curlers. She'd put the curlers in carelessly. Some had fallen to the bedspread. Some yawned half-open, dangling from her wispy hair.

"What's wrong, Mommy?" Gus said.

Flora closed her eyes. "Wrong? Nothing's wrong." Her voice was dreamy and removed, like a spirit voice at a séance.

FDR came into the room. "She's been like this since yesterday," he said. "I gave her two Milltowns."

"Are the Milltowns doing this to her?"

"I don't think so, Gussie."

"Maybe we should take her to the hospital."

"I don't think it's very serious. Her bowels are regular and her heartbeat is strong. This will pass in time."

Gus didn't press the issue.

FDR cleared his throat. "We'll go out for dinner tonight, Gussie," he said. "Mommy isn't up to cooking. Soon as she gets herself together, we'll go. I'm thinking of the Townhouse. They have a decent menu there."

Flora's pasty white thighs were round as kegs. Her calves were webbed with blue veins. She struggled to a sitting position then leaned forward to pull up her stockings. She couldn't reach them over her stomach.

She looked at Gus. "I hardly recognize you, Gussie," she said. "You've changed somehow. You don't seem happy. Are you unhappy Gussie? Are you going to have an unhappy life?"

There was something obscene in her appearance—her naked legs against the brown bedspread, her collapsing hair.

"I'm doing okay, Mommy," he said.

"Are you? I don't think so, Gussie. A mother knows these things. I doubt very much that you are doing okay."

She reached down for her stockings again but her hands got no further than mid-thigh. "Come here, Gussie," she said. She patted the bed. "I have something to tell you."

Gus sat down next to her. The air in the room was heavy with the smell of rancid body oil and stale cologne. There was a half gallon of Rhine wine on the floor next to the night table. "They say a child remembers the womb," she said. "I don't know if that's true, but I remember carrying you. You were tucked safely inside but moving restlessly as if you were afraid of confinement. You moved my water like a drowning swimmer who had lost his stroke. I don't think you were meant for dentistry, Gussie."

"That's what you wanted to tell me?" Gus said.

"I'm sorry we pushed you so hard. But no, I do not think you would be a happy dentist. And I want you to be happy, Gussie. If you can't be a happy dentist, then I just want you to be a happy something, not an unhappy nothing, not an aimless swimmer far from shore. Whatever you choose to do in life, I will support. Your happiness is all I've ever wanted."

She reached up and touched his face. Her hand went to the back of his neck. Her pull was weak but Gus didn't resist. He allowed her to bring his face down to her puckered lips which were dry as paper. "Are you still mama's miracle baby?" she said. She gave Gus a sidelong look, her expression sly and coquettish.

FDR, standing in the doorway, cleared his throat. "You want to get dressed now, Mommy?" he said, looking at his watch. "I'm starved, and I'm sure Gussie is starved, too. Right, Gussie? The men of the house are ravenous!"

"Give me a few minutes," Flora said. "Can you ravenous men wait a few minutes? Gussie? Can you wait for me? Or is your mother too much of a burden for you to bear?"

She still wasn't dressed an hour later. FDR and Gus went out and ordered hamburgers at the Burger Shed Café in downtown Milk River.

"She's losing it, FDR," Gus said. "You'd better take her home."

"She won't go," FDR said. "Not as long as you're here."

"So all this is my fault?" Gus said.

"No, son. I didn't mean it that way."

"It's the wide open spaces," Gus said. "This flat cow country gets to you."

FDR sighed. "Yes, I know. I'm feeling it, too."

"She's drinking a lot," Gus said.

FDR sighed again. He drummed the table with his fingers. "It gets her through these long afternoons. Back in the frontier days, many women depended on the constipating opiate laudanum to help them endure monotony and hardship. Some died of impacted bowels because of it."

Gus wanted to tell him that he'd also been drinking a lot. He wanted to tell him that he loved the big empty country, his special view of it atop his radio masts, and how, on certain days, he'd seen the horizon arc with the earth's curvature. He wanted to tell him that this great endless ocean of silent flatland was beyond beautiful and at the same time too awful for a non-native to deal with. He wanted to tell him that he had momentary glimpses of something in the landscape he couldn't define. Ray Springer's "It" wasn't an explanation Gus could offer since he himself didn't understand what Springer meant. "*It*" was barely a word! More words didn't help. Springer said there was an inverse relationship between "It" and words. Gus asked what he meant by inverse. "The more words you play out the less you get back," Springer said. "You can talk yourself into a coma, Gate."

"It," Ray said, had nothing to do with yesterday or tomorrow. "It" was off the clock. "It" was not related to success or failure. Success and failure were the Siamese twins of life. There was failure in success and success in failure. Same coin, two sides. Ray Springer called this the shithouse rule. "Say you take a healthy dump," Springer said, "but if there's no toilet paper in the shit-house you leave feeling cheated. Your work didn't get rewarded with a nice roll of wipe. On the other hand, if you're bound up tight as an overwound clock a fat roll of quality toilet paper won't be any use to you at all. It just sits there fat and happy while you grunt and groan."

Springer formulated the shithouse rule twenty thousand feet over Dresden with the help of the piece of flat shrapnel that spun through his guts like helicopter blade. He showed Gus the grooves and craters in his belly where the piece of steel had tumbled in and tumbled out before settling in his sheepskin flight jacket.

"I'm sitting in a pool of my own blood and shit, looking down on a burning city," Springer said. "We're shot up pretty bad but it looks like we'll be able to get home. Then the radio op finds this station in Zurich playing American music and he pipes it into the intercom and it's Frank fucking Sinatra singing "All or Nothing at All," the song that gets the bobby-sox girls gooey. You get the picture, Gate? Forty thousand German civilians burning in white phosphorous hell, and *me*? I'm praying to some god I don't even believe in—Don't let me fucking *die* goddamnit!

Don't let my dick go floppy!—while Frankie croons his Hit Parade fuck-song in my ear. On one side of the coin a city full of cremated Germans; on the other side, my roscoe's future. All to the tune of Frankie's number one fuck-song. You believe some god has a say in it, then you got to believe he's a badass jokester with one bodacious mean streak. I could almost hear his horse laugh shaking the ribs of our shot-up plane while the side-gunner above me starts chuckling, *like he gets it*. He was just crying himself to death, but it sounded like chuckling. Silly-ass situation, Gate, don't you think? Does it get more silly-ass than that? But silly-ass is what you need to get used to if you want to see things straight. You need to look at yourself in the funhouse mirror every morning and say, I am one silly-ass son of a bitch going out to do some silly-ass son of a bitch thing with a bunch of other silly-ass sons of bitches. You see what I'm saying?"

"Yes. No. Not really," Gus had said.

"Give it a few more years, Gate. Get married, get a job, have some babies—in short do the All American three-step boogie. You'll eventually figure it out if you don't get brain-lock first."

Gus poured ketchup on his burger. "When I died they washed me out of the turret with a hose," he said, recalling a short poem about a ballturret gunner Ray had once recited.

FDR looked at him. "A riddle? I don't care for riddles, Gussie," he said.

"Maybe your life is a riddle, FDR," Gus said.

Gus had meant to provoke FDR and was immediately sorry but FDR only nodded in tacit agreement which made Gus feel worse.

FDR leaned back in his chair. The waitress came by and refilled his coffee. He thanked her and stirred some sugar into his cup.

"I'm sorry," Gus said.

"For what?" FDR said. "For telling the truth?"

PART TWO

10

Winter arrived early and all at once. It knifed south from the arctic and through the Canadian plains killing any vegetation that had survived previous frosts. Ice crystals like tiny acetylene torches were suspended in the stark afternoon sky. The sun, dull as a nickel, perched on the rim of the frozen earth. It was forty-seven below and ordinary jackets were useless against the killing wind. Gus wore his hooded sheepskin parka over his civvies and insulated "bunny boots" on his feet. He wore thermal long johns, a cable-knit sweater, and heavy wool pants. Windchill dropped the virtual temperature to minus seventy-seven.

People were advised to carry food, blankets, kindling, and matches if they were driving any distance. Water pipes in the outer walls of unprepared houses froze then burst, flooding basements, bathrooms, and kitchens. The engines of ungaraged cars would not turn over unless warmed overnight by electric head-bolt heaters. Batteries froze, crankcase oil thickened to the consistency of tar, windshields iced over, rubber lost flexibility. Some lit dangerous fires under their engine blocks in desperation.

Cottonwood trees, greedy siphons of ground water that grew along the riverbanks, cracked open. The woody explosions were loud as rifle shots as water froze and expanded within their trunks. Cattle that could not be rounded up in time and moved to shelter froze where they stood in the drift lines along fences. Despondent ranchers, facing another year of financial loss, dreamed of tropical escapes.

Spit froze in midair and skipped on the sidewalk like a flat white stone. Miniature icicles formed in noses on the inhale, thawed on the exhale, then froze again with the next breath taken. Eyes filled with protective tears, unsalved lips cracked and bled, and ears, uncovered too long, darkened with frostbite.

Gus found refuge in the Athenian ice cream parlor, where he met Tracy Winshaw. She was sitting in a booth by herself, drinking coffee and reading a hardback book. Next to her coffee cup a lipstick-stained cigarette sent a thread of smoke straight up from a tin ashtray. She was thin as a twig but her face, Gus thought, could have been on the covers of glamour magazines. She wore her black hair long and tied in a loose ponytail. When she turned her head quickly—and she did this often to see who came into the Athenian and who left—the ponytail would toss prettily. Gus was taken by the way her ponytail flounced to her quick movements. Her pale unblemished skin was drawn tight over her cheekbones and her dark eyes behind the lenses of her cat-eye glasses had the deep visionary luster you see in photos of starving refugee children. Her full lips, though, saved her from looking completely ethereal. She was beautiful in the soulful way of Audrey Hepburn or Gene Tierney. A song, "Angel Eyes," by Nat King Cole played in Gus's mind as he watched her from his stool at the soda fountain.

He slid off the stool and went to her booth. "Well, now there, then," he said, using the phrase James Dean made famous in *Rebel Without a Cause*. The hip California style of casual speech made these small town girls giggle. She didn't. He sat down opposite her; she kept reading.

"You look kind of down, sitting here by yourself," Gus said. "I thought I'd come over and cheer you up."

She regarded him with severe indifference. "How thrilling," she said, "but I don't need cheering up."

The book she was reading was titled *Common Sense and Nuclear Warfare*.

"Pardon me for breathing," Gus said.

"Everyone has a right to breathe. Just don't do it in my booth. Distribute your cheerful germs somewhere else."

Gus managed a twisted hayseed grin. "Hey, how about this here gol-dang cold front?" he said. "By golly, she was forty above just yesterday. Looks like I'll have to chip my cows out of the ice. And my tractor? Couldn't get Old Fireball out of the barn unless I primed her carb with nitroglycerin."

She picked up her cigarette and blew a stream of smoke across the booth. "You're very funny," she said. "Do you invent your own material or do you get it out of that *How To Be The Life Of The Party* book?"

Someone came into the Athenian and Tracy turned quickly to see who it was. Gus watched her ponytail lash left then right.

Gus tried another approach. "I see you dig Bertrand Russell," he said. Russell's picture was on the back cover of her book. Gus had seen his picture in the newspapers. Russell had been leading a protest against the atomic bomb at some American military base in England. He even remembered the caption under the photo: Better Red Than Dead. What crap, Gus thought at the time, but now had enough sense to keep his opinion to himself. The Chinese Reds were shelling poor little Quemoy again, but Gus didn't want to bring this up and maybe spoil whatever chances he might have with her.

"You've read Bertrand Russell?" she said.

Gus hadn't, but said, "He's one of the great thinkers of our time."

"I'm trying to read *The Principia*," she said. "It's pretty heavy going, though. I'll try it again after I've taken more science and math at the college."

"College?" Gus said.

"I'm a sophomore at Northern Plains State."

"There's a college in Milk River?"

"We even have electricity and indoor plumbing."

She studied Gus, his olive drab parka with squadron markings on it. She said, "You've never read a word of Bertrand Russell, have you?"

"Maybe I could take some classes at Northern Plains State."

"Before you go any further with this, I have to tell you something. I do not date flyboys."

"On principle?"

"Principles are all we have, don't you think?"

Gus saw her again a few weeks later. Both Flora and FDR were down with the flu and FDR asked Gus to do the grocery shopping. He gave Gus twenty dollars and the keys to the Buick.

It was still cold out, fifteen above, but the wind was blowing hard enough to make it feel like fifteen below. Gus saw Tracy walking down Main Street wearing a jacket that was far too light. He pulled up ahead of her and got out. "It's way too cold to walk," he said. "Hop in, I'll give you a lift."

She recognized him after a few seconds. She was wearing a gray wool skirt and long black stockings and carrying a book. She was cold, but hesitated anyway.

Gus said, "I'm just offering you a ride. I'm not asking you to go dancing."

Her smile triggered glandular reactions in Gus.

"Okay," she said. "I'm on my way to school. But I need to drop by Daddy's office first."

Her daddy's office was in a two-story frame house on the south side of town. "This is a dentist's office," Gus said, reading the sign out front.

"Daddy's a dentist," she said. She seemed suddenly shy and apologetic.

Gus laughed, then groaned.

"What's *that* about?" she said, annoyed.

"My daddy's a dentist, too," Gus said.

It was her turn to laugh. "If this is karma," she said, "then I'm going to stick with materialistic atheism."

She went into her father's office and came out a few minutes later. She'd gone in laughing, but now she was frowning. Gus started the car.

"Your old man give you a hard time?" he said.

"Always, on allowance day," she said. She pulled out a wad of paper money from her clutch purse, riffled through the bills. "He's a fascist and a bigot. Or is that redundant?"

Gus nodded, but kept silent. Family warfare wasn't an ideal topic of conversation to begin a relationship.

"I'm a hypocrite, I guess," she said. "I take his money but reject his so-called ethics, or lack thereof."

"I know what you mean," Gus said.

"You do? No, I don't think you do. My daddy's a super extreme case. For instance, he won't do dental work on Indians, Negroes, or Jews—though there aren't many Negroes or Jews in Milk River, except for the radar base. Even Eisenhower is too liberal for him. He thinks Ike is a tool of the Communists!"

"And you'd rather be Red than dead," Gus said.

"Of course I would! Wouldn't you? Do you even have to think about it? Dead is dead. It's final. Political regimes are never final. And besides, what's so wonderful about the capitalist system? We'd still be in the depression if it weren't for the war. The capitalist system *depends* on war. The cold war is a capitalist invention. When it ends, and if we're not all dead by then, they'll think of some other way to keep the war factories going."

"Wait a minute," Gus said. "I forgot my notebook."

"You think it's a joke? Capitalism and war are symbiotic with one another. If one vanishes, so does the other."

"I can't believe that never occurred to me," Gus said.

"You don't know what symbiosis is, do you?"

"I've heard the word, I think. In high school biology."

"It's simple: War makes money so money makes war."

Gus didn't remind her of the wad of war-making money in her purse. He'd never been interested in politics and didn't intend to become interested now. If he echoed her opinions he might have a chance with her, but she'd see through his false endorsements.

"You're military," she said. "You think what you do is a justified moral crusade, correct? You've been thoroughly brainwashed. If they told you to go into a nursery and shoot all the babies you'd do it because they've taken over your moral character and reshaped it. You belong to them. You—who*ever* you are—have ceased to exist as an independent entity. Tell me I'm wrong."

"I'm Gus Reppo, former independent entity," he said. He offered her his hand.

She accepted it, smiling. "Tracy Winshaw," she said.

Gus pulled the Buick into the college parking lot. Tracy looked at her watch.

"In ten minutes," she said, "Professor Gordon will be lecturing on the worker's movement since 1880. Doctor Gordon is a visiting speaker from Minnesota. He's written books on the subject."

"Is he a Red?"

"Technically, no."

"What does *that* mean?" Gus said.

"He's not a card-carrying Communist, but he sympathizes with socialist philosophy. I think it's safe to say that Professor Gordon is a Marxist. You see, Gus Reppo, the people have got to be looked after, and the capitalists won't do it because there's no money in it. To the capitalists, human labor is a commodity to be bought on the open market for the lowest price, like pinto beans or sorghum. That's why they hate unions or any legislation that protects workers, like the child labor or minimum wage laws. If they could move their manufacturing plants to Mexico or India where people work for pennies a day, they'd do it."

"People wouldn't let that happen."

"*People* have nothing to do with it."

"Are you a Marxist?" Gus said.

"Technically, peripherally, I'd have to say yes."

"You're a peripheral Marxist."

"I'm certainly not a capitalist. But my education is far from complete. So, yes, I guess you could call me a peripheral Marxist."

"So I guess I'm a peripheral warmonger, right?"

"Do you feel a need to make jokes about everything?"

"It's part of the military's brainwashing program," Gus said. "We make the enemy die laughing."

She opened the door and started to get out of the car, then hesitated. "Come to Professor Gordon's lecture with me, Gus Reppo—for your own edification."

"My edification?"

"It means enlightenment."

"I know what it means."

"So?"

"You don't date warmongers," Gus reminded her.

"Don't flatter yourself. This doesn't qualify as a date."

Gus thought of the practical benefits. She might think differently of him if he managed to stay awake during the entire lecture.

"Okay," he said. "I'll go."

The seats in the auditorium were small and set close together with shared armrests. Attendance was good, and the audience, dressed in winter coats, wool hats, and heavy fur-lined boots, were packed into the seats, shoulder to shoulder and thigh to thigh. The air was dense with the aroma of wet wool.

Tracy and Gus were jammed together directly under the speaker's podium but Gus's attention was fixed on Tracy, not on Professor Gordon. Gus lost track of the professor's argument after he described the coal strike of 1902.

Gus spent the hour breathing her perfume, feeling the strands of her electrified ponytail finding his ear and the back of his neck.

The press of her thigh kept his adrenaline flowing. Dozing off was not an option, in spite of the relentless drone of Professor Gordon's voice.

"Well, what do you think?" Tracy said when they were back outside the auditorium. She lit a cigarette.

"I thought it was very profound," Gus said.

She studied Gus's face for traces of sarcasm.

"Doctor Gordon is a brave man," she said. "He stands up for what he believes. He refused to sign the loyalty oath his college requires of its faculty and got fired for it. The House Un-American Activities Committee has subpoenaed him. He'll probably go to prison. They've made a mockery of the First Amendment. Do you find *that* very profound, Gus Reppo?"

"You want to get a cup of coffee?" Gus said.

"I've got a class," she said.

"How about after class?"

"Well, you're not in uniform, so I guess it would be all right. Get a table in the Student Union. I'll meet you there. You can tell me more about how profound you thought Professor Gordon's lecture was."

When she came into the Student Union an hour later, she was not so fierce. She was with a group of other students. They were all smiling and laughing, but she came to Gus's table alone and pensive.

"If you have the time, you might take some courses here," she said.

"My parents would like that," Gus said.

"They don't want you in the military?" she said.

"They want me to be a dentist."

"Oh my God," she said, laughing.

"What about you? What do your parents want you to be?"

"Normal," she said.

"What's normal?"

"For them it's marriage, kids, bank accounts. Nice house, nice car. Husband in the Rotary Club. The usual mindless fluff."

"And you want something else."

"I want to go to law school, at the University down in Missoula. I don't want to bring kids into this world. They'd just become gun fodder or lockstep consumers. I want to help change the world so that people some time in the future can bring kids into it with a clear conscience."

"A thousand years from now," Gus said.

"You're a pessimist. I'm not. By the next century things will be different. Fifty years at most. I look forward to the year 2000. Things are going to be wonderful in the twenty-first century. War and capitalism will be history. People then will look back at us and say, What were they *think*ing?"

"You'll be a grandma in 2000," Gus said.

"No I won't. You've got to be a mother before you can be a grandmother."

"You won't ever get married?"

"God no! Marriage, like most bourgeois institutions, is finished."

Gus took a chance. "*The White Tower* is playing at the Orpheum. Want to go?"

"I don't date flyboys," she said automatically.

"Is that part of your freethinking attitude, or are you just prejudiced?"

This seemed to shock her. "God, I'm *such* a hypocrite," she said.

"Under this brainwashed warmongering façade, I'm really a nice person," Gus said. "Façade" was not a word he would normally use, but it made her laugh and that was justification enough.

"All right," she said. "I'll go. Pick me up for the early show, so we can have dinner afterward. I'll buy."

"I can buy," Gus said.

"You pay for the movie, I'll pay for dinner. Those are my terms."

She took a small notebook out of her purse and tore out a sheet of paper. She wrote down her address and phone number and handed it to Gus.

11

"What sort of name is *Reppo*?" Dr. Winshaw wanted to know.

"Sir?" Gus said.

"What nationality?"

"I'm not sure, sir," Gus said. "I think one of my grandfathers came from Wales."

"No. It's not Welsh. It could be a shortened version of some Slavic name, such as Reponovich or Repovanya. Roman Catholic Slav or Eastern Orthodox. Am I correct?"

Dr. Winshaw scraped his tongue against his front upper teeth after he said "Slav," as though the word left a layer of scum on it.

"I don't think it's Slavic, sir," Gus said. "You mean like Russian? No sir, I'm pretty sure it's not Russian."

"There are Slavs other than Russians, my young friend," Dr. Winshaw said. "The Balkan states are packed with backward Slavs—Polacks and bohunks. Ignorant, troublemaking people. A very undesirable sub-race."

Gus and Tracy were standing in the entryway of the Winshaw house, a large three-story brick situated on Saddle Butte, over-looking the city lights. Gus glanced at his watch several times while Dr. Winshaw quizzed him, hoping that either he or Tracy would get the idea that they had to get out of there to catch the seven o'clock showing of *The White Tower*.

"What do you make of it, Tracy?" Dr. Winshaw said. "You've studied languages and comparative cultures. Where do you think the roots of Mr. *Reppo* were engendered?"

"Equatorial Africa," she said. "Probably the Congo. I believe he's an albino African of Ibo descent."

Gus almost laughed. He faked a cough.

"Not likely, Tracy," Dr. Winshaw said. "However, I wouldn't rule out the Middle East. Perhaps Syria or Lebanon. Mr. *Reppo*'s nose doesn't look particularly Semitic; his complexion, while pale, is not especially sallow, and the blue eyes are quite Nordic, but I suppose it is possible. Do you have a German-Jewish strain in your lineage, Gus?"

Dr. Winshaw, a tall angular man, bent down to study Gus's profile closer. His nostrils flared, as if he was able to smell family origins. He was well over six feet and his back had a permanent curvature from years of leaning down to look into the mouths of reclined patients. FDR had once told Gus about this particular hazard of dentistry. FDR had solved the problem by working on patients while seated on a rolling stool.

"We don't belong to any church," Gus said.

"The Jew, as a member of a racial subspecies, is not *only* defined by the practice of religious ritual, Gus." Dr. Winshaw spoke slowly, sonorously, savoring each inflected word. "The Jew, you see, has a way of life, or rather a way of *apprehending* life, that is quite at odds with *our* way."

"*Our* way?" Gus said.

"Indulge me, Gus. That's why I'm asking these questions. I'd like to know more about the family background of the boy who is taking my daughter out on a date."

"We can't stand here all night, Daddy," Tracy said. "We've only got fifteen minutes before the first show."

"Reppo, Reppo, *Reppo*," Dr. Winshaw mused. "Turkish? Kurdish? Perhaps Armenian, as in Reposian? Or French, as in *Repos*. *Repos* is French for lazy, I believe. Ah, have I hit a nerve?"

"I'm part Indian," Gus said, remembering something Flora had told him about her grandfather, a half-blood trapper from up north by the Truckee river. Gus didn't recall the tribe.

"Very amusing," Dr. Winshaw said. "I suppose Tracy put you up to that, Gus. You two seem to share a common sense of humor." He gave Tracy a hard meaningful look, letting her know that a sense of humor had better be the only thing she and Gus shared. But as far as Gus was concerned, Dr. Winshaw couldn't have issued a sweeter warning.

"What sort of name is Winshaw?" Gus said, mimicking Dr. Winshaw's overbearing inflections, as they drove to the movie.

"Who cares?" Tracy said. "People who research their family genealogies are usually trying to prove they're related to the old European aristocracies. It gives them unearned importance. They've never heard of the French Revolution, or grasped its implications."

"Maybe it's Chinese," Gus said. "Rickshaw, Winshaw—pretty close."

"You should have asked him."

"Uh-huh. And I'd never see you again."

"You might not see me again, anyway."

"I get the feeling your daddy isn't a lot of laughs."

"That's the insight of the century."

"He thinks I'm a French Indian named Lazy."

"If that's all he thinks, you're lucky."

Gus parked the Buick in front of the Orpheum. *The White Tower* wasn't drawing a big crowd that evening.

"Maybe I *am* lucky," Gus said.

"I don't believe in luck, Gus," Tracy said.

She said it too seriously. Gus hoped there were some laughs in the movie.

There weren't.

12

George Walters, a radio operator, had a problem with the Hammarlund receiver. Gus was in the radio shack doing scheduled maintenance on the VHF transmitters when Walters called him on the intercom system.

"What's wrong with it?" Gus asked.

"If I knew, I'd fix the fucking thing myself!" he said. Walters, who was hard of hearing, shouted every word as if he had to make himself heard above the noise of an airplane engine. "Bring a flashlight! I can't see dick in here! Flashlight, Reppo! Flashlight!"

Gus put on his parka, grabbed his toolbox, and walked against a sub-zero gale to the radar blockhouse, a thick-walled concrete and steel structure built to withstand a non-direct hit from an A-bomb. A "non-direct" hit meant any nuke one-megaton or less landing outside a two-mile radius of the radar site.

It was dark inside the blockhouse. It took a minute before Gus's eyes adjusted to it. The glow of the radar consoles and the faint light coming from the Plexiglas plotting board at the back of the blockhouse were the only sources of illumination.

George Walters' radio gear—the backup communications system to the landlines—was cubbyholed to the right of the plotting board. Two airmen, taking coordinates from the radar operators, marked directional arrows on the board that signified the flight-paths, speed, and altitude, of all aircraft in the area.

"What's the problem?" Gus asked Walters.

"I got this goddamn hum! It's fucking near driving me nuts!"

Gus took Walters' headphones and listened. "House current," he said. "You're picking up AC from the blockhouse wiring. Probably a blown RF filter of some kind."

Gus unplugged the Hammarlund, unscrewed and pulled out the front panel along with the chassis. He turned the chassis over and tested the low frequency discriminator circuits. He replaced a filter, put the Hammarlund back together, plugged it in.

"I'll send you the bill," he said to Walters.

Walters, not known for his sense of humor, said "Stick the bill up your ass, Reppo!"

Walters was called "Shakey" by some of the airmen, but not to his face. He'd been an artillery spotter in Korea, sitting in the observation seat of an L-4 "Grasshopper." The L-4 was a Piper Cub rigged for military service. Its top speed was about eighty knots, its engine a little four-cylinder toy putting out all of sixty-five horsepower.

Flying behind North Korean lines, Walters radioed the position of artillery batteries and troop movements. The L-4 took NKPA small arms fire on every mission. The little plane always returned home with a dozen or more bullet holes in the fabric of its wings and fuselage. The worst were fuel tank hits, but the pilot always managed to nurse the little plane back to American lines. The pilot, a Nebraska crop duster in civilian life, was good at making the L-4 hard to hit, but for Walters it was a daily, gut-wrenching experience. Walters came home to the US with ulcers, a permanent case of the shakes, and a foul, hair-trigger temper.

Most steered clear of Walters, but Gus liked and admired him. He knew Walters had been a college student before he enlisted. Walters had two years of graduate work in political science and history.

"Why did you quit college, Walters?" Gus asked as he packed up his tools.

"Why do you fucking *think*?"

Gus had no idea, but didn't press it.

"Three units short of my master's at CCNY," Walters said. "Then the money ran out. I'll go back and get a PhD on the GI Bill. Why do you care about my fucked-up academic career?"

"Well, I was wondering. What do you know about Marxism?"

A small desk in front of the Hammarlund supported a logbook, microphone, and a mug of steaming coffee. Walters picked up the coffee mug with both hands and guided it with difficulty to his lips.

"Jesus, Reppo. What do you think we're doing up here in this godforsaken shithole? The Marxists are the fucking enemy!"

He set his coffee down, concentrating hard not to spill any on his logbook. In the chow hall Gus had seen Walters chase a steak around his plate, his knife and fork rattling like machine fire against the Melmac.

Gus tried to keep his eyes off Walters' palsied hands. The palsy grew worse when he was agitated, and even worse when someone noticed the palsy.

"Marxists are Commies?" Gus said.

"The other way around. Commies are Marxists, but all Marxists aren't necessarily Commies."

"They're not the same thing?"

"What did I just say? You're pissing me off, Reppo! Go read a book on syllogisms."

"What kind of gism?"

"Listen to me you goddamn moron. What they've got in Russia is Leninism, the Bolshevik form of Marxism, cooked up by the raznochintsy revolutionaries of the 1860s. Dictatorship of the proletariat in a *non*-industrialized country! Are you *kidding* me? What a fucking joke! You get it, Reppo? You even know what the goddamn proletariat *is*?"

"No," Gus said.

"It's uneducated pudpounders like you! Turning an *industrialized* country over to the proletariat is like giving your car keys to a retarded five-year-old! You haven't read Ayn Rand, have you?"

"No."

"Jesus! They don't teach jack*shit* in high school! They ought to require *Atlas Shrugged* instead of that piece of Commie crap, The Grapes of Trash!"

Gus figured he meant Wrath, not Trash, but he didn't want to get Walters more worked up than he already was by correcting him. Walters picked up his coffee cup with one hand and lost control of it. Coffee sloshed into his lap.

"*Fuck* me!" he screamed. The airmen behind the plotting board looked at Walters, yellow markers suspended. Radar operators looked up from their scopes. The shift boss said, "Let's watch the language, fellows."

"There's this girl in town," Gus said. "Calls herself a Marxist. I went to a lecture with her. The speaker was a Marxist from Minnesota who's getting called up before the House Un-American Activities Committee."

"You better watch your ignorant ass, Reppo. Remember that loyalty oath you signed when you enlisted? It's got teeth, brother! You fuck around with those people you could find your clueless ass in Leavenworth! Remember this—if she says she's a Marxist, then she probably belongs to one of those Commie front organizations that have words like 'world peace' and 'justice' and 'the people' in their titles. You stuffing her chicken yet?"

"No."

"Good. My advice? Do *not* get involved with a half-assed apparatchik. She will break your balls. If you're smart you'll stay the fuck away from these junior league Jacobins. Listen to me for a goddamned minute, Reppo! If the Reds had B-52s instead of those lame Tupolev turbo props, we'd be eating borscht and singing 'The Internationale' by Christmas!"

Gus felt dispirited. This wasn't how he wanted to think about Tracy. Apparatchik? Jacobins? He'd have to look them up.

"There's something else you should know," Walters said. "This part of Montana is packed with Commie spies."

Because this was too crazy to believe Gus felt better about Walters' warnings: The man was nuts.

Walters read Gus's smile. "You don't think so? You think I make this shit up, Reppo?" he said. "I'm telling you what a lot of people already know. We're headquartered at Malmstrom, right? But do you know why Malmstrom was built in the first place? I'll tell you why. They built it during the war as a base to ferry equipment to the Soviets! Planes, trucks, jeeps, guns, ammo— you name it. Malmstrom to Russia via the north pole. The Vladivostok Express. Ask anyone who's lived around Great Falls for any length of time. The Russians planted agents all around the base knowing that one day we'd be their worst nightmare."

"Thanks for the info," Gus said, unable to restrict his smile.

"And fuck you too, you ignorant piece of shit!" Walters said.

Gus put his parka on. He left Walters sitting there adjusting the dials of the Hammarlund with his trembling hands.

13

Gus caught a ride into town that night with Lyle Dressen, an off-duty radar operator. Dressen was a big, friendly kid from LA. He combed his hair in a duck's ass held in place by a gel thick as transmission grease. His dad owned a Cadillac agency in Studio City, and his mother was a former showgirl and actress. Lyle had been a football star for North Hollywood High.

"You want to go to LA for a few days, Reppo?" Lyle said.

"What are you talking about?" Gus said.

"Major Darling is taking a C-47 from Malmstrom to LA. He's going to pick up some brass in LA and ferry them to Texas. It's his chance to kiss some important ass. A one-star general from NORAD and a couple of bird colonel desk jockeys from the Pentagon. Darling's already been passed over twice for light bird. If he's passed over again, he's finished. They call it the three-strike rule. He'll have to retire as a major. So he's going to kiss the ass of anyone he thinks can help his cause. Here's what I'm saying, Reppo: We can go with him as far as LA."

"How do you know this, Dressen?"

"Anyone can catch a hop anywhere, any time, just so long as there's space on the plane and we have time off. I'll use a few days of leave. You could do the same."

"I'll think about it," Gus said.

"Don't think too long. There's only room for a few more hitchers."

It was snowing by the time they reached the viaduct and the

bridge was icy. Once he reached the crest of the bridge, Dressen slowed down for the descent into Milk River. There was a traffic jam at the bottom of the bridge. Cars were blocking access to Main Street.

"There's been a wreck," Dressen said.

"Look, they're dancing," Gus said.

The dancers were clumsy in their heavy parkas and boots. Some dancers fell together in a heap then rolled around in the snow. Dressen hit the brakes and yanked the wheel, and the car slid sideways all the way to the bottom of the bridge. The car stopped inches away from a parked pickup truck.

"They're not dancing," Dressen said. "It's a brawl."

Gus got out of the car. Someone punched him in the face before he could find his footing on the ice. Someone else threw him down and kicked him. Gus's parka absorbed most of it but the impact still knocked the wind out of him. Lyle Dressen came around the car and blindsided the kicker with a forearm shiver to the side of his head. "How about picking on someone your own size, turd knocker," Dressen said.

Gus got up wheezing. "What's going on?" he said.

"It's the town boys," an airman said. Gus didn't know him. His nose and mouth were bloody. He was looking at a tooth in his hand, one he had just spit out. "They blocked the viaduct to stop airmen from coming into town. They outnumbered us at first but now we outnumber them. We're about to fuck some people up."

Gus saw half a dozen cars with squadron stickers on their windshields parked sideways on the bridge. All of them had braked hard, coming to rest against the barrier of town boy cars.

Gus sat on the hood of Dressen's car, handkerchief held against his bleeding nose, and watched the fight. An airman from Mississippi, Jimmy Rails, was clubbing town boys with the steel shaft of a foot-long torque wrench. Willie McFee, a kid from Chicago who'd been a regional Golden Gloves champ, was fighting a huge town boy, popping him with snappy lefts and slashing rights. The town boy's head looked like it was on a hinge. Most of the fighters had stopped to watch the boxing skills of Willie McFee. Their interest switched to the wrestling skills of the town boy when he grabbed Willie in a bear hug.

A town boy yelled, "Squeeze the grits out of that coon, Vuko!"

"Thumb his eyes, Willie!" an airman yelled.

Gus slid off the hood and walked through the crowd toward town. No one challenged him, much of the fight having gone out of both sides.

He walked up Main Street to the Milk River Hotel. The hotel had the nicest bar in town. It was frequented mainly by businessmen and professionals. Gus went into the men's room and washed up. He combed his hair with his fingers.

"You ignorant proletarian bastard," he said to the mirror.

"Capitalist war loving swine," the mirror said back.

He sat at the bar and ordered a pint of tap beer and wondered if he'd ever see Tracy Winshaw again. But then, why wouldn't he? She seemed to like him a little. He'd been a good audience for her ideas. He didn't think she found him dull or stupid. He looked forward to using the word "proletariat" in conversation with her.

"Maybe a dictatorship of the proletariat wouldn't be a totally bad thing, if the top people were decent human beings and knew what they were doing. Apparatchiks like yourself could make it work." He enjoyed the thought of saying apparatchik to her.

"Yes," she'd reply, impressed by his unexpected seriousness, "the changeover might involve some hardship at first, but in the end we—I mean the intelligentsia—would reorganize society to maximize cooperative freedom, limiting, of course . . ."

Limiting of course *what*? Alcohol consumption? Religious holidays? The major league baseball season? Sex on bingo nights? *Non*-cooperative freedom?

And what was *cooperative* freedom, anyway? Professor Gordon had used the phrase in his lecture, and Gus didn't understand it then, either.

Inventing this conversation with Tracy was not helpful. Gus couldn't extend it beyond these few lines. His was a half-pint intellect with a thimble full of knowledge: a working definition for a fool. Instead, he thought of how she might look naked. Tiny but perfectly shaped breasts. Like scoops of ice cream topped with cherries. Thin but well-shaped legs. Ribs showing, yet the torso nice to look at and hold.

Tracy looked nothing like Beryl Lenahan. No one looked like Beryl. Beryl Lenahan probably didn't look like Beryl Lenahan. Memory and need exaggerated her beauty. But that didn't have the effect of making Tracy less desirable, or Gus less needy.

It was not a good idea to think of either girl naked. He had enough money to find relief but didn't want to go to the whorehouse behind the Moomaw Dairy to get it.

"I want love, not just sex," he crooned into his beer.

"That's because you're still wet behind the ears, son."

A heavy man in a wrinkled suit had taken the stool next to Gus. An ebony cane with an ivory handle leaned against the bar next to him. The man's nose was mapped with gin blossoms. His doughy ears sagged from his fleshy skull like chewed biscuits. One eye was blue the other milky gray. The milky eye seemed more startled than blind, as if its sole purview was impending calamity.

"You put a premium on romance because you lack vital experience," he said.

"Excuse me?" Gus said.

The man leaned close to Gus. He had the sickroom smell of a man indifferent to personal hygene. "No offense, laddy buck. But regarding the situation you were referring to, I am the voice of experience."

"Glad to meet you, Voice," Gus said.

"No need to be rude, young man. I was about to offer you the benefit of what I, Solomon Coe, have learned in fifty-odd years of dealing with the weaker sex."

"And to think I almost blew it," Gus said.

"First of all, my vitriolic young friend, they are not the weaker sex. Stop thinking of them as weak. It will improve your chances for a sane life. Secondly, none of them believe in love. Or rather, their notion of love is far different than that of a lad such as yourself, who no doubt was brought up on sentimental movies and lugubrious novels, as well as the absurd opinions of the poorly informed. Your notion of love, you see, is an idealistic fantasy while theirs is practical. Their foremost requirement is security, not knights-errant in chain mail atop noble steeds."

As he spoke, the man's voice changed without warning from basso to alto and back again, as if each intonation signified an alternate meaning.

"Love is love," Gus mumbled.

"That sort of blind faith will lead you into the sloughs of emotional despond," the man said. "A woman can become a harridan overnight. Married in June, young men become ruined suicidal puppets by Christmas. When the bride says, 'I love you,' what she means is, 'I possess you and now will shape you to my special requirements.' You see, my boy, women alone bear the downside consequences of sex. Thus, their day-to-day state of mind is governed by practicality. They can be ruthless when it comes to redirecting the heat of passion into a cool plan for survival. They may not be conscious of this age-old process but they carry out its demands nonetheless."

"Nice talking to you, sir," Gus said. He swiveled away from the man. The man put his large hand on Gus's knee and swiveled him back.

"Hear me out, son. You won't regret it." His voice gave way abruptly to a musical alto singsong. "There's a further problem with your notion of romantic love, a problem you, as yet, have no inkling of. Consider this: It is well-known that a woman takes nine times the pleasure from sex as does a man. Nine times! This is a proven fact! The Greeks established this ratio three thousand years ago. Small wonder, then, that the Greek male was not averse, in intimate locker-room encounters, to playing the part of the female. Pythagoras himself determined this radical nine-to-one differential. He was good with ratios. He would have invented the calculus had it not been for Zeno's paradox, which remains unchallenged to this day."

"I've got to go," Gus said.

The commanding basso held him back. "Here's the upshot, laddy buck! Romance has the half-life of a housefly! It's a moneymaking concept deliberately foisted upon the public through movies, magazines, popular song, and the chocolate candy industry. The reality is rather different. And it is this: You either can please the ladies or you cannot. If you cannot, it's bye-bye Charlie. Some will stay with the unsatisfactory man for family, religious, or security reasons, but these ladies, even though the matress they lie on is stuffed with money, will eventually turn away and face the wall, if you get my drift. You will not enjoy them, nor they you, and life goes on, a dull and dismal pantomime making one wish for early death. But hark! Beware the man who can turn the key in her ignition! The one who can unlock the door to her soul!"

"But *hark*?"

"In some cases you can deal with them through discipline. Regardless of your feelings about such things, you must bite the bullet and *spank* her. And no, I do not mean a playtime spanking. No sir! Nothing of the sort! You will need to make those rosy cheeks glow in the dark! Warm up her little scooter! Does she refuse to beg for mercy? You *must* make her beg for mercy. Spanking, you see, is more than a preliminary erotic exercise, it is man-to-woman communication of the most basic kind. It establishes the polarities of submission and control.

Some will appreciate the wisdom in this harmless practice, some will not."

"Jesus Christ! Leave the kid alone, Sol," the barkeep said.

"There you go again, James," Coe said. "Imposing yourself rudely on my conversations. Fascist swine that you are, would you nonetheless have the courtesy to allow the unencumbered exchange of ideas and opinions?"

"How about you having the courtesy of not annoying the bejesus out of my customers," James the barkeep said. James was a slow-moving giant who, in spite of himself, looked amused.

"The old fruitcake comes in here two, three nights a week and lectures my clientele," he said to Gus. "Boys like you mostly. You don't have to listen to his bullshit, kid. Take your beer over to a booth. Sol can't fit in a booth."

"I wish you wouldn't characterize me in that unfortunate way, James," Solomon Coe said.

He turned his wounded alto persona to Gus: "My boy, I have been married five times. I know whereof I speak." He held his fist up and extended his fingers one at a time starting with the thumb. "One, two, three, four, five," he said. "Five wonderful and dismal and enlightening times. Should you find value in this remarkable history, I'd be glad to take you to my home where we can explore the many vicissitudes of the female sex, in more—ah—isolated and therefore *friendlier* circumstances."

"Don't go with him, kid," the barkeep said. "Sol's got more vista-a-tudes than you want to know about."

"I'll take my argument a step further," Solomon Coe said. "I contend that *all* love, whether romantic, carnal, or spiritual, is nothing more than self-interest. The religious martyr, for example, who so publicly suffers the slings and arrows of persecution for love of his God, is merely ensuring his place in the celestial city. What could be more steeped in self-interest than that? Especially if he covets and enjoys pain."

"You're making a martyr out of this kid, Sol," James said.

"On another, but related subject," Coe said, "what is mankind's most destructive invention?"

"Barroom bullshit artists," James the barkeep said.

"The H-bomb," Gus said.

"Both of you are wrong. It is the *mirror*!" thundered the irrefutable basso.

Solomon Coe gave Gus his business card. He was a lawyer, with offices in Milk River, Chinook, and Box Elder. "You find yourself in a sticky situation vis-à-vis a young lady," he said, "give me a call. I fight them mano-a-mano. I fight fire with fire, son. And I take no prisoners. You'll see."

Gus slid off his stool and headed for the door.

Coe, having found his second wind, boomed, "Beware of the crazy one, laddy buck! She is the one you'll never figure out! She will take your mind apart screw by screw and leave you stuttering nonsense to the woodwork. Like Lupina Sissler, my third effort to achieve matrimonial bliss! Or Deena Jo Blackstone, my fifth, both odd numbers, both numbers prime! She will teach her insanity to you and once you've learned it you will descend with her into unplumbed depths of dissolution and misery! Watch out for her! Soul of a spider, she winds you in her web and offers no way out!"

Gus was almost to the door when Coe shouted, "How will you know her? That's just it! You won't, not until it's too late! You will have turned your hole cards face up, but suddenly she wins the day with a hidden royal flush! Game over, my friend! Game over!"

Just as Gus reached the door Coe slid off his stool and stared at him. His milky eye shimmered in its socket like a gray lamp. "I wouldn't go down that path, son," he said, slipping into a third tone, a sympathetic tenor. "Though, in all probability, you have no choice."

"What path is that?" Gus said.

"The one you're on, my boy."

Gus got out the door into a stinging wind. He looked back. The wind momentarily stopped the door from closing. Coe, silhouetted in barroom light, was stooped over his cane. His legs and cane formed a tripod to hold up his bulk. Gus pulled his parka hood up and cinched it tight. Even after walking three blocks Solomon Coe's rising and falling voice echoed in his head.

14

Gus walked to the Athenian. Before he went in he looked into the front window to see who was there. He saw Tracy sitting in a booth with two other people. Next to her was a boy in a beret and turtleneck sweater. He wore a trim goatee and Elvis-style sideburns. A girl sat opposite them. Her short red hair looked liked combed fire. Their talk was animated in a way that made Gus feel out in the cold. Which he was. He took a deep breath and went in.

"Well, now there, then," he said, doing James Dean again and then feeling ridiculous now for doing it.

"The airman!" Tracy said. "What's the airman doing here?"

The others looked at him with benign contempt.

Gus thought: The airman. She's forgotten my name.

"Uh, coffee," Gus said, his voice almost inaudible. "Need to warm up."

"Sandra, move over," Tracy said. "Let the airman sit down. He might have something to contribute."

Gus, realizing that he'd been holding his breath, exhaled. The boy in the beret offered him a cigarette. Gus didn't smoke, but accepted it. Sandra, the girl with the fiery hair, gave him a light from her butane Zippo. Gus drew in the hot smoke, held it in his mouth, then let it out.

"So this is your airman, Trace?" Sandra said. Her saucy jokes-on-you laugh made Gus feel as though she'd spotted a flaw in his appearance—unzipped fly, a zit on his nose. She picked up her cigarette from the communal ashtray and took a deep drag. The ashtray was overflowing with cigarette butts, most of them with red lip prints.

"So what's your story, Peter Lorre?" Josh said.

Josh smiled in a way Gus didn't like. Gus didn't like Josh calling him Peter Lorre, either. It was a public put-down. Gus remembered Peter Lorre whining like a whipped dog as Humphrey Bogart slapped him around in *The Maltese Falcon*.

"This is Gus Reppo, Josh," Tracy said. "He's from the radar base."

"Aha," Josh said, "a noble defender of the faith."

"And what faith would that be?" Sandra said.

"The only faith we have," Josh said. "We worship the great unholy trinity—Many, Much, and More. Gus is its disciple and defender. Right Gus?"

"Could I talk to you for a sec, Tracy?" Gus said.

"Sure. Talk away," she said.

"I mean alone."

"You can say whatever you want right here. These are my friends, Gus. I've known them a lot longer than I've known you. I don't think we have any secrets between us that they can't hear."

"Speak up, Gus," Josh said. "Hell's bells, don't mind me. I'm a congenital smartass. If I've ruffled your feathers, I apologize."

"It can wait," Gus said.

"Maybe Gus would like to join the protest," Sandra said.

Gus looked at Sandra to see if she was setting him up. She looked like the type who could do that. She had attractive features but for some reason that Gus could not fathom she wasn't exactly attractive. It had to do with the unattractive thing that was going on behind her attractive features.

"How about it, Gus?" Josh said.

"I don't know what you're talking about," Gus said.

"We're going to Richland, over in Washington," Tracy said.

"Richland is where they make the plutonium for atom bombs. Isn't it curious that its called *plutonium*, after the god of the underworld? The Satan bomb. We're going to chain ourselves to the main gate of the Hanford works. We hope to discourage the Satan bomb."

"Why?" Gus said.

"Why not? If you believe in something, you do it. Otherwise you're just taking up space."

"You're not going to stop them from making plutonium," Gus said.

"That's not the point," Josh said. "The point is to *make* a point. We might spur others to take up the cause. Look what's happening in England."

"Bertrand Russell is leading the way," Tracy said.

"I don't think I'm allowed to protest plutonium," Gus said.

"Our hero!" Sandra said. She lit another cigarette. Gus's cigarette was in the ashtray with an inch-long ash. He hadn't picked it up since his first puff. Sandra looked at Gus through threads of smoke, her green eyes opaque as jade.

"We can't give up making our bombs while the Russians keep making theirs," Gus said.

"The age-old recipe for disaster," Josh said. "Pure and simple."

"They'd be playing the tune that we'd have to dance to," Gus said.

"Good God!" Josh said. "The poetry of the apocalypse, straight from the mouth of an American defender of the skies!"

Gus ignored Josh. "I don't think you should do this, Tracy," he said. "You could go to jail."

"I'm not afraid of spending a few days—months even—in jail. In fact, I hope they *do* arrest me. Can you just see the headlines? Coed Jailed Protesting Nukes. That would generate sympathy among the undecided, don't you think?"

Gus was sorry he'd said anything. He felt like an idiot, and worse—he felt that he was ruining his chances with Tracy.

"If you came with us wearing your cute uniform," Sandra said, "that would *really* cause a row."

"They'd put me in Leavenworth," Gus said.

"What's Leavenworth?" Tracy said.

"A federal prison in Kansas," Gus said. "The government doesn't fool around. I'd probably get ten years, maybe twenty. Hell, they might hang me for treason."

"Okay, count Gus out," Josh said.

"Ten years isn't much when you consider that the half-life of plutonium 239 is twenty-four thousand years," Tracy said. Gus watched her lift her coffee cup to her full lips. She seemed almost cheerful about what could happen to him.

"I'll call you, Tracy," Gus said.

"We're leaving this weekend for Richland," she said. "We'll probably be back by Monday, unless they decide to imprison us."

"Should score big points with your dad," Gus said.

"Is *that* what you think?" she said. "You think I'm doing this to humiliate my dad?"

"He doesn't figure into it?" Gus said.

"You bastard," she said.

"Sorry," Gus said. "I didn't mean it the way it sounded."

"Maybe you should go back to your radar base and hunt for phantom Russians," she said.

"They aren't phantoms," Gus said weakly.

"The flyboy has foot-in-mouth disease," Sandra said.

Gus left the Athenian, trying not to slink. Out in the street, the time-and-temperature sign on the First Intermountain Bank said -11.

He headed down Main. The city looked deserted. He was the only human being out on the streets. He looked at himself in the plate glass window of a hardware store.

"Good work, you idiot," he said.

15

A pink and white car pulled up to the curb ahead of Gus. The car, a Mercury Turnpike Cruiser, looked showroom new. The driver rolled the window down. "Want a ride, flyboy?"

Gus got in. "Nice car, Sandra," he said.

"It's my dad's. I get to use it when he's not. He likes to drive his old Studebaker. He won't let me touch that. Where to, airman?"

"No place special."

"Hell, we're already *there*," she said, laughing.

It was the same laugh, but this time Gus liked it. He didn't feel put down by it. In the Athenian, he decided, she'd been performing for her friends at his expense. Her laugh now was openly friendly and good-humored. Her features, which he'd seen as individually attractive but collectively unattractive, had relaxed into ordinary good looks. Gus marveled at the transformation. Was the change in him or in her? What triggered it?

"Where are your friends?" he said.

"Still in the Athenian, saving the world from itself."

"You don't sound convinced."

"The world is going to hell and people like Tracy and Josh are going to hell with it. It's like we're all in this big leaky boat headed for the falls and we're bailing with teaspoons."

"But you're going to Richland with them anyway."

"It could be fun."

"So with you it's a fun thing, not political?"

"It's always a fun thing. You were right on the money about

Tracy and her old man. She's going to have great fun watching him get steamed. People work out their kinks in ways that satisfy."

"What kinks are you working out?"

"Boredom. Boredom is the first circle of hell."

"I think you're too deep for me," Gus said.

"I'm not deep. I just try to stay on the qui vive."

"The key what?"

"It's French for staying alive to the situation."

"You go to college, Sandra?"

"Call me Sandy," she said.

"Your friends call you Sandra."

"My friends are incorrigible snobs. I love them dearly, but they're kind of uppity. Maybe you noticed."

"So *do* you go to college?"

"I'm a third-semester sophomore in philosophy and French at Northern Plains. What are your plans for the future, Gus? Going to make a career of the air force?"

"I don't have any plans," Gus said.

"Stay that way. People who plan out their lives are bores. Life just happens, plan or no plan."

"My life was planned out for me. That's why I joined the air force. I'm an escapee."

"A fugitive from boredom! But now you're stuck for what—four years in Milk River? How ironic."

"A little over three now," he said.

"A lot could happen in three years, even right here, in boredom's capital city."

"A lot has already happened."

She smiled at this, but didn't ask Gus to elaborate. "Ever been to the Milk River dam?" she said. "It's one of our famous tourist attractions."

They drove west on US Route 2. A few miles out of town she turned onto a narrow unpaved road. The almost-full moon turned the bare fields into flats of gray pewter. Sandy had the heater turned on high, but Gus could feel the outer cold pull heat from his body.

"Supposed to get down to twenty-five below tonight," she said. "After I finish my degree at Northern Plains, I'm going to find a job in Florida or California."

"Looking for paradise?" Gus said.

"Nope," she said. "I just want to be warm."

"Being warm isn't everything," Gus said. "I think northern Montana is pretty neat. I mean, there's nothing like it anywhere else."

"Good! There shouldn't be anything like it anywhere else! How many hells do we need? Maybe some place in Siberia comes pretty close. No one lives voluntarily in Siberia! People get sent there to be punished for crimes against the state." She looked at Gus and grinned. "Is that what happened to you, Gus? Are you being punished for crimes against the state?"

"I don't have anything against the state," Gus said.

"You might before you leave the air force," Sandy said.

"What's that supposed to mean?"

"Just a thought. Sometimes a thought just comes to me."

"Like you got a crystal ball?" Gus said.

"You just seem like the kind of guy that attracts trouble. You don't look for it, but it finds you anyway."

The road they were on suddenly sloped down to a gritty beach. Frozen sand crackled under the Mercury's tires. The big V-8's roar rose and fell as the rear wheels searched for traction in the cold sand.

The lake formed by the Milk River Reservoir stretched out flat and black under a waning gibbous moon. Sandy parked a hundred feet from its edge. She reached across Gus and opened the glove compartment and pulled out a pint of Southern Comfort. She uncapped it and offered it to Gus. Gus swallowed some and gagged.

"Too sweet," he said. "It's like cough syrup."

Sandy took the bottle from him and raised it to her lips. She tilted her head back and Gus watched her fine throat work as she swallowed. He leaned toward her but checked the impulse to kiss her throat while she was drinking. Too early for that sort of move.

She lowered the bottle. "All set?" she said.

"For what?"

She laughed and started the car. She gunned the engine and slipped the gear lever into drive.

"Whoa," Gus said.

"Hang on, flyboy," she said.

The car waffled, gained traction, then gathered momentum. It sank on its springs as it left the sloped beach and dropped onto the iced-over lake. The car slid sideways a hundred yards as the wildly revving engine suddenly had no load.

"Jesus Sandy!" Gus yelled above the roar. "The ice could break!"

She took her foot off the gas pedal and let the car idle in gear so that it moved more or less forward with some yawing as they skated toward the middle of the reservoir.

"It's been below zero for three weeks," she said. "The ice should be thick enough by now to hold us."

"You don't know for sure?" Gus said.

"That's why it's fun," she said. "If it doesn't get your blood moving, what's the point? You might as well stay home playing Chinese checkers in front of the fire."

That didn't sound so bad to Gus.

"Sometimes you eat the bear, sometimes the bear eats you," she said.

"Is that what you learned in your philosophy class?" Gus said.

"My grandpa used to say it. It used to seem dopey to me."

"But now it doesn't?"

"It seems clearheaded. Worthy of Sartre."

Gus didn't ask who Sartre was.

"Give the bear leeway," he said.

"Is that your philosophy of life?" she said.

"I don't have a philosophy of life."

"Sure you do. You just haven't faced up to it yet."

"You know what?" he said.

"What?"

"You're scary."

Ice crackled under the car. Gus felt the car lean left, as if the ice was softer on that side. The thought of drowning under the ice made him nervous. He imagined sinking to the bottom of the lake, the car slowly filling with icy water. The thought gave him the jitters but he wasn't about to beg her to go back.

Sandy seemed calm. Her calmness scared Gus more than the cracking ice did. She said, "Last winter a couple of high school kids drove a pickup out here and the ice opened up. The lake hadn't been frozen long enough. They weren't hauled out of the water with grappling hooks until spring. Their bodies were half eaten by pike."

"How do you know what's long enough?" Gus said.

"Stay cool, Gus. If you've lived here all your life, you get to know what's long enough by instinct."

Gus could sit atop a swaying hundred-foot radio mast in a gale without a whisper of fear, but the thought of drowning under the ice, his body feasted on by pike, chilled him to the marrow.

He picked up the pint of Southern Comfort and took a long pull. When he finished, he gave the bottle to Sandy. Her lips parted, stayed parted a moment, then accepted the bottle. Gus thought: She's going to kill us but she's got great lips.

She put gradual pressure on the accelerator and the car picked up speed in a more or less straight-line direction. When she got the car up to forty miles an hour she hit the brakes and turned the wheel a full revolution and the car went into a wild spin that made her shriek with laughter.

Centrifugal force crushed Gus against the door. The car rotated like a helicopter blade and she slid toward Gus on the slick plastic seat-covers, raising a static charge that lifted strands of her hair. Gus put his arm around her, his hand found a breast, he tried to kiss her. A blue lip-to-lip spark snapped between them. They both jumped.

"Forget it," she said. "That's not what this is about."

"What *is* it about?" Gus said.

"Thrills, flyboy."

When the car stopped spinning Sandy pressed down on the accelerator again to build up speed. They were headed for the dam's spillway at thirty miles an hour.

"I think I've been thrilled enough," Gus said.

He thought he could hear the ice separating under the tires. His right foot stomped the floorboard as if the car had an extra brake pedal.

"There's a hundred foot drop on the other side of the dam," she said. "We can't go over it because the dam's nowhere near full, but we can make a run at it and maybe ride up the berm and get close to the top. Maybe close enough to look down the spillway."

"Why?" Gus said.

"Why not?"

"Why don't we just shoot ourselves and get it over with."

"Don't think that hasn't occurred to me, but where's the fun in that?"

She let up on the gas and the car gradually slowed down. When they were a hundred feet from the damn, she hit the gas again and turned the wheel hard and they slid sideways, coming to rest against the upsloped berm. "I guess this will have to do," she said.

She turned on the radio and searched the dial for music. She found a station in Canada playing polkas, another one in Wyoming playing Patti Page's "How Much is that Doggie in the Window?" She made a face and twisted the dial until she found a Denver rock and roll station. She turned up the volume, pulled a hooded fur-lined parka out of the back seat and put it on. They got out of the car and climbed up the ice-crusted berm to the top of the dam. Gus walked to the edge and looked down at the spillway, about a hundred feet of steeply sloped fill.

"Be careful," Sandy said.

Gus laughed.

"What's funny?"

"You drive two tons of steel across a frozen lake and you want *me* to be careful?"

"Touché," she said.

Gus walked the length of the dam. At one point he did a handstand, then walked on his hands on the edge of the spillway's hundred-foot drop.

"You don't have to prove anything to me, Gus," Sandy said.

Gus was happy to hear her voice tighten with concern. "Stay cool, Sandy," he said. "I'm part monkey."

They sat down on the berm and finished the bottle of Southern Comfort. Gus tossed the empty down the spillway. He pulled off his hood and tried to kiss her again. Sandy turned her head aside.

"What's wrong?" he said.

"I can't believe you don't know," she said.

"Know what?"

"Men can be so damn thick."

"What are you talking about?"

"I'm not going to move in on Tracy. I'm her best friend, for God's sakes."

"Tracy? What's Tracy got to do with it? She thinks I work for Satan. I'm the plutonium kid."

"You've got a sizeable blind spot, Gus. Tracy likes you a lot, in spite of your drawbacks."

"Not after tonight."

"Don't make too much of that," she said. "Tracy's got a temper, but she doesn't hold a grudge."

Somehow that didn't make Gus feel better.

"What if I said I was more attracted to you than to Tracy?" he said.

"I'd say you were lying."

"Maybe you'd be wrong."

"Any whichway your compass needle points, is that it?"

Buddy Holly was singing "I'm Looking For Someone to Love."

Sandy stood up, found her footing, then pulled Gus to his feet.

"Let's dance," she said.

Hooded in their parkas, they danced to Buddy Holly on top of the Milk River dam under the moon and stars.

16

Sandy took Gus to the Beanery, an ancient Chinese restaurant next to the railroad yards. Gus had a skull-cracking headache. They ate noodles in hot sauce, sweet and sour pork, and spring rolls. Sandy ate with chopsticks. Gus twirled his fork through the noodles, watching her eat. She ate as if it were her first meal in days. Like a Chinese rail-splitter, Gus thought. No self-consciousness, no delicacy, no reluctance.

"What other suicidal pastimes do you have besides driving your father's new car across frozen lakes?" Gus said. He touched the lump on his head, the source of his headache.

"Sometimes I fall for losers," she said.

"I'm either lucky or screwed or both," Gus said.

He meant it as a joke, but she didn't smile. They looked at each other so intensely that they both blushed.

"I didn't peg you as a loser," she said. "I could be wrong. I hope I am."

Sandy dropped Gus off at his parents' house. He didn't explain why Flora and FDR were living in Milk River. She had to be curious, but didn't ask. He was thankful for that.

He'd hurt his head by banging it against the Turnpike Cruiser's roof. Sandy had gunned the car as it approached the beach to make sure it didn't get stuck halfway up. The shock of hitting the sand catapulted Gus off the seat. His head slammed into the padded headliner of the steel roof. It knocked him out for a few seconds. By the time they got back to town he had a tender lump on the top of his skull and a headache he felt down to his teeth.

Sandy consoled him with a goodnight kiss. It started as a heatless brush of lips, but it lingered several seconds and then developed into a full engagement of energetic tongues.

She broke away first. "Uh-uh, no way," she said.

"Maybe I'm one of your losers," he said.

"Whatever you are, this stops here."

Gus got out of the car, thinking he really might be one of her lucky losers. That seemed twisted enough to qualify for Ray Springer's shithouse rule.

"Where have you been?" Flora said. She was seated at the kitchen table, a glass of Rhine wine in her hand. The record player was on. Mantovani's "Charmaine." "We waited dinner on you, then went ahead and ate it cold."

"Something came up," Gus said.

"Something always comes up, it seems," she said. She was more than mad, she was distant, as if a line had been crossed and there was no going back.

"I'm sorry, Mommy," he said. "It was a crazy night. I got involved with some people. I couldn't get out of it."

"I don't expect you to explain, Gussie," she said.

She poured herself another glass of wine. "Charmaine" ended and another Mantovani piece came on: "The White Cliffs of Dover." It sounded just like "Charmaine" to Gus. Beatless music to lull you into a coma.

"Where's FDR?" he said.

A choked-off laugh stuck in her throat like a chicken bone. She cleared it out. "FDR? He went to bed an hour ago. His stomach was sour and he had to take a bicarb. There's a sliced roast in the fridge. You go ahead and eat something, Gussie."

"I'm not hungry," he said.

"You really should eat. You're skinnier than ever. You're skinnier than *he* ever was."

She raised her glass. She kept her eyes on Gus as she drank, making an effort to keep him in focus.

"Skinnier than FDR?" Gus said. "FDR's never been skinny."

"Did I say FDR? I didn't mean FDR."

"Who *did* you mean?"

She sat up and straight in her chair. "I don't know if this is the right time to tell you. There may never be a right time."

"Tell me what?"

"About Orson Gunlocke. My God how odd that name sounds. I haven't said it aloud in years."

"Someone we know?"

She emptied her glass and then refilled it. Her eyes lost focus again and seemed to be looking at something beyond the kitchen wall. She smiled fondly, then frowned, then started crying. Tears spilled down her plump cheeks.

"No," she said. "We don't know him. He was a figment of time and foolishness."

"You're not making a lot of sense, Mommy," Gus said.

"It's never made a lot of sense."

"*What* hasn't made a lot of sense?"

"You look so much like him, my darling boy," she said. She reached her hand toward Gus. He leaned away.

"Maybe you should stop taking Milltown, Mommy," Gus said. "I think the drug is messing you up. You're not tracking."

"What can I do about it?" she said. "What can anyone do about anything? Sometimes things happen and it's like an avalanche. You try to get out of the way, but you can't. How can flesh and blood be expected to stand against an avalanche?"

"Jesus Christ," Gus said under his breath. He went to the fridge and took out the sliced roast. He made a half sandwich with tomato, onion, and lettuce. He wasn't hungry. He was still full of noodles and sweet-and-sour pork and spring rolls and the memory of Sandy's mouth on his, but he thought it might make Flora feel better if he ate something she had prepared. And as she watched him eat she seemed to gather strength.

"When you're young," she said, "you're all good looks and confidence, isn't that so? Age and time, and all the stupid mistakes, shape your final self. The one you were meant to be. Don't you agree?"

"Why are you asking *me*?" Gus said.

"Don't you know? No, you don't. You *settle* into what you really are and what you've always secretly been. Yes, secretly! It often isn't pleasant when it comes out. You didn't want this ugly gosling, did you? So you adopt a version of yourself you can live with."

"By you you mean you, right?"

"And everyone else. The easiest person to lie to is yourself, Gussie. It's true! Great men in high places lie to themselves and so become great fools, or great monsters. But this is well-known. They've documented it and they will document it again and again in the years to come. It's not a news bulletin."

She refilled her glass, drank half of it, then filled it to the brim again.

"Maybe I shouldn't be saying these things to you, Gussie. I don't mean to frighten you into a solitary and loveless life, away from all the complications and miseries of mistaken involvement—never knowing the joys and disasters of a life fully lived. No, that's not what I mean to do at all. I just want you to know that I'm human, human as you, human as your father."

"And therefore fucked up," Gus said.

Her face, which had been bravely unmoved by her speech, suddenly collapsed. She began to sob silently. She fought against the emotion and didn't recover until another record dropped on the spindle. Mantovani's soaring strings played "I'll Be With You in Apple Blossom Time."

"Oh! Isn't that lovely!" she said, dabbing at her tears with a paper napkin. "This song speaks to my heart every time I hear it. It's so sad, so hopeful, and such a damn *lie*. You know they'll never see each other again, in apple blossom time or in any other blossom time. I mean the lovers. But they had their time, their moment." She reached for Gus again and this time he didn't back away from her touch. She stroked his cheek with her damp fingertips.

"Who is Orson Gunlocke?" he said.

"He was a penniless sharecropper from the Oklahoma panhandle. The terrible drought ruined the land he worked. The winds carried the good soil away. Nothing could be planted, and if it was planted it did not sprout. And then the landowner told him he had to leave, the bank was taking back the land. He was left with nothing, not even food. He ate out of garbage cans and for fresh meat he killed squirrels and doves with a slingshot. He hitched rides to California with just the clothes on his back, eventually stopping at our door hoping to find some kind of work. I gave him a sandwich—roast beef, like the one you're eating now! I watched him eat with tears in my eyes, his hunger was so terrible. He was so thin and gaunt, so ruined by things that were not his fault. I hired him to take care of our lawn and shrubs, and for odd jobs around the house. He excelled at plumbing and electricity. This was before the war."

"Orson Gunlocke," Gus said, testing the syllables.

"He called me Queenie, because I was like a queen to him. 'Queenie, might I have a glass of water?' he would say. 'Queenie, my shoe leather is so thin I can see my toes. Does your mister have an old pair he won't miss?'"

"Queenie," Gus said, trying out the word. He hated it, but in a comical way it fit. He stopped a grin twitching like a tic at the corners of his mouth. "Really, Mommy. You should back off on the Milltown."

"At first it was ordinary human compassion. Then I made my mistake: I fell in love with him. I so wanted to make him happy. I even considered leaving FDR, but when it came time to decide I couldn't bring myself to do it. I was a coward caught between love and comfort. I didn't think I was a coward at the time. I thought I was being sensible. Now I know. I know exactly what I was then and what I am now. A sensible woman, a coward."

The bread and beef in Gus's mouth was dry as cardboard. He couldn't swallow. He took a beer out of the fridge. After a minute he said, "Does FDR know he's not my father?"

"We never discussed it. What would be the point? He's a very good man. I think he's always known you couldn't be his son, but he raised you as if you were. He loves you, Gussie."

"I look like an Okie named Orson Gunlocke," Gus said, more to himself than to Flora. "Where is Gunlocke now?"

"I don't know. The last I heard he was married and living in Chula Vista. He sent me a letter informing me that he'd found work in a defense plant. I wrote that he had an infant son named Gus. I never heard back. Then came Pearl Harbor, and the world was never the same."

"So everything worked out more or less for the best," Gus said.

"Please don't be mean, Gussie. Yes, it all worked out. We made our separate lives. Sadness and regret were part of those lives. But that's the way of the world. You'll see."

"The shithouse rule," Gus said.

She looked stern for half a second, then she hid her face in her hands and sobbed. "Please don't hate me," she said, her voice tiny and wet as it bubbled between her fingers.

"Tell you what," Gus said. "Why don't you take some Milltown and go to bed? Take the whole damn bottle."

Gus felt ashamed of his outburst but not ashamed enough to say he was sorry. He went to his room and flopped down on his bed. His skull ached. He put the pain out of his mind and thought of Sandy. He relived their parting kiss, improved on it, then fell asleep.

He woke before daylight, thinking: *They've kept me in the dark, all of them.* He understood that he needed to find out who he was, who he was not, and who he might have been.

17

They deplaned into the hot Santa Ana winds of Southern California, then dragged themselves and their B-4 bags out to the freeway to hitch a ride to Lyle's place in North Hollywood. They were wearing their sheepskin parkas over their winter blues. The plane was a bare-bones C-47 left over from the war—no heat in the back compartment, no insulation. Steel bucket seats lined the fuselage wall. At altitude, the temperature had been sixty below. Overheated and sweating in their arctic gear, they looked as out of place on Sepulveda Boulevard as elephants on the moon.

Curiosity and pity got them rides. Two hours later a farm truck loaded with citrus dropped them off at Tujunga and Weddington, six blocks from Lyle's house. The driver gave them a sack of oranges. They peeled and ate oranges as they trudged through the neighborhood.

"Fantastic place," Gus said when they reached the Dressen house, a flat-roofed modern structure. A grand bougainvillea vine with its million blooms covered one wall of the house. Lemon trees, birds of paradise, and oleander bushes filled the front yard. Ice plant with yellow and orange flowers lined the walkway to the front door.

"They can't afford it," Lyle said.

The house was empty. They went to Lyle's room and got out of their winter gear. "Let's go for a dip," Lyle said. He rummaged around in a dresser for swimming trunks. A pair Lyle had worn in grade school were small enough for Gus.

The pool was behind the house, just beyond a brick patio big enough to play tennis on. The pool was shaped like a kidney and had two diving boards, one three-feet above the water, the other ten feet up. Lyle climbed the ladder to the high board and cannonballed into the pool. Gus jackknifed in from the low board.

"Who the hell is violating my goddamned swimming pool?" The voice came from behind an oleander bush.

"Hey, Pop," Lyle said. "It's me. This is my buddy, Gus Reppo."

A man stepped out from behind the shrubbery. He was big-bellied and bald, wearing Bermuda shorts and a Hawaiian shirt. His sweating face was florid and thick. He had a martini in one hand, an electric hedge clipper in the other. "Aren't you supposed to be in the army defending the nation somewhere?" he said.

"Air force, Pop. We got some leave time and caught a hop from Malmstrom. We go back in three days."

"I've got the afternoon martinis made. You boys can have one. I guess if you're old enough to bleed for your country, you're old enough to have a martini."

Gus and Lyle climbed out of the pool. They went into an atrium off the kitchen to dry off. Mr. Dressen went into the house and brought out the pitcher of martinis.

"Where's mom?" Lyle said.

"Don't have the slightest idea," Mr. Dressen said. "Probably trading lies with her fancy Brentwood friends. I thought you joined the army, Lyle."

"No sir. I joined the air force."

"Not that it matters a hell of a lot," Mr. Dressen said.

"Matters to me, Pop," Lyle said.

Mr. Dressen looked at Gus. "What about you, Gus? You gung ho like Audie Murphy here?"

"I guess so, sir," Gus said.

"Well good for you," Mr. Dressen said without interest. He picked up his clippers and went back into the bushes.

Gus and Lyle carried their martinis into the kitchen. Lyle opened the fridge and took out a plate of cold cuts—cheese, sliced tongue, and deviled eggs.

After they ate Lyle showed Gus around the house. The living room was white carpeted and big enough to house a semi trailer. It was full of light from the floor-to-ceiling windows that filled an entire wall. A grand piano occupied one end of the room.

There were some framed photographs on the piano. A platinum blonde with metallic skin and blood-red lips looked out of an ebony frame. The woman didn't look real to Gus. She looked like a manufactured product—one of those movie star photos anyone can buy at Woolworth's. The photo was signed, "Best Wishes, Lorena Lamb."

"Believe it or not," Lyle said. "That's my old lady. She's even scarier in real life."

"She's kind of beautiful in a way," Gus said.

"She was in movies for a while, twenty years ago. Bit parts, mainly. She was a body double for Jean Harlow once. She hasn't worked much since then, but she keeps an agent. Lorena Lamb is her movie name."

"Who plays the piano?" Gus said.

"Nobody. It's decoration."

Lyle took Gus out to the garage. Two identical pale blue 1956 Cadillacs sat side by side. It was a three-car garage. One space was empty.

"Mom's got the Bentley. She won't drive a Cadillac, even though Pop sells them. 'Ordinary people aspire to the Cadillac. Uncommon people aspire to the Bentley.' That's her philosophy of life in a nutshell."

"I thought *my* family was fucked up," Gus said.

"You don't know the half of it, Reppo," Lyle said.

Gus saw a motorcycle parked in front of one of the Cadillacs. "Whose bike?" he said. It was blue and had a chrome gas tank.

"Mine," Lyle said. "It's a BSA Goldstar. The best damn bike

ever. It'll beat any stock machine on the road. I've had it up to a hundred ten and the tachometer was still climbing. I didn't come close to redlining."

They went back into the house.

"I hate to desert you, Reppo," Lyle said, "but I'm not going to stick around. I've got a girlfriend in Van Nuys. I'm going to spend my time over there. I don't like leaving you with my folks, but it can't be helped. You get hungry, grab what's available. Or you can walk out to Tujunga. There's a few small restaurants close by. We had a cook for a while, a Swedish woman, but she couldn't deal with Mom and took off. Mom can't boil water without scorching it but she'll tell a professional cook how to stuff a squab. Go figure."

"You hate your folks?" Gus asked.

"You see something here not to hate?"

"They're your *folks*, Dressen."

"I don't hate them. I hate what they do. Or what they don't do. Or how they think. That doesn't leave much, does it? Yeah, I guess I hate them. What about you, Reppo? You hate Mr. and Mrs. Reppo?"

"No."

"No? That's it?"

"I don't hate them. I pity them."

"Pity's worse. Is that why you enlisted? Because you pity them?"

"I enlisted to get away from them."

"But you don't hate them. Sounds like hate to me. You run from the things you hate. Am I missing something here?"

Gus got on the BSA. "Let me use this while you're in Van Nuys," he said.

"You know how to ride?"

"How hard can it be?

PART THREE

18

Gus let himself into the house with a spare key hidden in the garden shed. The deserted house was, and was not, as he remembered it—everything the same but somehow not the same. Recognizable, but part of a past the details of which he'd have to rethink and reconstruct. He felt he'd been away for ten years, not less than one. He'd grown up here, sheltered from Flora's secret. Maybe it was FDR's secret, too. The secret that now cast a new and darker light on every word that had been spoken and every gesture that had been made within these walls.

He looked out the sliding glass doors that opened to a patio. He imagined Orson Gunlocke leaning on a rake, looking through the glass doors at Flora, the grin on his face familiar to her now. He imagined her unlocking the door and the door sliding open and Gunlocke saying, "Queenie, might I have a glass of cold water?" and Flora taking him inside where Gus, a nonentity—less even than a forethought—became a physical presence in the world.

He searched the Chula Vista section of the San Diego phone book and found only one Gunlocke: M. A. L. Gunlocke, on a street that intersected Kearny Avenue. He thought about it for a while. He thought about it while he showered. Thought about it again while he shaved. He thought hard, thought maybe this was a mistaken impulse and that he should end his side trip into the past and go back to LA.

He went through his closet looking for something to wear. He picked a decent pair of bleached Levis out of his stash, a soft cotton shirt, white gym sox, and a pair of penny loafers he hadn't worn since high school graduation.

He brushed his teeth and combed his hair. He walked through the house twice, turning wall switches on and off and checking the windows to make sure they were still locked. He went outside and stood in the patio and looked down at the ocean and the tide that rode into the rocks of La Jolla Cove. The house was on a high cliff and the thunder of the incoming waves was baffled by distance. He took a deep breath, smelled the cool briny air.

The ocean was gray, the sky above it was gray. On the horizon the sun was wrapped in a silver scarf of fog. He decided to walk down to the beach, to revisit the sound and feel of it, and in the same instant realized he was stalling. Back in the house he dialed the number for M.A.L. Gunlocke.

"What now?" a weary female voice said.

"I'd like to speak to Orson Gunlocke," he said.

"So would I," she said. "Orson Gunlocke was killed in the war. If you think this is a smart thing to do or that I am amused by it then you are sorely mistaken, whoever you are."

"My name is Gus Reppo."

"You and the vipers you work for have no hold on me."

"Mrs. Gunlocke? Is this Mrs. Gunlocke? Orson Gunlocke's widow?"

She hung up.

That should have been enough. It wasn't. It only increased his curiosity. Gus redialed the number but she didn't pick up. He jotted down the address on a scrap of paper. He locked up the house and headed south to Chula Vista on the Goldstar.

The house just off Kearney was a 1940s tract house—small, shallow-roofed, visibly out of plumb, and in need of paint. A hastily made government-financed bungalow built with barely cured wood, one of many in the area meant to house the influx of defense plant workers during the war and returning veterans after. A weedy patch of dirt that passed for a lawn fronted the house. A bent TV mast rose from the middle of the roof like a long skeletal finger. There was no antenna on it. Black cable, like a rotten vine, swung out from the mast in the ocean breeze. An old lopsided two-door Ford sedan sat in the driveway. The front right tire was flat, the windshield on the driver's side was cracked. The tire looked like it had been flat for months. Stickers in the back window of the Ford said, "Jesus is Lord" and "He is Our Mainstay."

Gus took a deep breath and knocked on the door.

The woman who opened it said, "No again to you sir, I do not want . . ." Her mouth yawned open. A meaningless sound came out of it. She swayed and staggered. Her eyelids fluttered. She took a step back. Her knees locked, unlocked, buckled. Her arms flew out from her sides like windblown rags. Gus reached for her, grabbed a handful of her dress. The dress tore and she sat down hard and flopped, knocking her head on the carpetless floor.

Gus crossed the threshold and knelt down beside her. Her eyelids fluttered open; her breathing was noisy and fast. Gus got an arm under her shoulders and raised her to a sitting position. He got behind her and hooked his elbows under her armpits, dragged her toward a sofa. He propped her up against it. She reached up and touched his face.

"Orson," she said.

"Gus," he said into her searching fingers.

"I must have toppled," she said.

"Yes, ma'am, you sure did."

He helped her get to her feet, then eased her down on the sofa. She leaned back into the cushions, staring at him. Her breathing was audible. She was a slight woman in her early forties with pale hair cropped unevenly below the ears. She had the face of an undernourished Dust Bowl refugee—angular, thin-lipped, sharp featured. Her eyes were a startling arc-welder blue, uncomfortable to meet for more than a few seconds. The skin around them was etched with deep crow's-feet. Gus believed her crow's-feet did not come from habitual smiling.

"Orson," she said. "You come back."

"I'll get you a glass of water, ma'am, then I'll go," Gus said. "I'm sorry to have bothered you."

Gus found the kitchen and let the cold water run for a minute before filling a glass. There was a picture of Jesus thumbtacked to the wall above the sink, the standard picture available in most five-and-dime stores. A neighborly, kindhearted Jesus with perfect Painless Parker teeth. His beard was trimmed and combed as if someone had gotten him ready for the portrait painter.

Gus went back to the woman in the living room. He handed her the water. She set it aside and stood up. There was another picture of Jesus on the wall above the sofa. It was almost the same as the one in the kitchen, except this Jesus was not smiling. This Jesus was troubled, and less comfortable having his portrait painted.

The woman took a framed picture off a radio console and showed it to Gus. The man in it was small boned, his smile more smirk than smile, his flinty eyes hard but also touched with amusement at someone else's expense. He was standing next to the Ford out in the driveway. In the photograph the car looked new. Gus was looking at himself in a navy blue jumper and bell bottom pants. The picture was signed, "Orson."

"Was Jesus brung you back," she said.

Gus took a step toward the door. "You're not thinking straight, ma'am," he said. "I'm Gus Reppo. Airman Gus Reppo. I'm stationed at an air force radar squadron in Montana. Seems that Orson, uh . . . worked for my mother, before the war."

"Orson," she said.

"Gus," he said. "Gus Reppo. Me and my friend, Lyle? We took some leave-time to spend a few days in LA and so I thought I'd drop by and say hello since I had the opportunity."

She turned her head sidelong and studied Gus aslant, her eyes narrow. "I bet you're hungry," she said. "I'll get up some eggs and grits. Don't have much else in the house right now."

"That's okay, ma'am," Gus said. "I had something to eat before I came here."

"They told me the *Fisk* went down off Guadalcanal," she said. "It was torpedoed by a Jap sub. All they was doing was taking supplies to those poor bogged-down marines. The Japs had no reason to sink the *Fisk* since it was unarmed. But that's how they was back then."

She waited for Gus to agree. "I guess they didn't split hairs over such things during the war," he said.

"The King of Heaven took him for his own reasons," she said. "That's how it was and how it still is. So if he was brought back to me, there must be a reason in that, too. Nothing happens in this world without the Lord put his stamp on it."

"There's no reason needed for things that can't happen, ma'am," Gus said.

She laughed harshly. "You talk like an idiot," she said. "I guess you're just joking me like you used to. Is that right, Orson?"

"Gus," he said.

She whirled around and stalked into the kitchen. The thin cotton housedress she was wearing flared and light from the kitchen windows silhouetted her skinny legs.

Gus headed for the door. There was no need to prolong this. But she came out of the kitchen on the run and grabbed his arm. Her grip was strong. "No sir," she said. "You can't just up and go. That would not make *any* sense, can't you see? Come sit at the table with me. Don't be afraid, if that's what you are. Is that what you are, *afraid*? Do you feel that I am haunting *you* instead of you haunting *me*? Is that how this is going to work?" She laughed at this preposterous idea. Her laugh made Gus want to bolt.

Gus said, "I'm not afraid, I just—"

"Then come set. Where's the harm?"

She towed Gus into the kitchen and pushed him down into a

chair. She fried him an egg and dipped warm grits out of a tin pot. She poured him a cup of coffee.

"Eat up," she said. "You come a long way, Orson."

Gus searched for something to say that would make things seem ordinary.

"Something happened to your TV antenna," he said.

She touched her thin lips with her finger and narrowed her eyes as if deciphering the hidden meaning of his words. "TV is a tool of Satan," she said.

"But you have a mast on your house," he said.

"I sometimes wanted to see what he's been up to," she said.

"But you can't, with no antenna. Do you even have a TV?"

"The TV is in the bedroom closet," she said. She said this with deliberate indifference and Gus could tell she wanted her TV out of the closet and working again.

"I can get it working for you," Gus said.

"Is that so?" she said. "And why would you want to do that?"

"Because I can," Gus said. "No other reason."

"You think not? Reasons sometimes hide themselves in the dark, unbeknownst to them that thinks they got it all figured out."

"It's still light" Gus said. "I can probably get it working before dark."

"That's not half of what I meant," she said.

"I can do it," Gus said.

"Do what you will, if you think it's you who wills it."

Gus found the wind-wrecked antenna in a backyard shed along with a wooden ladder. The antenna—a big one designed to pick up distant stations—wasn't in bad shape. He straightened the elements as best he could, then brought it out into the yard. The double X-style antenna was bulky but not very heavy and Gus carried it up the ladder to the shallow roof. He loosened the turnbuckles that held the guy wires tight, unseated the aluminum mast from its roof mount, then telescoped the mast into itself so that he could get at the section that needed to be straightened. The rubber exterior of the coaxial cable was weathered but the copper wire inside, and the braided shield that protected it, look serviceable. Gus clamped the double X antenna to the top of the mast, aimed the array in the general direction of Los Angeles, then raised the entire apparatus to its dominant position above the house. The job took less than an hour. "Satan's back in business," Gus said, looking up at the quivering elements.

Gus went into the bedroom and opened the closet door. The TV set was buried under a pile of laundry. It was a late 1940s Crosley table model with a seven-inch screen. Gus carried it out to the living room and set it on top of the radio console after removing the picture of Orson Gunlocke. He brought the coaxial cable into the window closest to the TV.

He plugged in the Crosley and turned it on. It hummed as filaments and cathodes turned red. Dust, rising on convected air from the heated vacuum tubes, made him sneeze. A warped gray-on-gray picture sidled gingerly into the screen. Gus adjusted the horizontal stabilizer and contrast controls, then turned the channel selector until he found a stronger station. He rotated the fine-tuning knob until there was more picture than snow, more sound than noise.

He called her into the room. She'd been on the telephone, arguing with someone.

"You can get five channels now, Mrs. Gunlocke," Gus said. "Three local, and two from LA. All but one comes in real strong."

"I won't have you calling me Missus. You call me Marva, as is proper," she said.

"Marva," he said.

They sat down together on the sofa and watched *Kukla, Fran, and Ollie.*

"Satan's work," Marva said, but her eyes belied her words. She was spellbound by the fuzzy puppets.

19

"They wear bow ties and talk like they are your friend, but I know them for what they are," Marva said. She meant the bill collectors who had been harassing her over the past few weeks. The phone rang again but she didn't answer it. It rang a dozen times before it stopped. It was early evening, not dark yet, but Gus hadn't been able to leave. She'd found other chores for him and, for reasons he could not identify, he felt obligated to comply.

He got the spare tire and jack out of the Ford's trunk and replaced the flat. The spare had only a few pounds of air in it but would probably hold up until she could get to a filling station.

Her toilet leaked. The reservoir tank lost its water a few minutes after flushing. Gus fixed that by reseating the flapper so that it nested on the drainpipe squarely, and by adjusting the rusted chain that pulled it up and lowered it. He unscrewed the ball cock from its corroded shaft and reset the float angle so that the tank would not overfill.

She asked him to look at the bedroom door. The jamb was out of plumb and the door wouldn't close. It stayed inches ajar even if you put your shoulder to it. Gus couldn't do anything about that, short of taking the door off its hinges and planing the edges to match the warp. Gus didn't ask her if she had a plane. He was sure she didn't. The kitchen table needed to be repainted, but he was sure she didn't have paint, either.

"You always been a good man around the house, Orson," she said.

"Gus," he said.

She snapped a dishrag at a fly then sat down at the kitchen table. She peeled chips off the flaking paint with her fingernail. "I don't know what I am going to do," she said.

"I need to get back on the road before dark," Gus said.

"They're coming over with the truck," she said.

"It's not my motorbike. Lyle won't want me riding it in the dark."

"They got wind of my new Shelvador. They got people who find out such things, like what you got and when you got it and what it might be worth."

"I'd hate to wreck it," Gus said. "The Goldstar's a beautiful machine."

"They got no *conscience*. They take it away, no matter how sorely you need it. You listening to me?"

"What?" Gus said.

"The *church* got me a new Shelvador refrigerator on sale for a hundred dollars," she explained. "I had a old wartime icebox, but you can't hardly get a twenty-five pound block of ice anymore, and then you got to go ten miles to fetch it. Even then stuff spoils. Milk will turn after four days. Bacon will show mold in two weeks. If you forget to empty the drip pan, like I often did, the overflow warps the floorboards. The good people of my church took up a collection and got me the Shelvador."

"And the bill collectors want to take it?" Gus said.

"Agency men are on the way over with a truck. Those are the ones who don't wear bow ties and don't pretend to be your friend."

Gus met the collection agency men at the door. "She can't give up the Shelvador," Gus said. "Her food will spoil."

The collector was a big man in work clothes. His name was stitched over the shirt's single pocket: Frank Keller. Another man in denim stood behind him leaning on a yellow hand truck.

"You her boy?" Frank Keller said.

"He is my husband," Marva said, stepping next to Gus and taking his arm in hers.

The agency man looked at Gus, then at Marva. A grin struggled at the corners of his mouth. He turned to look at his partner. His partner covered his mouth with his hand and looked away.

"How much does Mrs. Gunlocke owe?" Gus said.

Frank Keller opened a leather-bound account book. "Nineteen dollars and ninety-seven cents on three accounts. Five months past due on all three."

"So you come into her house and take anything of value you want?"

"That's how it works, Bud."

Gus took out his billfold. He had twenty-six dollars. He gave the man twenty.

"There's another payment due in a month," Frank Keller said, digging in his pocket for pennies.

Gus closed the door.

"You were directed to do that," Marva said.

"A simple thanks would do," Gus said.

"You took on the responsibility like you were meant to, even if you did not mean to. You going to deny *that*?"

She pulled Gus into the living room and made him sit down next to her on the sofa. The TV set was still on. "The Show of Shows," a comedy revue, had just started.

"There's nothing funny about that man," Marva said of the TV comedian. "He makes me want to bite the heads off nails."

Then someone was at the door, tapping out what sounded like the rhythm of a secret code.

"That'll be Josiah Comfort and Becka," Marva said. "I forgot to remind you. This is the night we take stock."

Gus started to get up but Marva pulled him back down. "Wait," she said. "I want to watch this first."

It was a beer commercial. A man and a woman sitting in deck

chairs under palm trees drinking Lucky Lager while Mexican trumpets played a hat dance. The announcer said, "Really now folks, can life get any better than this?"

"You see?" Marva said. "They make it seem God-sent instead of what it is, hell-sent."

Josiah Comfort at the door tapped out the coded rhythm again. The commercial ended with the beer-drinking couple toasting the good life by clinking bottles. They lit cigarettes, and turned to the camera, their smiles inviting the viewer into their pleasant world.

Marva got up and went to the door. Josiah Comfort, in black suit and hat, stepped into Marva's living room—a craggy man with furious eyes set in dark hollows. His wife, an exhausted-looking woman, with a worried forehead and sparse white hair, followed him in. Behind them an overweight boy of six or seven bulled his way over the threshold. The boy wore short pants and knee-high socks. His lips were cherubic but he had the sour expression of an old man with gout. The Comforts went directly to the kitchen and sat at the table. Marva drew Gus into the kitchen after them.

"This is our Saturday evening Take Stock meeting," Marva explained to Gus. "We're Mainstays of the Lord. Josiah is our pastor. This here's Becka, the pastor's wife. They visit the flock one door at a time, Saturdays. I would not have the Shelvador if it was not for Josiah and the flock."

She pulled out a chair for herself and sat down.

"Do we have a new supplicant?" Josiah said, looking, finally, at Gus.

"It's Orson come back!" Marva said.

Josiah weighed the possibility. He studied Gus, studied Marva. "It's *like* Orson come back," he said.

"Yes," Marva said. "That's what I meant to say."

"There *is* a semblance," Josiah allowed.

Marva, unable to contain herself, said, "When I first laid eyes on him I toppled! It's a miracle!"

"It's *like* a miracle," Josiah corrected.

"Yes, that's what I meant to say," she lied. "It's just *like* a miracle."

"The time of miracles is long gone," Josiah said. "We are at the end of times. Chaos and desecration are upon us, not miracles. Mankind is played out, and God has turned his back. We need to take stock. The day is coming when things will be put right."

Becka Comfort whispered "Amen."

The child looked into the Shelvador without asking. He helped himself to a slice of American cheese which he folded into quadrants. He brought the folded cheese to his mouth and his mouth yawned open mechanically like a hinged trap. He had more teeth than seemed natural—tiny blunt pearls that would have looked more at home in the jaws of a large rodent. He finished the cheese and went back to the Shelvador, his salivating mouth anticipating another slice.

"Corky Comfort!" Becka said in a shouted whisper. "You must always *ask* sister Marva before you take!"

Marva held back comment as she watched the boy peel a second slice of cheese out of the cellophane wrapper. She wanted to take the cheese away from the boy, wanted to tell him that he was not to open the Shelvador, but she also wanted to seem generous to the Comforts—after all, there'd be no Shelvador without them. The boy ate the second slice of cheese, ignoring his mother, who seemed to live in a state of permanent distraction and was no longer focused on Corky's unabashed snacking. Having finished with the American cheese, Corky opened the bread box and removed a hard dinner roll, which he quickly nibbled down to crumbs.

When he was done foraging, Corky planted himself on his mother's lap. His ample flesh made him seem larger and heavier than Becka but he snuggled up to her as if he were a two-year-old. Becka appeared uncomfortable under the child's weight but she did not push him away or complain. Corky laid his head on her chest and sucked his thumb noisily. Becka stroked the boy's silky locks—an open act of adoration. Corky seemed to drowse, though under their half-closed lids his eyes were active. He studied Gus and Marva, making secret appraisals. He watched Gus for a time, then shifted to Marva, then back to Gus, then back to Marva. The knowing eyes, satisfied with what they saw, closed.

Marva said, "Orson here fixed the television."

"Do not call him Orson, daughter," Josiah warned. To Gus he said, "What is your name, son?"

"Gus Reppo," Gus said. "I'm in the air force, on leave."

"And you are not attempting to deceive Mrs. Gunlocke for personal gain?"

"No sir. Not at all."

"He fixed the Ford like he knew it from having done it before," Marva said with guarded defiance. "He also fixed my leaky commode—ball cock, flapper, and all. Orson always was a expert with the plumbing."

Josiah weighed Gus's worthiness a second time, again finding him innocent of poor intentions. He turned to the Bible he'd brought with him. He opened it and read:

"'A great star fell from heaven blazing like a torch and it fell on a third of the rivers and on the fountains of water. The name of the star is Wormwood and a third of the waters became wormwood and many men died in the waters because it was made bitter.'"

Josiah looked up from the page. "Could it be any clearer than that?" he said. "Could the Lord's final disposition of fallen humanity be laid out more plain?"

"Amen, amen," Becka whispered.

Corky stirred in Becka's lap. He withdrew his glistening thumb from his mouth and opened Becka's blouse. His chubby fingers worked the buttons with practiced speed. He reached in, retrieved a thin, elongated breast. He raised the dark nipple to his lips and began to suckle. Becka allowed this without resistance or embarrassment, as if Corky receiving his mother's milk on demand was commonplace and never contested.

When Corky had satisfied himself he sat up straight and said, "Can we go home now? When we gonna pray? I wanna pray *now* so we can go *home*." Becka buttoned her blouse. She tried to hush the boy in constrained whispers but Corky arched his back defiantly and slid between her knees to the floor where he bellowed his displeasure.

With the others distracted by Corky's tantrum, Gus sidled out of the kitchen, recognizing an opportunity to escape. He went out to the front yard where he'd parked the Goldstar.

The weather had changed. It had started raining and a hard wind was coming off the ocean, which gave him second thoughts. Riding the Goldstar was easy enough, but the roads now would be wet and slick. And it was dark. Not good conditions for an experienced rider, much less for a novice. He went back inside. He turned on the TV and watched a boxing match.

While he watched he could hear Josiah talking. His voice was full of trembling intensity. "'. . . the beast that ascends from the bottomless pit will make war upon them and conquer them and kill them and their dead bodies will lie in the street of the great city which is called Sodom.' In our day, my fellow suppliants, *all* cities are called Sodom!"

As if perfectly timed with Josiah's emphatic words, one of the boxers knocked out the other.

Josiah said a brief prayer, then declared the Taking Stock meeting over. Josiah, Becka, and Corky filed out of the kitchen and out of the house.

Marva saw them out, then turned to Gus. The session had affected her. She looked radiant, as though taking stock had heated her blood. "Tomorrow," she said, "we are going to the Mainstay Tabernacle over in Lemon Grove."

"Mrs. Gunlocke . . ."

"I told you before, do not call me Mrs. Gunlocke. You *know* my name."

"Marva, you've really got things mixed up," Gus said.

"You're the one mixed up!" she said.

"Josiah thinks *you're* the one mixed up."

"Josiah don't *know* what I know. He can't see you like I see you. You maybe fooled him, but you do not fool me."

"I'm Gus Reppo."

"So you say, but a lie is a lie whatever name you put on it."

"You're telling me I don't know who I am," Gus said.

"I'm telling you, you will know who you are before this night passes."

Gus shrugged. There was no arguing with the convinced.

"We won't have any trouble getting there now we got the car," she said. "Listen to me, Orson. You hear Josiah preach in the tabernacle, you will flat topple. People topple every Sunday. It is a thing to behold! After they topple they are cured. You will be cured of your doubt."

"I don't think so," Gus said.

"You don't listen too good, do you?"

"That's what my mom says."

"Your mama got you figured!"

She put her hand on his arm. She squeezed his biceps in spasms timed to underscore her words. "Let's not talk about it for a while," she said. "We have time, and things will sort out by morning, you'll see. You are tired after your long journey over the waters. You need to rest your mind, which is stuck in the mudflats of confusion just now."

She opened the sofa into a bed and brought out sheets and pillows from her bedroom closet. "You sleep here tonight," she said. "I'll make grits and eggs tomorrow and then we can drive to Lemon Grove."

Gus didn't argue. He figured he'd get up early and whether it was still raining or not, he'd make good his escape on the Goldstar.

Marva went into her bedroom and closed the warped door as best she could. Gus watched the little TV until after midnight. Then he made up the sofa bed and turned in.

The sofa bed had a steel crossbar under the thin mattress, level with his kidneys. He kept waking up with sharp back pains. He turned sideways to avoid the steel bar, legs drawn up in fetal repose. When he finally fell asleep it was almost dawn.

The dream started as a thought, a plan of escape. He felt the Goldstar under him, throbbing powerfully. He saw landscape flying by. He cut through traffic but it wasn't southern California traffic, it was US Route 2 traffic, coming into Milk River from the west. He could see the river on his right, grain elevators on his left, the tall sky above. He twisted the throttle and the bike went airborne on the viaduct and then he was with Sandy in her Turnpike Cruiser sliding broadside across the ice of the Milk River reservoir.

"Kiss me, Orson," Sandy said. And he kissed her in front of his parents' house, his mother's face grieving in the window, only now Sandy did not make him stop. Her lips were surprisingly hard and dry and he was surprised again when he reached under her dress and found she was not wearing anything underneath it.

This discovery excited him further and Sandy said, "You go on and work her good, for it is your right! I knew this was goin to happen, it was fated! I foretold it for I have the gift of prophecy!" Though puzzled by the way she spoke, he entered her thrusting hard, and her lean thighs pressed with uncommon strength against his kidneys. Her hands clamped his neck, squeezing his jugular, and he saw wheels of light turning in the dark air. When she started uttering non-words like a certain sect of believers speaking in tongues, he realized that he was not dreaming and that it was not Sandy under him clawing his neck and back and pulling his hair and ears and slapping at his shoulders and buttocks, it was Marva Gunlocke, his dead father's insane wife. He stopped mid-thrust, stunned by the horror of it, but she locked her legs on him and wouldn't let him pull away. She said, "You keep on workin it! You *got* to keep on! It's your right and *duty* to finish what you begun!"

He made his mind blank and kept on until it would not have been possible to stop, and when it was over she let him rise.

"You see now how *right* that was?" she said. "There can be no question in your mind! You don't just look like him, you *are* him! You are Orson come back to me! You even *do* like him—all rabbity like. I got chillbumps down to my feet! Looky here, my toes are still splayed out like they was cramped. You done me *right*, Orson, like you always did!"

"Orson's dead, Mrs. Gunlocke," Gus said. "I am Gus Reppo."

"Go ahead. Say it a thousand times. Make *me* out the one can't see things straight. It won't change the truth."

"I am Gus Reppo, I really am Gus Reppo," Gus said.

"*I* know who you are! It's you that don't know who *you* are!"

Gus showed her his dog tags. "This proves it. My name and air force serial number are stamped on them. Call the Pentagon, tell them my serial number. They'll tell you who I am."

"Show me anything you want. Show me pictures of you in baby clothes. Show me your school picture. Show me pictures of the gal you left back in Cimarron County. It don't mean nothing. Orson come back the only way he could figure to come back— as himself in body and soul, but taking a false name."

"I am Gus Reppo," Gus said. "Always have been."

"Reppo!" she scoffed. "Who ever heard of such a thing? It only shows how the Lord deals out hints and clues. There is no Reppo, never was. After the *Fisk* went down Orson's spirit rose up out of the darkling waters and he spanned the great ocean itself and he found you, his spit and image, and then he went down *into* you, like the *Fisk* went down into the deep, and some years later when he figured the time was right he made you come to Chula Vista to fulfill what he was intended to fulfill but couldn't because of the Jap torpedo. That's why you did what you did. And that's why you are wrong to think you are some fool boy named Reppo when the *facts* say you are Orson Gun-locke—heart, body, and mind."

She stood up and smoothed her wrinkled nightgown around her narrow hips. "Anyhow, it's sealed now. You can't undo what you done. Maybe you think you can, maybe you think you just had a good time with a poor helpless widow, but that's because you are blind as a doorknob and can't see the truth underneath the deed. That's where the truth lies, *underneath the deed.*"

"It was a dream . . . I don't see . . ."

"That's right! You don't see! You're blind to the truth!"

"I was with Sandy in the dream, and then she wasn't Sandy, and you were there . . ."

She covered his mouth with her hand. She said, "Dream is just another side of waked-up which itself is part of a bigger dream too big to ponder by the likes of you and me."

She stroked his hair. She picked up his hand and kissed it. There was nothing in her eyes to suggest insanity except for this sudden uncharacteristic tenderness.

"I am going to get us up some breakfast now," she said. "And then we are going to the tabernacle. You get yourself into the bathtub. I don't want the smell of rut befouling sanctified air."

20

Gus stepped on the starter. The weak six-volt battery barely turned the crankshaft and the carbon-caked spark plugs fired indifferently. When it finally caught Gus kept the accelerator pinned to the floor listening to valve clatter and fan belt screech. The car shook like an old dog rising out of dream. Gus revved it until it moaned.

He backed it out of the driveway and into the street, then shifted into first. The car bucked ahead in neck-snapping jerks. Marva's Sunday hat fell off twice. When Gus forced the shift lever into second the going was smoother, but it backfired and balked in third. The engine had no power in third.

He drove to Lemon Grove in second, never exceeding twenty miles an hour. The car left a blue haze of smoke behind it. Gus stopped at the first gas station he saw. He told the attendant to fill the tires and to put a dollar's worth of gas in the tank.

"After church I'll have to go back to LA," Gus said.

Marva smiled, as if humoring a stubborn but unclever child.

"Lyle will be worrying about his motorcycle," Gus said. "And then we have to be on the plane Tuesday morning or be counted AWOL."

"Those lost at sea are not considered willful absentees," she said. Her tone suggested a superior knowledge of such matters.

Gus felt lost at sea. He felt seasick. Marva's grits were greasy and her partially cooked eggs were strung with clear mucous. For toast she blackened slices of stale bread under the oven's broiler. Her coffee, made from twice-used grounds, was bitter and gritty with an acidic aftertaste. Some eggshells she'd packed into the percolator's basket to restore flavor and clarify the coffee found their way into the pot. Gus choked on a fragment.

Another aftertaste, one from the previous night, soured his thoughts. None of it was his fault—he needed to believe that. Marva had planned it. She was the instigator. But he hadn't pulled away from her after he realized what was happening. He'd needed to finish it. Needed to hear her unchecked gibberish rise in pitch and volume as she worked herself up to a sharp climactic yelp.

He thought: I'm so fucked up.

Not as fucked up as she is.

But that's not an excuse, is it?

Do I need an excuse?

Everyone needs an excuse.

Not everyone. Just the fucked up.

"I hear voices," she said cheerfully. "Is that you talking to yourself, Orson dear?" She put her hand on his knee. The hand traveled to his thigh.

"If I stay, they'll come and get me anyway," Gus said. "They'll lock me up for the rest of my enlistment and give me a dishonorable discharge."

"If it came to that, I would wait for you. But you musn't worry about things that are not ordained. You are safely home now, Orson. Please try to understand that."

The car sputtered along, the engine revving and failing to rev, the steering wheel shaking violently and transferring the shake to Gus's hands, chest, abdomen, and legs. He felt overpowered and invaded, his grip on sanity pried loose, finger by finger.

Marva pointed out a plain, one-story flat-roofed building made of whitewashed concrete blocks. "There's the Mainstay Tabernacle," she said. "We're right on time! You see? You are running on a schedule you didn't even know you had! Things are coming to a head, Orson! See how things turn out? Are you beginning to understand what is happening to us?"

"I am not," Gus said.

He slipped the gear lever into neutral and the car stopped shaking. They coasted smoothly into the parking lot. Gus set the brake and they got out of the car and went into the church.

Josiah was sitting motionless in a high-back chair next to a lectern. His head was bowed and his large-knuckled hands were clasped. Marva and Gus took seats in a middle pew. There were about forty people in the church. Becka and Corky sat up front, facing the lectern, along with several other women and their fussing kids.

The organist, a piously smiling fat man in black-rimmed glasses and tangerine suit, struck a note. He held the note longer than needed then added a second note. It was the first chord of a hymn. The congregation recognized it, and they stood up and began to sing:

> Oh weary soul the gate is near
> In sin why still abide?
> Both peace and rest are waiting here
> And you are just outside
> And you are just outside.

After several more choruses, Josiah stood up behind the lectern and cleared his throat. The music died. "Everyone deceives his neighbor," he said. "And no one speaks the truth."

His voice was barely audible—a practiced technique—and the congregation, some with the hymn's lyrics still on their lips, leaned forward. Some elderly worshippers cupped their hands behind their ears or fiddled with the buttons on their hearing aids.

"Their tongue is a deadly arrow," Josiah continued, a little louder now. "Each speaks peaceably to his neighbor . . . but in his heart he plans an ambush!"

This last phrase fell on the ears of the flock like a thunderclap. Josiah raised his head now and for the first time leveled his scouring eyes on the assembled. An emotion twisted his austere features into a mask of contained fury. A woman gasped. A man coughed as if he'd been struck in the throat. Josiah closed his text.

"What is the street address of hell?" he asked.

He waited, as if someone might be foolish enough to answer such a question.

"I'll tell you what it is, although you already know it! Hell is right here in Lemon Grove! You—*you* brought it in with you! I can smell it on you!"

The shocked congregation looked at one another. Josiah's voice quelled their mumbling confusion.

"This could not be true, you say! We are God's beloved, you say! You ask, has Reverend Josiah Comfort lost touch with reality? Is that what you are thinking? Of course that is what you are thinking!"

He waited until the congregation regained its composure.

"*Hell*, my dear brothers and sisters, my fellow sinners, is *possibility*," he said. "You—and me—are all inheritors of possibility. One step this way, one step that way, and you are in it, up to your neck!

"The white worm curled about the cherry's stone—this is what possibility brings. The worm thrives at the core of flesh! Death, dear friends, *inhabits* life! I say to you destruction *lives* at the core of great accomplishment! And eternal life is *present* in the *core* of what must decay!"

Gus thought: The shithouse rule.

Josiah began to read again from his prepared text and Gus stopped listening. He drifted into a reverie of the previous night, almost believing that it was all a dream, a sexual nightmare, and that none of it had actually happened.

The last few months of his life took on a dreamlike feel. The radar squadron—did it exist? Did Milk River exist? Flora and

FDR—were they his parents or did he belong in some nonlegal but binding way to Orson and Marva Gunlocke? Why was he named Gus? How odd was it to think of your baby as Gus! Who in their family was Gus? None of his uncles, great uncles, or grandfathers was named Gus. Who was he named after? Why wasn't he Henry or Roger or Paul? Those were popular names among his high school classmates. What was wrong with Larry, Jeff, or Walt?

Gus, still unaware of the increasing pitch and power of Josiah's sermon, looked at Marva. She seemed possessed. Her eyes were wide and her lips trembled. He touched her hand but she didn't seem to notice. "I am going to topple," she said quietly. Gus looked around him. The congregation, on their feet now, swayed like reeds in a punishing gale. It was an undulating sway—to the right then to the left then back to the right—a swaying governed by the rhythm of Josiah's driving sermon. Some of them swayed too far and lost their balance, and the pews and aisles began to fill up with toppled worshippers.

Marva caught Gus's shirtsleeve, ripping a stitch at the shoulder seam. Then she lost her grip and she sank to the floor next to his feet, her face twisting helplessly in a fit of ecstasy as her body twitched.

Her hat rolled away. Gus went after it and saved it from being crushed by another toppler, a large woman in enough blue gingham to equip a small boat with sailcloth.

Marva gabbled as she had gabbled in the sofa bed the night before. He wanted to cover her mouth with his hand, thinking that her gabbling was a coded confession of forbidden acts that everyone, even the toppled, could hear and decipher.

Then something happened. Gus was rocked by a tidal wave of sorrow. He was sorry for Marva, sorry for the Mainstay flock—most of whom were poor people looking for their weekly topple that somehow sustained them through their dreary lives. He felt sorry for Josiah, who, every week, had to bring forth the spirit that made them topple. He felt sorry for burned-out Becka, beleaguered mother of the dreadful Corky.

And he felt sorry for himself for having stumbled into their world. Sorry—and fearful—that he might not break free of it, and that if he did, sorry for the wreckage he'd leave behind.

He helped Marva to her feet and she leaned weakly against him. He felt moved to do something for her, some final gesture before he left for Los Angeles, a gesture that would make her feel her fantasies had some basis.

"I feel strange, Marva," he said.

"You do? Then let it come *on*, Orson! Don't you fight it!"

Gus stepped out into the aisle and toppled, careful not to hit the floor too hard. He heard Marva chortle and clap her hands. Gus faked a herky-jerky convulsion embellished by twitches of his arms and legs. He let his eyes roll back, let spittle form on his lips.

"Jesus God Almighty!" Marva said. "My unbelieving husband done toppled!"

Gus heard Josiah's passionate exhortations rise above the gabbling crowd. He watched through slit eyelids the swaying of those who had yet to topple. He heard their gabble and gabbled a little himself. When he felt he'd been down long enough to please Marva, he decided to get up.

But he couldn't. His legs wouldn't bend at the knees and his arms wouldn't bend at the elbows. He felt nailed to the floor. His eyes fluttered shut and stayed shut and he couldn't reopen them. He took in huge sobbing lungfuls of air but that did not end his paralysis. Somewhere above him Marva said, "Let it work itself out, Orson, you stop fighting it. Do you no good to fight it."

He made himself relax by taking slow, easy breaths. As he relaxed he felt himself sink through the tabernacle floor. He was still afraid, but his fear now was manageable. He sank through the concrete floor of the basement, and then into the interior dark of the earth, and he kept sinking until he was suspended in watery green light.

His fear was replaced by curiosity, the curiosity replaced by expectation. What he expected was not clear to him until he saw that the green light he was suspended in was the ocean, and on the floor of the ocean, half a mile away, was a sunken ship. He walked toward it until he could see its markings.

"The *Fisk*," he said.

He entered the old Liberty ship by the torpedo hole that sent her down. In the engine room, sitting on a ruptured steam pipe, was Orson Gunlocke.

"You come a long way for this, son," he said.

Much of Orson had been blown away by the torpedo blast. Shredded flesh like white seaweed undulated from his exposed bones. Half his head had been shorn neatly off on a vertical axis as if by a table saw. Small fish came and went, taking what they wanted of what was left of him. What hair he had looked like it was still on fire.

"Why am I here?" Gus said to the empty bones.

"You tell me," Orson said.

"You're my father."

"Maybe you've come to claim your inheritance."

"I'm responsible for your death."

"How do you figure that, boy?"

"You had a safe job in a defense plant. They weren't going to draft you. You joined the navy because of me."

"You're half right, but that aint the whole story."

"Flora wanted you to marry her even before you knocked her up. But you were already thinking of marrying Marva. After you found out about me you enlisted."

"You got that plumb wrong, son. Your mama would never give up her rich dentist and her La Jolla house. No way."

"She admitted that. I didn't believe her."

"Believe her, kid. I was born to be poor. Look at Marva. What'd I give her except a hard time?"

"She never said that. She loved you."

"She's crazy, maybe you noticed. You put the blocks to her, didn't you? Banged her like you meant it. You must be a bit off the beam yourself. Looks like you got a little of me in you, boy. Maybe more than a little."

"You're not mad at me?"

"The dead don't get mad."

"And you've been dead a long time."

"No, only since this morning. We got torpedoed ten minutes before breakfast."

"That was in 1944."

"This is 1944."

"No, it's 1957. I was five in 1944."

"You don't get it, do you? It's always 1944. Time stopped for me right here. It'll stop for you some day. If that doesn't kill you, nothing will."

"That doesn't make sense."

"Work it out boy. It comes up on you fast. You only get a short time to figure it out."

Someone touched Gus's eyes and they opened. It was Josiah, leaning down. "Get up," he said.

Gus sat up, movement in his arms and legs restored. He got to his feet with Josiah's help. "What happened?" he said.

"You toppled, son," Josiah said.

"He toppled like he was meant to topple!" Marva said.

"He flat double toppled!" someone added.

A crowd gathered around him as if he'd done something unusual. As if they hadn't seen such a toppler as Gus. Their voices came to him like a single voice:

> *The young unbelieving agnostic flat toppled!*
>
> *Boy howdy! The stranger dropped like a rock!*
>
> *He bears the weight of a momentous guilt.*

For doing WHAT we may never know or want to.

I surely would like to learn the truth of it.

Must be a deadly thing to put him down like that.

But that was a healing topple if I ever seen one!

I wonder though if this boy made the grade.

Corky, leaning against his mother, smiled his yawning rodent smile. "I seen *way* better topples than that," he said.

Gus and Marva left the church. In the car Marva said, "What did it feel like, what did you see?"

"I was under a mile of water," Gus said, shifting into second gear.

"A mile of water!" Marva said.

"But I could breathe and walk. I walked to the *Fisk*."

Marva turned white.

"Yes," Gus said. "I saw him. I mean, in the dream."

"Was no dream," she said, her unsteady voice somber.

"He was blown apart, but could talk. How could that not be a dream?"

"It was a visitation."

"Whatever," Gus said.

Gus was not happy with himself. He'd toppled like any other ignorant member of the flock. You had to believe what they believed to succumb to toppling, and he didn't, or at least had no opinion one way or the other. He'd toppled deliberately, to please Marva. But then his topple became genuine. He felt he'd been conned as he once had been on the Mission Beach pier, losing two dollars in five minutes to a blind shell game artist.

"I told him I was responsible for his death," Gus said.

"You told *who*?"

"Orson."

"Why did you say *that*?"

"You don't know?"

She squirmed in her seat. She looked out at the passing scenery as if it interested her. She fidgeted. She sat on her hands to keep them still. She bit her lip. "'Course I don't know," she said.

"He worked for my mother, the dentist's wife, in La Jolla. She fell for him and he knocked her up. When he found out about me a couple of years later he joined the navy. Orson's my father. Because of me he's at the bottom of the ocean feeding the fishes. I killed him, more or less."

She gave Gus a narrow look then offered him a riddle: "How can a man be his own father by another mother then cause him, more or less, to die at sea? Answer me that and I'll give you a dollar!"

"Not possible," Gus said.

"So quit your nonsense, Orson! I never could abide your fool notions!"

"You didn't know about the dentist's wife?"

Marva sneered. The corner of her lip rose, exposing a long eyetooth. Her nostrils flared and quivered. "That fat old harlot!" she said. "I knew about her! When you couldn't find regular work, she took you on for four dollars a day. After two years of trimming her hedge you wanted to be shut of her. You wanted to go back to Oklahoma but there was nothing there for you. When the war came you got the job at the airplane plant for eleven dollars a day."

"Why do you think Orson went to war when he had a safe defense plant job?" Gus said. "Was that one of his fool notions?"

"It always grieves me to think about that."

"He wanted to get away from all three of us. The dentist's wife is my mother, and Orson is my father. And you are a certified nutcase."

Marva seemed not to have heard Gus. She said, "Oh, you should have seen you topple, Orson! You went down like you'd been knocked on the head!"

Gus touched the back of his head, feeling for lumps. He'd rather believe he'd been sapped from behind by an overzealous parishioner.

"Things are going to go back like they was," she said. "You going down like that was a sure sign that things are changing for the better."

Marva told the story she wanted to hear. She amended or deleted the parts that threatened the outcome: "We'll gas up the car and go to Mexico," she said. "We'll get married again in Tijuana, like before. There's a Justice catty-corner from the Fronton Palace where they play that High Lie game. That's where we got hitched the first time for two dollars. Then we'll drive down the coast to that big hotel at Rosa Rito Beach. We'll sell that motorbike of yours, maybe get a hundred dollars for it. That will pay for our honeymoon. It'll be like it was before, those Mexican boys in white jackets bringing us pork chops and Coca-Colas in that balcony room that looks out on the ocean. We'll have us a child this time. I'm not too old to bear. The seed I have in me now should take. We'll name him August, after your great granddaddy who fought in the Civil War. We're getting our second chance, Orson! What more could a normal human being want?"

It was not a question Gus felt qualified to answer. He pulled the sputtering Ford into her driveway, set the brake, and shut off the engine.

Marva got out and went into the house. Gus sat there for a while, listening to the hot engine tick.

He thought: Wasn't Gus a nickname for August? If she had a child and named him August wouldn't the child be called Gus? Would that child somehow be *him*? He felt a weakness come over him stemming from a collapse in his ability to think things out in an orderly way.

He laid his forehead on the steering wheel.

He thought: I can't allow such ideas to put down roots.

21

Gus didn't follow her into the house. He got out of the car and went directly to the Goldstar. He switched on the ignition and stood on the crank. Marva came out of the house on the run, the baleful whites of her eyes bright with madness, her lips compressed into a thin bloodless line. She had an eight-inch kitchen knife in one hand and a claw hammer in the other. Gus jumped on the crank again and the engine caught once and died. He pulled out the choke. He rocked the bike side to side to shake out possible air locks in the gas line.

"No you *don't*!" Marva yelled. "*No* sir!"

The Goldstar was cold; it was reluctant. It didn't want to start. Gus slapped the gas tank. "I've got to go, Marva," he said. "I can't be AWOL."

"You aint in the navy anymore, Orson! Get that out of your head! You come home to me best way you could! Home is here, Orson! The war is over and done with! God gave you and me a second chance. Can't nothin be done about that! Or do you think you can gainsay the Lord? Listen to me, Orson, you ran off to war for some fool notion but you are back now and you are going to stay back!"

Gus pushed the choke back in and stood on the crank again. The engine caught. It grumbled as if aroused from sleep then gave a throaty cough and roared. Gus toed the gear lever into first and eased out the clutch. Marva trying to deliver a blow snagged the back of his shirt with the hammer's claw. She ripped it down to his waist. He lost his balance and stuck out a leg to keep the bike on its wheels. The bike carved a dirt-spraying circle around her yard. Marva walked through the spray swinging the hammer at him. It glanced off the back of his head. The world went instantaneously green. He thought he was back in deep water, on his way to visit Orson Gunlocke again at the bottom of the Pacific, but he shook off the effects of the blow and gunned the engine.

"Topple!" she screamed. "Topple him Jesus!"

Gus ran another circle around the yard trying to keep the bike on its wheels. Marva closed in on him and stuck him twice with her kitchen knife, high on the shoulder and down on the arm. Gus held the bike upright by keeping one foot in the dirt. He straightened the wheel and gunned it. The bike leaped out into the street.

Marva threw the hammer at him. The hammer sailed past his head and came to rest across the street. A man who had come out of his house to pick up his Sunday paper, did a clubfoot tap dance to avoid the spinning hammer. "Crazy goddamn bitch!" he yelled, then carried his paper back to the safety of his front porch.

"I'm done toppling!" Gus yelled over his shoulder. He stood the Goldstar on its rear tire and almost lost it again. He slowed down, then looked back to see if she was still after him. She was in the street, hopping on one foot and then the other, waving her bloody knife.

Gus headed north at high speed as if pursued by the Furies. He roared through National City then slowed as he passed the Naval Station on Harbor Drive. He took Pacific Highway to La Jolla Boulevard then turned into the street he grew up on, Spindrift Drive.

The house was damp and cold from the recent rains. He turned on the furnace and went into the master bedroom. He peeled off the remnants of his bloody shirt and checked out the cuts on his back and arm. She hadn't put her weight to the knife. Either she'd lost her grip or a remnant of sanity made her soften her thrusts. But she had a strong grip, strong as a man's. Gus concluded that the halfhearted stab was a consequence of sanity temporarily diluting her madness.

The bleeding had stopped. He wet a washcloth and mopped up coagulated blood around the cuts. He found a bottle of iodine in the medicine chest along with a roll of gauze and adhesive tape. He cleaned the cuts with soap and water then swabbed them with iodine. Her knife might have been clean but there was a good chance it was not. Marva Gunlocke did not keep a spotless kitchen.

Gus taped bandages over the cleaned cuts then touched the tender spot at the back of his head. No blood there, just a small lump. He found an ice pack, filled it with ice cubes from the fridge and went into the living room. He turned on the TV, then found an unopened bottle of brandy in the liquor cabinet. He cut the seal with his thumbnail, unscrewed the cap, filled a tumbler to the brim.

He carried the brandy to the easy chair—FDR's chair—opposite the big Capehart TV. He set his brandy on the antique trestle stand next to the easy chair, careful not to spill. He turned on the TV, then held the ice pack on the back of his head. He pressed his head against the chair's padding, holding the ice pack in place that way.

The Lucky Lager commercial he and Marva had watched on her little Crosley came on. The attractive couple under the palms were more attractive in full color. Their welcoming smiles and relaxed manner presented a vision of sane living that made the selling of beer incidental. "Really now folks, can life get any better than this?" said the smooth announcer.

"Probably not," Gus said.

He got up and went into the kitchen where the telephone was and called her.

"My husband paid up the collection people," she said.

"It's me, Gus Reppo," he said. "I wanted to tell you that I'm all right. The cuts didn't go deep."

No response, just her little TV in the background with the voices of a religious forum all talking at once.

"Marva?"

"You still don't know, do you?" she said.

"It was a mistake, my coming down there to see you."

"You will go to your second grave ignorant," she said.

She laughed—the dry cackle of a wise crone who'd taken the measure of a fool.

"I guess this is another mistake," Gus said. "I just wanted you to know I'm okay, in case you were worried."

"Worried? About *you*? I have better things to worry on."

"Tell me something I don't know."

"You sound stupid drunk."

"I was stupid for coming to your house," Gus said.

"You can't walk away from it sinless," she said. "Did you think of *that*?"

"I'm sorry," he said.

"Sorry won't undo the child."

"Child? There is no child."

"You can add that to the store of things you don't know."

"Marva, I'm sorry . . ."

"Sorry is the hypocrite's favorite word."

"Sorry's all I got."

"You'll be a far sight sorrier when the reckoning comes. And it will come, you'll see. The child will see you dead."

She waited a few seconds, then hung up.

Gus slept in FDR's and Flora's overstuffed bed that night and got up late the next morning. A dense fog had rolled in from the ocean. He took a shower, rebandaged his cuts, put on clean clothes. He turned off the furnace and locked up the house. Then headed north on the Goldstar.

Visibility on the highway was less than fifty feet. The fog was so thick Gus felt he could part it with his hands like drapery. When he turned the Goldstar into the Pacific Coast Highway north of Torrey Pines he lost all sensation of speed even though the speedometer said fifty. Fifty was too fast in such conditions. He backed off to forty, then thirty. Thirty felt no different than fifty. He looked down to see if the pavement was moving under him. This bit of foolishness made him laugh at himself. Even so, he could have been riding a treadmill on a stage with no scenery. There were no visible objects, left or right, to give him the sensation of progress.

He worried about cars coming up behind him blind. They might see him too late. He pulled off the road to let traffic pass. He stopped to assess his situation but left the motor idling.

Stopped felt no different than not-stopped. Zero felt no different than thirty. The looming shapes of cars slipped by, soundless except for the hiss of tires on wet pavement. Like dreams of cars, they appeared and disappeared in uncertain intervals. The cars—gray blurs with nondescript human shapes behind the steering wheels—seemed made of fog, not steel.

A plump child in the back seat of a slow-moving sedan waved at him. The child pressed its face against the window and smiled. The red mouth against the glass was like a gastropod attached to a hull. The mouth had an abundance of small teeth. The fat tongue moved like a pink eel against the glass. For a moment Gus thought the child was Corky Comfort. He shook off the thought. When he looked again to make sure, the car was re-swallowed by fog.

Gus eased out the clutch but kept the Goldstar on the highway's shoulder. He held his speed to thirty, even though he could not sense motion. Gus thought: I'm going to be killed if I stay out here.

He left the highway at Encinitas and stopped at a café called the Breakwater. He went in and took a seat at the counter and ordered the seventy-nine cent breakfast special—two eggs, two strips of bacon, toast, and hashbrowns. Coffee was ten cents extra.

Other drivers had the same idea. They filed into the café like the survivors of a shipwreck. Gray shapes outside the café became recognizable human beings in the fluorescent lights that hummed like hornets above the tables and booths. They all ordered the seventy-nine cent breakfast special.

"Pea soup out there," one driver said to another.

"I've seen worse," the other answered.

"The hell you say. Where?"

"San Fran. London. Erie PA."

"What about you, gorgeous?" the first man said to the waitress. "Good looker like you seen worse?"

The waitress took offense at the man's flattery. She was not gorgeous. She was short and stocky and had a large, red-spotted nose. Gus thought: She's had her fill of liars.

She gave the man his food then turned her back on him and went into the kitchen. It was an open kitchen. The customers could watch the cook fry eggs. The waitress said something to the fry cook. The cook, a large solemn man, looked at the man who had offended her.

"Touchy as a prima donna," the man said, ducking away from the fry cook's stare. He chuckled and wagged his head bashfully so the fry cook and others would see that he'd meant no harm by his remark. He was a good guy, a harmless wit.

After that they all fell too silent eating.

Gus mopped his plate with a piece of toast and finished his coffee. He put a dollar on the counter and headed for the door.

"Good luck, kid," said the man who'd seen worse fog in San Fran, London, and Erie PA. "If I were you I'd wait it out. It should burn off by noon. Take a stroll on the beach. Do a little beachcombing. No telling what you'll find. My wife once found a Distinguished Flying Cross some joker left behind. We use metal detectors."

Gus didn't take the man's advice. At Newport Beach he turned east and got on the Santa Ana Freeway hoping to escape the fog but the fog had moved inland. If anything it was denser. In Anaheim the only visible objects were the towers and spires of Disneyland. They rose out of the fog ominous and white, like spell-casting fingers.

In East Los Angeles the sun had burned off the fog. Gus twisted the throttle and the Goldstar roared with unrestrained relief. The world was simple and clear again, weighted with massive slabs of concrete and steel and dappled with bright patches of color all the way to the snowcapped San Gabriel Mountains. He got to Lyle's house in the early afternoon.

"Where've you been?" Lyle said, inspecting the Goldstar for nicks.

"San Diego," Gus said.

Satisfied that his motorcycle hadn't been marred, Lyle said, "Welcome back to the war zone. Ricky and Lucy are at each other's throats again."

They went inside. Mr. and Mrs. Dressen were sitting in the dining room. A platter of pinwheel sandwiches and a pitcher of martinis were on the table. The martini pitcher was less than half full. The sandwich tray was untouched.

"I've wasted my life," Mrs. Dressen said. She lit a cigarette, blew smoke dramatically toward the ceiling.

"That's what life's for—to waste," Mr. Dressen said. "It's our one absolute no-strings-attached luxury. How have I wasted thee, let me count the ways."

"I don't want to hear your nihilistic bullshit today," Mrs. Dressen said. "My fatal mistake was marrying a self-justifying cipher like you."

"And yet my income is substantial, your comfort uncompromised."

"Dumbfuck luck," she said.

"My favorite Chinese dish," he said. "Dumbfuck luck with

potstickers. Seems to me you've done all right for a no-talent stand-in for Jean Harlow."

Lyle and Gus escaped into the patio before Mrs. Dressen could mount a counterattack. They sat in wicker chairs facing the pool. The sunlight reflecting off the water was green and cool.

"I'm never getting married," Lyle said. "How about you?"

"I'd rather be a priest," Gus said.

"Too drastic. If you were a priest you'd never get laid. You'd have to pound your pud twice a day to get some relief or butt fuck a fellow padre and then tell your confessor all about it. All that pussy out there would be off limits. You stray one time, the pope deep fries your cojones."

"If getting laid means getting all tangled up in stuff you didn't know was there and never wanted any part of, then I'd *ask* the pope to deep fry my cojones."

"Jesus, Reppo. You're what—eighteen, nineteen? How tangled up can you get at nineteen? You have a bad experience in San Diego?"

"It's not about how old you are," Gus said.

"You just don't know the ropes, Reppo. I think you got it into your head that getting laid has something to do with obligation. You got to stop thinking that way."

"Obligation is just the beginning."

"OK, you got laid in San Diego, and now she figures she's got controlling interest of your ass. Does that about sum it up? Take it from me, airman. She doesn't."

Gus thought: the only woman I've ever satisfied belongs in an insane asylum. A trend? Takes a nut to screw a nut?

Mr. Dressen came out and sat down with Lyle and Gus. He opened a pack of cigarettes and offered one to Lyle. To Gus he said, "How about you, kid? You care to smoke with a nihilistic cipher?"

It seemed like a good time to start. "Sure," he said.

Mr. Dressen lit the cigarettes with his gold lighter. Gus choked on his first inhale. The second puff was easier.

"Ciggies," Mr. Dressen said. "Jesus how I love them. Too bad they return your devotion by killing you. Very much like women."

"The shithouse rule," Gus said.

Mr. Dressen looked at Gus.

Gus shrugged.

22

The plane was empty on the flight back to Great Falls. The other passengers had either found alternative transportation or had more leave time to kill. Major Darling was drunk. Gus didn't realize this until Darling started singing "Clementine" above the Mojave Desert. He called Gus to come up front and take the copilot's seat.

"Look down there, airman. That's pure Clementine country. Lost and gone forever. Make you feel lonely? Makes me feel lonely as hell."

"Where's your copilot, sir?" Gus said.

"'Ruby lips above the water, blowing bubbles soft and fine, but alas I was no swimmer, so I lost my Clementine.'"

"Sir?"

"Lieutenant Rothstein you mean? He fell in love—got his head up some girl's dress in Culver City. The boy had another week of leave time so he didn't have to go back with us. So here we are, airman—up the creek without a copilot. Take the yoke, will you? I've got to get some sleep."

"Excuse me, sir?"

"You attended flight school for a while, before your bad breeding caught up with you, isn't that right airman?"

"No sir. I didn't go to flight school."

"Half you enlisted bastards washed out of flight school, otherwise why would you be stuck in Milk Fucking River? Answer me that, airman."

The cabin darkened as they entered a cloud. "Major, sir, I don't mean to contradict you, but you're not making sense."

"I figure you had a few hours in a PT-19, maybe even some T-33 time, so holding this old boat on course should be no big deal for you. Am I right or am I right?"

"You're not right, sir," Gus said.

"Listen to me, you insubordinate son of a bitch. I could teach a red-ass baboon to keep this airplane on course, and you're telling me you *can't*?"

"Shit, sir," Gus said, weakly.

"I warn you, airman. Don't give me any of your nonsense just now. I've had a very bad weekend and I'm not in a jocular mood. You continue to disobey my orders, I'm likely to have you put to death. Does that strike you as jocular?"

"Put to death, sir?"

"For mutiny. I am the captain of this ship, and therefore I am the absolute law here. Judge, prosecutor, jury, and executioner. You keep giving me static, airman, I'll have you up on charges, after which I will personally shoot you and throw your lifeless body into the Great Salt Lake where you will be eaten by the carnivorous brine shrimp. No one will ever find your remains."

"You're just kidding around, right sir?"

"No more of this treason, airman. I'm going to take a nap and you are going to hold this fine old bird on course. I'm very tired. I've kissed so much upper echelon ass, male and female alike, my lips are brittle. Now, take the goddamned yoke and apply what you learned in flight school before you washed out."

Gus took the yoke in his hands. He felt the vibration of the engines all the way to his shoulders.

"Keep your eye on the directional arrow of the Omni," Major Darling said. "You drift left or right, make the appropriate course change. The arrow needs to be pointing straight ahead. You learned this VOR stuff in week one of flight school, if you weren't asleep."

"Major Darling, sir. I didn't . . ."

"Did I ask you for your input, airman? Now shut your pie hole and listen to me. When we pass over Salt Lake City, the arrow will flip-flop. The next Omni station radial will come from either Pocatello or Idaho Falls, I forget which. It doesn't matter. All you have to do is keep the twitchy little arrow pointed straight ahead. Got it?"

Major Darling picked up a set of headphones and handed them to Gus. "Put these on. Listen for a steady tone. You hear a dot-dash, you've drifted left. A dash-dot, you've slipped right. Or maybe it's the other way around. Either way you'll know you've drifted off your vector. Keep your brogans off the rudder pedals. Just turn the yoke right or left a skosh, she'll change course for you a degree or two as needed. The winds aloft are negligible so you won't have much correcting to do."

Major Darling climbed out of his seat then leaned down to Gus, his face inches away. Gus smelled bourbon. The major's eyes were red, the lids heavy. "Whatever you do, don't mess with the throttles," he said. "I've got the power set at thirty inches of manifold pressure and the fuel mixture at auto lean. Leave the friction wheel alone, she'll stay put. We're cruising at fourteen thousand feet at 140 knots, so there's no need for you to play around with the power or the trim. Just keep her level. She's a faithful old bird, airman. You treat her with respect, she'll be true to you. Or is the concept of reciprocal fidelity alien to your family background?"

Major Darling stumbled back into the rear of the ship. Gus gripped the yoke and stared at the Omni arrow. He listened to the steady tone in his earphones.

The plane broke out of the gloom into an explosion of light. The Mojave Desert spread out like a beige carpet, weighted at the edges by snowcapped mountains. Overhead the sky was striped with pink herringbone clouds.

Lyle came into the cockpit. He sat next to Gus. "Do you know what you're doing, Reppo?" he said.

"What do you think?"

"Great. Just fucking great. He's sitting back there singing and drinking Old Taylor. He told me he really fucked up at Lackland and that he'd never get promoted to light colonel."

"What happened?"

"He put the blocks to a general's wife in a coat closet during a full-dress party with a lot of brass hats in attendance. There was some serious drinking involved. The general opened the closet door and found his wife smoking the Major's purple panatella."

"No shit?"

"Caught her inhaling. The general can't bring charges against Darling—too embarrassing. But Darling will never see the oak leaves on his collar turn to silver. He'll go from one boondock assignment to another until he retires or gets riffed."

"Riffed?"

"Reduction-in-forces. The air force is top-heavy with field-grade brass. The future is grim for these leftover heroes from the war. They don't fit the modern air force—too fucking wildass to kiss desk-jockey ass and behave themselves. I think Major Darling half hopes you'll bring down the curtain for him by sticking this old crate into the side of a mountain."

"He thinks I went to flight school," Gus said.

"Fuck. Do you know *any*thing about flying an airplane?"

"Just what he told me."

"Let me take over, Reppo. I took flying lessons for a while in Pasadena, almost got to solo."

"This isn't a Piper Cub, Dressen."

"A plane is a plane. Wings, motor, pedals, stick."

"Be my guest. Just leave the throttles at thirty inches of manifold pressure and don't fuck with the mixture controls or the friction wheel. Keep the VOR needle on the Salt Lake radial. It'll flip when we approach Idaho Falls or maybe Pocatello."

Lyle frowned. "I didn't understand a word of that, Reppo. I'm going to put on a parachute."

When the plane passed over the Great Salt Lake, Major Darling came back into the cabin. "Jesus Christ, you've got us over the Pacific Ocean!" he said. "Where did you plan to put down, in Hawaii?" He looked normal to Gus, well-rested and sober.

"No sir, we're over the Great Salt Lake."

Gus looked out the windows left and right. Mountains to the right, empty space to the left. More mountains straight ahead. The mountains straight ahead were dark under winter clouds.

"We're passing over Ogden right now, sir," Gus said.

"I was just pulling your leg, airman," Major Darling said. "Now get your ass out of here. Thanks for your good work. I might put a stripe on your sleeve for the effort. Remind me when we get back to the squadron."

"Yes, sir. Thank you, sir," Gus said.

PART FOUR

23

Gus—bulky in parka, two layers of clothes, bunny boots, and with his B-4 bag in tow—squeezed through the front door of his parents' house. Arctic wind moaned in the eaves like the baying of a lost dog. All the lights in the house were on, suggesting a social occasion in progress, but Flora was alone, seated at the dining room table drinking Rhine wine.

"My God Gussie, where have you been?" she said. "I've been worried sick."

"You've got all the lights in the house turned on, Mommy," he said.

"I don't like dark rooms. Answer me. Where have you been?"

"I caught a flight to Los Angeles. I didn't have time to tell you."

"How long does one telephone call take?"

"I'm sorry, Mommy."

"Los Angeles? Why Los Angeles? You're not making sense, Gussie."

Her face sagged with fatigue. Gus saw that she hadn't been sleeping. He pulled off his parka and boots and sat at the dining room table. Without asking if he was hungry Flora brought him a foil-wrapped ham sandwich from the fridge and a chocolate cake from the cupboard. She cut a moist wedge of the heavily iced cake and poured him a glass of milk.

"What's wrong?" Gus said.

A tear slid down the side of her nose coming to rest on her

upper lip. She dabbed at it with a napkin. Another started down the same path.

"Your father," she said, and for a moment Gus had a vision of Orson Gunlocke, broken and torn under a mile of water, strange, deep-water creatures gliding in and out of what was left of him.

"What happened?" he said.

"He's had a heart attack. I tried and tried to contact you, but no one knew where you were. Some sergeant I talked to thought you took time off to visit with us. The sergeant was under the foolish impression that you were close to your family."

"Where is he?"

"The sergeant?"

"FDR."

"In St. Bonaventure's Hospital. I've spent the last two days sitting at his bedside."

"Is it bad?"

"*Bad*? You think a heart attack can ever be *good*?"

A Mantovani LP was on the hi-fi. The army of tepid violins labored its way through "I Wonder Who's Kissing Her Now." Gus got up and went to the Stromberg-Carlson hi-fi. The machine was big as a coffin. He raised the groove-riding stylus from the spinning disk and turned the machine off.

"How did it happen?" he said. "I hope he wasn't shoveling the driveway. I told him I could do that. All he had to do was call me."

"Call you? You might as well be living on the moon, for all the good calling you does."

In the space between heartbeats, Flora's expression went from cross to pensive. She watched snow pellets, illuminated by the porch light, stream horizontally past the dining room window like thousands of crazed moths. Gus bit into his sandwich.

"It's my fault," she said. "We were discussing you and what we had planned for you once you were free of the air force. He still had dreams of you going to the UCLA dental school. But I told him no, my baby wasn't cut out for dentistry. I told him you were more suited to the agrarian life, farming in particular, since sharecropping was in your blood."

"You told him *that*? That sharecropping was in my blood?"

"It puzzled him. He asked me what I meant. I was feeling bitter at the time and full of self-pity. I don't know why I opened the subject."

"Let me see if I've got this right: You opened the goddamned subject but you don't know *why*?"

"Please, Gussie. Don't use such rough language to me. I'm not sure what I intended. But FDR hadn't a clue. He actually hadn't. I thought he'd had his suspicions, and that a full admission would be a comfort to him, but I was wrong. I told him all about Orson Gunlocke, our gardener. I told him of our secret trysts. Oh God, I must have been out of my mind!"

"He never guessed I wasn't his?"

"Never. It came as a complete shock. Oh, the poor dear turned so white he was almost blue! I realize now that was the beginning of his heart attack. He wasn't getting enough oxygen, but I kept on with the details of my affair with Orson as if he might understand and forgive! He must have felt that I'd put a knife into his heart! I didn't mean it that way, Gussie! I was only trying to be honest! Didn't someone once say the truth would set you free? What perfectly dreadful advice! The truth can throw you into hell!"

Flora got up and went to the hi-fi. She turned it on, started the disk spinning, then lowered the tone arm. "I Wonder Who's Kissing Her Now" started over again, from the beginning. Pleasant, genteel music about the agony of betrayal and the misery of loss. Gus wondered if Mantovani had ever heard of the Blues.

"When you were born," Flora said, "FDR wanted to name you Theo, after his successful uncle, Theodore, the oral surgeon who held the Painless Parker franchise in Arcadia, but I insisted on Gus, much to FDR's confusion. Do you know why I named you Gus?"

"You named me after Orson's great-grandfather, August Gunlocke, the Civil War hero."

"How did you know that? I've never told anyone!"

"Your competition told me."

"My what? What do you mean, Gussie?"

"Orson's widow. I went to her house."

Flora paled. Her lower lip trembled. "She has no claim on you!" she said. "None whatever! I am your mother!"

"For Christ's sakes, she didn't claim to be my mother or even my stepmother." What she claimed was far more bizarre, but Gus was not going to get into Marva Gunlocke's lunatic obsessions.

"Did you tell her about me?"

"Marva knew all about you."

"Marva! What an awful name! What did that woman say?"

"You don't want to know, Mommy. But it doesn't matter anyway. Marva Gunlocke is crazy as a bedbug. She should be in a mental hospital."

He got up from the table and searched the kitchen cabinets for something with alcohol in it besides Rhine wine. He found an opened pint of French brandy, among several unopened bottles. He drank some directly from the bottle, then poured the rest into his milk glass.

"You haven't finished your sandwich," Flora said.

"I'm not hungry."

"I see you've taken up drinking," she said, bitter but resigned.

"Smoking too," Gus said, lighting up.

"Blood will tell," she said.

"Half my blood is yours," Gus said.

"That won't be enough to save you, Gussie."

"I wasn't thinking it would."

24

Gus left the next morning before Flora woke up. The wind had died down and the temperature had dropped. Dry snow squeaked under his boots. The sky was a brittle porcelain blue. Heatless sun dogs burned on either side of the heatless sun.

He walked to town, then across town to St. Bonaventure's Hospital. FDR was on the second floor in a cardiac care unit. Gus found him reclining in bed reading the *Saturday Evening Post*. A Norman Rockwell painting had been reproduced on the magazine's cover: An overscrubbed family at prayer before the steaming holiday turkey.

"How you doing?" Gus said.

FDR looked at Gus briefly, without interest, then went back to his magazine. "I'm doing quite well, thank you," he said. "It was a minor infarction caused by a miniscule embolism."

There was no mistaking FDR's tone. Gus thought: Like this is my fault? And yet FDR's iciness made him feel guilty, as if he had been a coconspirator in his own illegitimacy.

"You're looking good, FDR," he said.

FDR was not looking good at all. He was pale as candle wax, his sweat-filmed jowls had a yellow sheen, and his lips were chalky. His voice was pitched high, as if his lungs couldn't supply the force needed to produce the timbre of normal speech.

"Considering everything," FDR said, "I suppose I should look worse than I do."

"Maybe you shouldn't believe her," Gus said. "She's flown her broom around the bend."

"Please speak of your mother with respect," FDR said, "whether she deserves it or not."

"I just meant her mental condition," Gus said.

FDR put the magazine down. "She doesn't have a *mental* condition," he said. "She's always had . . . eccentricities, but she's not insane. In any case she wasn't insane nineteen years ago, was she?" He made a strangling sound, then coughed to cover it up. "God!" he said with unrestrained bitterness. "To think how thrilled we were when you were born!"

Gus said what would eventually have to be said: "You're still my dad." It was the obvious thing to say, yet his voice wavered.

"Still? Still? How can *never was* become *still*?" FDR said. He picked up his *Saturday Evening Post*. He licked his fingers and turned the pages too quickly to read any one of them, his face hidden behind the impossibly sane Norman Rockwell family.

Under his breath, Gus said, "You'd better learn to live with it."

FDR dropped the magazine and raised himself on his elbows. "What did you just say to me?"

"Nothing," Gus said.

"It wasn't nothing. It was something. It was something very unfilial of you—but then what can I expect?"

Gus started to leave, but FDR called him back. "Mommy told me the fellow had bad teeth," he said.

"I'll come visit you tomorrow," Gus said.

"Hear me out. This is significant to me. Do you know what Painless Parker said of those who are indifferent to oral hygiene? He said, 'God hates those who do not take care of their teeth, and that is why they suffer.' I find satisfaction in that, though I do not hate the fellow myself. Mommy fed him breath mints when he came into the house. She could not endure him otherwise."

FDR's chest rose and fell under his hospital gown. He made a sustained sound, like gravel rattled in a stoneware jar. This alarmed Gus until he realized FDR was laughing.

"I trust that you brush at least twice a day, Gussie," he said. "You may not have dentistry in your blood, but you might have an inherited tendency toward dental neglect—common among rural farming folk, I understand."

"I'll see you tomorrow," Gus said.

"I expect to be going home tomorrow," FDR said.

"Is that a smart thing to do?"

"I am not medically illiterate," FDR said. "I know where I stand. This was not a major coronary. I know what I can do and what I cannot do."

Gus sat with him for another few minutes before he left the hospital. He would have said goodbye but FDR had dozed off with the magazine on his face. Gus removed the magazine and tiptoed out of the room.

He walked to the Athenian. The storm had moved south into Wyoming and Colorado having left three feet of snow in the streets of Milk River. Snowplows and snowblowers had been out since early morning, making automobile and foot travel possible.

The Athenian was empty. Gus ordered coffee and a cinnamon roll. He went to a booth where someone had left the morning newspaper. Gus read the headlines indifferently, then a story on the second page caught his eye.

STUDENT PROTESTERS BUFFALOED IN RICHLAND

Three students from Northern Plains State College were apprehended over the weekend at the Hanford Atomic Works near Richland, Washington. Tracy Winshaw, Sandra Ellison, and Josh Billings, were arrested as they attempted to handcuff themselves to the main gate of the Hanford compound. Criminal trespass charges are pending but the upstart trio was not detained. They were sent home to Milk River with their tails between their legs. When asked what they had hoped to accomplish, Miss Winshaw said, "We wanted to call attention to the mindless expansion of the bomb culture. We need to *talk* to the Russians, not play Who's Got the Biggest Pipe Organ." When asked about his daughter's motives, Miss Winshaw's father, Dr. Algernon Winshaw, a local dental surgeon and member in good standing of several benevolent fraternities, said, "The foolish girl needs a brisk spanking. What's wrong with these kids? They can't seem to grow up. I don't think their pinko professors do anything to teach them to respect the realities of life. When I was fourteen years old I had my own firewood business along with two paper routes. I helped my dad put food on the table. I shot a worn-out horse when I was ten." Authorities in the state of Washington would not comment on the case, but hinted that charges would be filed soon.

Gus wondered if the editors of the newspaper had understood the "pipe organ" reference. He decided they hadn't, since they'd printed it.

Gus went to the pay phone on the wall near the exit and dialed Tracy's number. A woman—Tracy's mother, Gus assumed—answered.

"Could I speak to Tracy?" he said.

"Who's calling? Are you from the newspaper? We have nothing more to say. We will pay her fine, and that's the end of it. Please stop this incessant calling."

"This is Gus Reppo. Tracy and I went to the movies once."

"You're the one from the radar base?"

"Yes, ma'am. I'm the one."

"I'm sorry, but I have to ask you—do you have radical ideas like Tracy's other friends?"

"The air force doesn't allow us to have radical ideas, ma'am."

"That's refreshing to hear, if it's true. Tracy needs normal friends who don't have these ideas. She's at the college right now. She'll be home later this afternoon. You can call her then."

Tracy's mother sounded reasonable but scared. Gus imagined Dr. Winshaw's thundering rages intimidating the whole family, although he didn't think anyone could intimidate Tracy.

He left the Athenian and walked toward the Northern Plains Campus. It was a good half-hour walk. When he reached the campus he went into the Student Union. He ordered coffee and picked up a copy of the student newspaper, the *Northern Plains View*, from a stack near the cash register. Tracy's picture was on the front page. It was a photograph taken while she was listening to a lecture. Gus thought it might be the lecture given by the Marxist Professor from Minnesota. He remembered a photographer moving through the crowd, flash bulbs popping. The photo was a good one. Unlike most quickly snapped newspaper photos, this one made her look as beautiful as she actually was. She also looked heroic, standing up and applauding the speaker, her smile angelic but determined. The article under the photo said pretty much the same thing as the article in the local newspaper, with one addition. The college reporter held a brief interview with Tracy.

> NPV: "Would you do it again, knowing what you know now?"
>
> TRACY: "Of course I would. And I will. Someone has to stand up for the dignity and survival of the human race."
>
> NPV: "But won't it cost your family quite a lot of

money in fines and in damaged reputations? What about your own future?"

TRACY: "It's a small price to pay, don't you think? What future do any of us have if this insanity goes on?"

Gus sat drinking coffee until noon pretending to read the paper but keeping alert to the come and go of students. He thought about Tracy and the dignity and survival of the human race. Dignity, in his limited experience, was in fairly short supply. Survival, on the other hand, would most likely depend on dumb luck. He thought about these notions: did they qualify as radical ideas, or even as *ideas*? He decided they fell short.

He studied each new influx of students as they entered the student union hoping that Tracy would be among them. Then it occurred to him that she was a celebrity now—admired or despised, but either way, in demand. He didn't think he wanted to talk to a celebrity.

He walked to the Milk River Hotel and waited for the afternoon shuttle that would take him back to the base. He needed to talk to Ray Springer.

25

Something was wrong. Ray Springer's bunk was bare: no blankets or sheets, and the mattress was rolled up. "Where's Ray?" Gus asked Lamar Harkey, the cook.

"You don't know?" Harkey said. "I figured y'all were buddies, going to the whores and drinking like you do."

Harkey was a genial freak. His legs were long and thin, his torso short and wide. His spine curved a bit making his torso seem even shorter, his chest a cavernous convex hollow. He had a geometrically angular head with massive black waves of brilliantined hair. He looked like Gregory Peck observed through an astigmatic lens. He also had the biggest feet Gus had ever seen on a human being. Size sixteen quadruple E.

"What happened?" Gus said.

Harkey, who had just finished a shift in the mess hall, sat on his bunk and took off his shoes. Gus caught a heavy whiff of foot odor.

"You missed chow, Reppo. I made my favorite—roast pork with cinnamon applesauce. You hungry? Mess hall's still open for the swing shift crew. Slow roasted pork and those little white taters about the size of monkey nuts afloat in a cream sauce. Plus butter beans with bacon bits and chipped almonds. Real peach pie for dessert. It makes my pecker stiffen up just thinking on it." Harkey grabbed his crotch affectionately.

"Sounds real appetizing, Harkey," Gus said. "But what happened to Ray?"

"Always knew he was touched some. He got shitfaced in town and when he come back he drove his hot rod smack into the AP shack. Mutt Runkle said he tried to run him over." Harkey picked black lint from between his toes as he related the story. "Then he took after Mutt with a tire iron and Mutt put his lights out with his stick. No one's blamed Runkle. Springer's the one gonna lose a stripe or better. How you figure a little peckerwood like that going after a big mean sumbitch like Mutt Runkle?"

Gus wondered about that, too. Drunk or not, it wasn't like Ray to go on a rampage.

"So where is he?" Gus said.

"Springer? They kept him in the hospital in town a couple of days, then shipped him off to the division hospital at Malm-strom. They say he's got a cracked skull and maybe a ruptured kidney. You see him, Reppo, tell him to back off on the John Barleycorn. He won't make it to retirement, he starts dropping turds on the squadron lawn like that."

Gus asked around but there were no witnesses to the incident except Runkle's partner, Jeff Sparks. According to Runkle, and backed up by Sparks, Springer came in at three a.m. from a night of hard drinking. He got pissed off that Runkle didn't open the gates immediately when Springer pulled up to them honking his horn. Runkle testified he did not take his time opening the gates, but Springer thought he had and went crazy. He drove his car into the AP shack once he was inside the gates, knocking some siding off. Then he got out of his car and came after Runkle with a tire iron. Runkle produced the tire iron for the Board of Inquiry. Runkle said he was forced to use the nightstick aggressively to defend himself. He had the sequence of events written down in his notebook. "I would have been within my rights to shoot him," Runkle said, "The way he was acting, I felt my life was in danger."

Gus didn't believe the story. He knew Runkle hated Ray's guts.

Ray, having seen action in the big war, had an aura that most respected. But some, like Runkle, felt Ray wore that aura a little too visibly. Runkle was the most vocal of these. Ray Springer was only a staff sergeant, but young lieutenants deferred to him because of his wartime experience as a ball turret gunner with three confirmed Focke-Wulf kills. Ray, in this sense, outranked everyone on the base except George Walters, the radio op, First Sergeant Burnside, and Major Darling.

After his shift Gus went into town and borrowed FDR's Buick without asking Flora and headed to Great Falls. Two hours later he parked outside Malmstrom's front gate. He identified himself to the AP guarding the main entrance. The AP checked the roster of airmen stationed at the 999th, found Gus's name, then gave Gus a temporary clip-on ID badge.

Gus asked the AP for directions to the base hospital. The AP drew a black "X" on an onionskin map then gave the map to Gus, pointing out the best route to take. The hospital was a ten-minute walk past the commissary, equipment sheds, the flight line, and several monolithic rows of gray, two-story barracks.

A flight of Scorpions, afterburners lit, scorched the sky on their way to intercept other Scorpions simulating attacking Tupolevs. Rows of KC-97 tankers were parked on the tarmac next to giant hangars. Two blue helicopters flying side by side passed low overhead. A squad of rifle-carrying APs in jump boots and white helmets jogged past Gus in double-time. There was a sense here of the vast and serious business of the United States Air Defense Command. Gus felt proud to be part of it. He thought: Too bad shitheads like Mutt Runkle were also a part of it.

Ray Springer was in the critical ward. There were only six beds in it and two of them were empty. A nurse showed him in. The nurse was a first lieutenant. Gus didn't know whether he was supposed to salute her or not. He opted not to. She seemed indifferent, one way or the other. Her nameplate said "Lt. Doris J. Dorio." She was at least five inches taller than Gus.

"Thank you, ma'am," Gus said.

First Lieutenant Doris J. Dorio, who looked to be in her mid-thirties, glanced at Gus with the interest she might have had for a moth. She yawned. "I've been on duty since six this morning," she said. "I'm ready to pack it in." She had the raspy voice of a heavy smoker. Her skin was shaded toward olive, her short black hair was lustrous under the ward's fluorescents.

"I know what you mean, ma'am," Gus said.

"No, kid, you don't. Not unless you've worked thirty-two beds of sick airmen fourteen hours straight with a twenty minute break to attend to your own bodily needs."

"Sorry, ma'am," Gus said.

"Hell, it's what I signed up for. But I'm a short-timer. I'll be out in another month. Twenty-eight days, to be exact."

She smiled. The smile transformed her from an overworked and hostile functionary to an overworked angel of mercy. She wasn't beautiful, but she didn't have to be beautiful to be attractive. Physical beauty, Gus speculated, probably had nothing to do with attractiveness, once you understood the difference.

"Didn't mean to bite your head off, kid," she said.

Gus liked First Lieutenant Doris J. Dorio. She was impressive in the seasoned way young girls could not be. She told Gus where to find Sergeant Springer, then left him standing there, mute with admiration.

Gus wasn't able to identify Springer. Three of the four airmen in the critical ward were heavily bandaged. A burn victim languished against the far wall of the ward. His ears were gone and his lips were shriveled. His nose was a wad of white putty. He glistened with unguents. An IV bag dripped saline solution and antibiotics into his unburned right arm. He seemed to be smiling, or grimacing, but that was because his upper lip was mostly nonexistent.

Gus looked at the legs of the other airmen. The one with the shortest legs had to be Ray. He sat on the empty bed next to the short legs.

The man with the short legs had a swollen head. His head looked like a melon wrapped in gauze. His own mother wouldn't have recognized him. His eyes were black slits surrounded by purple halos. He looked almost festive, as if he were wearing a crude mask for a costume party. Gus looked at the man's hand and saw Ray Springer's shrapnel pinky ring.

"You awake, Ray?" he said.

"Off and on. You meet my nurse, Gate?"

"Lieutenant Dorio?"

"Once I get my good looks back I'm going to ask her to marry me."

Springer's jaws were wired together. He talked in whispers through his almost closed mouth. Gus had to lean down to hear him.

"What the hell happened, Ray?"

"Nothing much. Runkle wouldn't open the gate. Let me sit out there in the cold for twenty minutes. When he got around to opening it, I lost it. Stupid. Even an old fart like me can be stupid as any fifteen year old."

"He had it in for you. He *wanted* you to lose it."

"And I took the bait. But look on the bright side, Gate. I'm going to marry my nurse." Springer made a hissing sound that Gus took for laughter.

"Lieutenant Dorio's agreeable to that?" Gus said.

"I'm working out a strategy. I'm going to quit the air force and settle down."

"Not take your retirement? You've only got another—what—four or five years?"

"Retirement's not what it's about."

Gus thought: "It" again.

"I've also got to quit pissing blood before I can ask for Lieutenant Dorio's hand," Springer said. "Marry a woman like that, your plumbing better be in good working order." He closed his eyes and dozed.

Gus waited a minute, then said, "She's been around the block a few times."

Springer whispered, "You got a sharp eye, Gate."

"Maybe she's too tough for you, Ray," Gus said.

"You mean for a fragile old dog like me?"

"I didn't mean it that way."

"How did you mean it?"

Gus shrugged.

"You don't know a whole lot about women, Gate. They all have a need, even the tough ones. The tough ones sometimes are needier. You just have to figure out the right strategy."

Gus was enjoying this conversation, in spite of the circumstances. "You make it sound simple," he said.

"I didn't say it was simple. There's a name for it. It's called courtship."

Springer dozed off again. Gus stood up. The burned man made a soft yodeling sound. Gus realized after a moment that the burned man was screaming and that the yodeling sound he made was all the scream he could muster. Gus looked for Lieutenant Dorio but couldn't find her. When he got back to the critical ward, the burned man had stopped screaming.

Gus sat down next to Ray Springer's bed. "I'll come back, next chance I get," he said.

"The shithouse rule, Gate," Springer said.

"How do you figure?" Gus said.

"I got my ass kicked, but here's the upside—I'm going to hook up with Lieutenant Doris J. Dorio, rhymes with Oreo. Wouldn't have happened without Mutt Runkle's help. Not a bad trade-off."

"What if she doesn't want to hook up with you?" Gus said. "Where's your shithouse rule then?"

"Then I'm just stuck in the shithouse, bound up but biding my time and hoping for a good outcome. It's not strictly either/or."

Lieutenant Dorio came into the ward. She replaced the drip bag hanging over the burned man, then joined Gus at Springer's bedside.

"They'll trepan his cranium tomorrow morning," she said.

"Ma'am?"

"His brain is swollen. They'll drill holes in his skull to relieve the pressure."

She took Springer's pulse and temperature, made a notation on the clipboard she was carrying. Then she did something that made Gus think Springer had a chance with Lieutenant Dorio. She picked up Springer's hand and studied the shrapnel ring.

"Is that a snake?" she asked.

Gus started to explain the ring but stopped himself. Ray needed to tell it. It would be a good way to begin his courtship campaign which, in any case, was going to be a long shot.

Out at the nurses' station, Lieutenant Dorio asked Gus what had happened to Springer. Gus told her what he knew about the incident.

"The AP used a nightstick on him," Gus said.

"Nightstick? I'd say he used a lot more than a nightstick. Your Sergeant Springer was *stomped*."

"That fuckhead Runkle," Gus said.

"Watch the salty language, airman. This isn't your barracks."

"Sorry, ma'am."

"Your sergeant might lose that kidney," she said.

"*What*?"

"It's possibly detached. There's blood clots in his urine. He also has two breaks in the lower mandible and three hairline cracks in the maxilla." She pointed to her jaw and face to let Gus see the areas she meant. "When they brought him in there was a boot print on his face."

"Jesus," Gus said.

"Someone danced on your sergeant's head, airman."

"I know who the son of a bitch is."

"You know what I like about the little guy? He never complains. Doesn't even seem to hold a grudge."

Gus went back into the critical ward. He sat down by Springer.

"You're really busted up, Ray," he said. "They'll probably give you a medical discharge."

"If I'm lucky I'll get disability pay, Gate," Springer whispered. "Maybe fifty percent. I could retire on that."

"Shithouse rule again?"

"Not a bad system, is it?"

Springer raised his head an inch off the pillow. "You been talking to Lieutenant Dorio about me?" he said. "What did she say?"

"She said you're hung like a donkey."

"Ah, romance," Springer said.

26

Gus couldn't look at Mutt Runkle. Seeing the AP made him sick. When he saw him, even from a distance, his heart would pound and his stomach cramped. His heart beat so hard he thought it might crack a rib. Gus was afraid of his adrenaline-fueled heart, what it might make him do.

He didn't feel this degree of hatred after Runkle beat him up. What was different here? Maybe he didn't think as much of himself as he did of Ray Springer. Ray Springer, to Gus, was like an older brother, a mentor. Gus was able to say it: He loved Ray Springer. He'd wanted to talk to Ray about Orson and Marva and what had happened in Chula Vista and where he stood with FDR and Flora. No chance of that happening now, maybe not for months, thanks to Runkle.

So he avoided Runkle. Which was easy to do since Runkle was unsocial and content with his own company. He ate by himself, lived in an NCO barracks with private rooms, conducted his gate duty with a bored indifference that was somehow menacing, barely checking out the shuttle-loads of airmen coming into the base or leaving it.

Gus didn't know he owned that much hate. Its acid burned his stomach like an ulcer. He looked at himself in the mirror and saw a face he didn't recognize. Ease off, he told his image. He made the image smile, but the smile was ugly in its falsehood. It made him look crazy.

He had a recurrent dream. Down in the ocean, walking through green water thin as air, he approached the *Fisk* and Orson Gunlocke. Sometimes Orson was spread out in pieces, sometimes he was whole. When he was whole Gus asked, "Am I responsible for your death?" Orson did not reply but tilted his head and scratched his chin as if working out the possibilities before he said, "Wrong question, son." Or Gus would walk toward the *Fisk* in that green light to find Orson torn up, small fish feeding on the ragged strips of flesh. And Gus would ask, "What am I so mad at?" And the mutilated apparition would answer, "At every God-damned thing." Gus said, "I did not launch the torpedo." Orson replied, "Don't matter who launched the torpedo. A torpedo is only an instrument." Awake, Gus asked himself: Was I born with this? Does it go back to August Gunlocke, the civil war soldier? Did this rage come down the years to Orson, then to me?

One night he followed Mutt Runkle to town. Mutt was on break and his first stop was the Milk River Hotel bar. Gus hid in a dark booth and watched Runkle drink double shots of house bourbon backed with mugs of tap beer. He drank alone. His sullen posture turned away any chance of genial company. After six shots and two mugs, Runkle left the bar and went to the whorehouse behind the Moomaw Dairy. Gus waited outside. Ten minutes later Runkle came out. He unzipped and pissed in the alley, rocking back and forth on his heels over the steaming spatter. As he rocked he hummed a sour tune. Gus stayed hidden behind a rack of garbage cans. A week later, Gus followed Runkle again, and Runkle repeated his routine as if it had been written down and memorized. Gus asked himself, So what? What's Runkle's stupid fucking habits got to do with me?

Gus, in his present state of mind, was not good company. Tracy Winshaw was the first to notice the change, or the first to say anything about it.

"Something's different about you," she said. "You look scuzzy.

Did you forget to shave? Don't they have rules about that? You need a haircut, too."

Gus forced a normal smile. They had just seen *The Invasion of the Body Snatchers* at the Orpheum. They were in FDR's Buick, the heater turned up high, parked on a unlit street by the high school football field on the outskirts of town. It was ten below zero and windy. Gus was sweating but Tracy was shivering.

"Nothing's different about me," he said, holding his manufactured smile in place. Runkle, his regular weekly routine, was on Gus's mind. You could set your watch by Runkle's routine.

"Yes, something is," she said. She tucked herself deeply into her winter coat.

Gus gave up on the smile. "That fucking Josh," he said, still thinking of Runkle.

"That fucking Josh?" she said.

"Thinks he knows it all."

"He knows a lot. He's kept a 4.0 in two years at Northern."

"Doesn't mean jackshit."

"What's wrong with you?"

"Nothing's wrong with me."

"Why are you picking on Josh?"

"I'm not picking on him. I don't give a shit about him. There's this guy I know, Ray Springer. I need to talk to him."

"Who's Ray Springer?"

"Someone who knows a hell of a lot more than Josh Billings."

"Does he read Kierkegaard? Does he read Nietzche?"

"He doesn't need to."

"Yet he knows more than Josh."

"Fuck Josh."

Gus didn't want this argument. He changed the subject. "Good movie, huh?" he said.

"In all respects but one," she said.

"How do you mean?"

"The obvious message."

"What message? It was science fiction."

"Oh please, Gus. Wake *up*. Didn't you understand who the invaders were supposed to be?"

"Martians?"

"They came from the Red planet all right, but they were not Martians."

"That makes a lot of sense."

"Commies, Gus. They were Commies, invading the brains of ordinary God-fearing Americans, turning them into agents of the Soviet Union."

"I missed that part. I guess I wouldn't keep a 4.0 at Northern."

"You've got to learn how to read between the lines, Gus. Things are hardly ever what they seem."

"I was never good at reading between the lines."

"Keep an eye on your neighbor. He might be a convert to Socialism. That's the message. They want to turn us into a nation of paranoid snitches doing the bidding of the capitalist war machine."

"Lord help us!" Gus said. He threw his hands up, feigning dismay.

"You're making fun of *me*?"

Gus saw his mistake. He'd lumped Tracy in with Josh. Not smart, even if it was more true than false.

They drove to his parents' house. It was only nine o'clock but both FDR and Flora were in bed. Gus made cocoa and they sat in front of the big Capehart and watched a snowy version of *The Philco Television Playhouse*, a show about an independent old lady wanting to go back to work in a New York garment factory but too old now to do the demanding labor.

"Slow death in America," Tracy said.

"I thought the son-in-law was a jerk," Gus said.

"Worse," Tracy said. "He had the sensitivity of pavement. It's the old story, the desperately ignorant bourgeois male unable to understand his own unhappiness."

"There's no quit in you, is there?" Gus said.

"Should there be?" she said.

He changed the subject. "You want a drink?"

"A drink? A *drink* drink you mean?"

"My folks keep the brandy handy."

"Clever," she said.

Gus found an unopened pint and broke the seal with his thumbnail. He looked at his thumbnail. It was black. When had he showered last? He couldn't remember. He poured brandy into two glasses. "It's good stuff," he said. "Imported from France."

"I've never had brandy," Tracy said. "I tried bourbon once and hated it."

"Brandy goes down easier," Gus said.

She sipped carefully. Then not so carefully. Showing off, Gus knocked his back then poured another. He refilled Tracy's glass before it was empty.

They went into Gus's room, taking an extra pint of brandy with them. Gus told Tracy how his folks had followed him around the country and made this room a replica of his room in La Jolla. Gus waited for the interpretation according to some world famous psychologist. She didn't offer one. She sipped her brandy, thoughtful and silent. Gus was grateful for her silence. She knew instinctively that Gus's peculiar family wasn't fair game for analysis, and he liked her for that. They sat on his bed. He put his arm around her.

"I'm freezing," she said. "I can't get warm."

Gus refilled her brandy glass.

Gus said, "I think I'm in love with you, Tracy."

She stiffened. "Don't. Use. That. Word," she said, her voice mechanical with suppressed fury.

"Why? You think it's dirty?"

"It's the dirtiest four letter word of all."

She looked at Gus, her eyes fierce with conviction, her lips trembling. He wanted to kiss her lips but she turned away.

"Do you understand me?" she said.

"About that word? Yes," Gus said. "Bourgeois bullpucky."

She allowed him to kiss her then. It was a long, physical kiss. When they emerged from it, Gus refilled the brandy glasses.

"Don't think you can get me drunk so you can have your way," she said.

"I'm not as bourgeois as all that," Gus said. He was beginning to like the stupid word.

"Let's get under the covers," she said. "It's cold in here."

Gus started to take off his clothes.

"No. Don't undress. I just need to get warm. I'm freezing."

"Won't that make things kind of difficult?" Gus said.

"There aren't going to be any 'things,'" she said.

"You're waiting for 'Mr. Right,'" Gus said.

"Don't be a shit," she said.

They finished the bottle in bed. Gus opened the other one.

"I'm so drunk," Tracy said. "But don't think that's an invitation."

"You're saving yourself for marriage," Gus said.

"Oh, you smart-mouth rat!" she said.

They necked for another hour. Gus developed a fierce case of lover's nuts. He grimaced. He groaned.

"You're angry with me," she said.

"No, I'm not angry."

"You're pissed off. You have been ever since the movie."

"I'm not pissed off. I'm hurting."

He tried to find her thighs under the blanket, under the layers of clothes. She squirmed away. Gus gave up.

"I'm not . . . experienced," she said.

"I know," Gus said.

"You do? How could you know?"

"It's obvious."

"But I know how to help you. I'm not a bourgeois tease. Give me some more brandy first."

Gus poured the brandy. She gulped it down. He put a hand on her teacup breast. She shoved it away.

She unbuckled his belt, opened his pants, worked her hand inside, found what she was looking for. She massaged him gently, then less gently. Gus gritted his teeth. He made noises he couldn't control. He pulled a pillow over his face.

When she finished, Gus said, "You've done this before."

"That is none of your business," she said.

"You start something going, then you put an end to the poor bastard's misery."

"You prefer misery?"

"I prefer you."

"Maybe I *am* waiting for Mr. Right," she said.

"That would be me," Gus said.

"The jury's still out, flyboy."

They eventually fell asleep and woke up to daylight.

The bedroom door creaked open. Flora stood in the doorway in her robe.

"How could you do this to me?" she said. She looked stricken. Her face warped, as if the skull behind it had turned to putty.

"We didn't do anything," Gus said.

"You," she said, pointing at Tracy, "This is my house! You are not welcome!"

"This is my friend, Tracy Winshaw," Gus said. "Her dad's a dentist, too."

"You think that's a recommendation? Get her out of here!"

"What sort of dentist?" FDR said, appearing behind Flora in his long johns.

"Where's the bathroom," Tracy said. "I've got to throw up."

27

They walked back to town. The wind had changed direction, from north to west. "Chinook," Tracy said.

"What's that?" Gus said.

"It's wind coming off the Rocky Mountain front. It's going to warm everything up. It's a ton warmer already."

"Like the Santa Anas back home," Gus said.

Gus explained the Santa Ana phenomenon—how, in fall and winter months, cool air moved west from the desert, compressing and heating as it roared down the western slopes of the inland mountains, raising the temperatures in the coastal cities to the eighties and nineties.

"I suppose it's like that," Tracy said.

She stopped as if she was going to be sick then started moving again holding on to Gus's arm. Gus turned windward, felt the soft warm air on his face. Even the sun's pale disk sent a miserly ray of heat earthward.

"Feels like spring," Gus said.

"Don't count on it," she said. "It'll get above freezing for a few days, maybe a week. Then go back to normal."

By the time they reached the Athenian, the temperature had climbed to above forty. They hopped over the brown snowmelt that ran in the gutter.

Josh Billings was in a booth by himself drinking coffee and smoking his pipe. He wore his red beret at a rakish slant. He looked like the professor he would most likely become. When Gus and Tracy came in he glanced up from the book he was reading and waved them over to his booth, white meerschaum suavely clenched in his smile.

"*Comment allez-vous?*" he said to Tracy. "*Bien, merci,*" Tracy said. To Gus she said, "Josh is taking French this semester."

"I'm thinking of taking a year at the Sorbonne," Josh said.

Gus saw the title of Josh's book: *Being and Nothingness.* Josh saw Gus looking.

"You've read Sartre?" Josh said.

"Nope," Gus said.

"*Quel dommage.* You'll find it a bit over your head, unless of course you've read your Hegel and Heidegger first."

"I'll put them on my reading list."

"Don't procrastinate, *mon ami,*" Josh said. "Being, you see, precedes essence, *non*? It only stands to reason, *d'accord*? You've got to invent yourself from scratch or the world will do it for you, *oui*? The challenge, you see, lies in inventing a self that is *authentique*, one you can live with day to day without shame or guilt. Have you ever thought about it, Gus?"

"How authentic can it be if you have to invent it?" Gus said.

Tracy started to speak but only managed a moan. She leaned forward and held her head in both hands.

"What's wrong, Trace?" Josh said.

"I feel sick," she said.

"She's hungover," Gus said.

"You've been drinking?" Josh said.

"I got stinko last night," Tracy said.

"I don't understand. You're not a drinker, Trace."

"It was brandy and we were cold."

"We?" He looked at Gus for clues.

Gus yawned. "We were at my folks' house. We killed a couple of pints of brandy playing double solitaire."

Josh relit his pipe. He pulled hard on it to get the tobacco crackling. When the tobacco was sufficiently fired up, he said, "*Maivaise foi*, Tracy. I'm disappointed in you."

"Don't be. It was fun. Now I'm paying the price."

"The shithouse rule," Gus said.

Josh ignored Gus. He gave Tracy a hard disciplinary look. "Getting back to Sartre," he said, "Acting in bad faith denies your authenticity. Getting drunk, don't you see, is a form of that denial. Beyond that, alcohol hampers your ability to process ideas in a clear and orderly way."

Tracy said, "You act differently when you're drunk, but that doesn't mean you're playing a role."

"What transpires between two people when they are intoxicated is false from the outset," Josh said. "You can't put any value on what people say to each other when they're not themselves." His eyes drilled this message home to Tracy.

"Just the opposite," Gus said. "Booze is like truth serum."

Tracy said, "I never pretend to be something I'm not. I don't do it when I'm sober and I don't do it when I'm drunk."

"And how often have you been drunk?" Josh said. "Once? You're fooling yourself, Trace." He tapped the air instructively with the stem of his pipe. "*En vin, il n'y a pas vérité*—there is no truth in wine."

"What's your point?" Gus said.

"The point is this. The world punishes you for being yourself. Getting drunk just numbs the pain. It's not the answer. The only answer is to hold firm to your inner convictions. *Très difficile, mais la recompense est le merité.*"

"Jesus Christ," Gus mumbled.

Josh gave Gus a sour grin. "Aren't you afraid of being seen with us, airman?" he said. "Won't your commandant put you in irons? You know—guilt by association with dangerous subversives?" He reached across the table and covered Tracy's hand possessively with his.

"I don't think you qualify as dangerous," Gus said.

"Ideas are the most dangerous things in the world," Josh said.

"Excuse me," Tracy said. "I'm going to the powder room."

When she was gone, Josh said, "You shouldn't have done this to her, Gus."

"She did it to herself," Gus said.

"With your help."

"I try to be helpful."

Josh leaned toward Gus confidentially. "Tell me, Gus. Did you . . . ?"

"None of your business, Josh old buddy," Gus said.

Gus left the Athenian and went to the Milk River Hotel to catch the morning shuttle back to the base.

He sat in the empty bar sipping coffee and smoking cigarettes, wondering if Tracy would be jacking off Josh Billings before the day was over.

28

A bird opened and closed its wings atop the UHF mast. A speckled barn owl big as a turkey. Gus had read somewhere that Indians believed a visitation by an owl was bad news. Owls had some kind of connection to unfriendly underworld spirits. They signified unhappy events to come. He climbed the mast without harness or lanyard to shoo the owl away. The big owl wouldn't shoo. Its unblinking yellow eyes met Gus's with unhurried curiosity. It flew away when it had seen all it wanted to see.

He went to the chow hall for lunch. They were serving Swiss steaks and mashed potatoes and creamed spinach. The Swiss steaks were glazed with gravy. The potatoes, formed into the shape of radar domes, steamed. Even the creamed spinach looked good enough to eat. The cook on duty was creative. He obviously enjoyed being a cook. Gus was glad Lamar Harkey wasn't on duty. An image of Harkey pulling wads of black lint from between his enormous toes occurred to him. He put the image out of his mind. Gus spotted Lyle Dressen sitting alone at a table. He joined him.

"I've gained twenty pounds since joining up," Dressen said. "I figure at this rate I'll weigh 260 pounds by the time I get out."

"I can eat twelve times a day and not gain a pound," Gus said.

"It's metabolism," Lyle said. "You got a metabolism problem. You're wired like a hummingbird. You know how long it takes a male hummingbird to fuck his woman? One millisecond. I bet you don't do much better."

They ate for a while without talking.

Mutt Runkle approached their table carrying an overloaded tray. He stopped and smiled at Gus. "How you doing, dingleberry?" he said. "Still going down on the local quim?" Runkle's smile went from nasty to nastier. His smile threatened bodily harm. Runkle moved on, looking for an isolated table. Conversations stopped as he passed by.

"What was all that about?" Dressen said.

"I've got to go," Gus said. "I can't stand to be in the same room with that prick."

Gus walked with Lyle to the radar operations blockhouse. Something was up. There were more officers in the blockhouse than Gus had ever seen. Mostly second lieutenants, crowding around a radar display. Major Darling was there, too. Lyle asked an airman at the Flight Plan Identification desk what was going on.

"Kruschev's plane is crossing Canada. We've got him just south and west of Moose Jaw. He's travelling in a fucking Tupolev. Division's got their tits in the wringer over it."

"They think Kruschev's going to bomb us personally?" Lyle said.

"It's supposed to be a goodwill trip. He's sucking up to Canada and the Canadians are letting him suck. We've scrambled a flight of Scorpions just in case. They'll shadow the Tupolev to Swift Current, Medicine Hat and Lethbridge, staying this side of the border."

"Let me know if they drop the bomb," Gus said to Dressen.

Gus started to leave. Major Darling saw him and caught his elbow. "Reppo," he said. "I want to see you this afternoon. Come by my office at fifteen hundred hours." Major Darling's smile was friendly but his jumpy red-streaked eyes said something else.

"Yes sir," Gus said. "What for, sir?"

"Just be there, Reppo."

Gus went to his barracks and plopped down on his cot. He dozed off and dreamed of an owl with Kruschev's face on it. Then it was Runkle's face. The face grinned, the owl flew off.

29

First Sergeant Burnside, broad shouldered, in crisp gabardine, a god of military correctness, was at his desk reading *Stars and Stripes*. He looked up at Gus. Gus started to salute then remembered you didn't have to salute master sergeants even if they were as impressive as Burnside.

"You look like you've been rolling in the sheep dip, Reppo," Burnside said. "You got any clean fatigues in your footlocker? You got a razor blade? I understand the Gillette company is putting out a good product these days."

Gus shrugged. "Major Darling doesn't care," he said.

"That shouldn't make any difference, airman. You wear the uniform, even fatigues, with some sense of pride. The air force is bigger than one easygoing base commander."

This conversation made Gus nervous. He hadn't realized he looked so bad. "What should I do, Sarge?" he said.

"Just go in, Reppo. You haven't got time to clean up. The major's expecting you."

Gus went in. He stepped up to Major Darling's desk and snapped a salute. Major Darling waved off the salute and pointed to an uncushioned wooden chair in front of the desk. "Sit your butt down, Reppo," he said.

Gus sat and endured a long silence while Major Darling looked at him as if he were looking at an empty wall. The major opened a bag of peanuts and poured some into his hand. He popped the peanuts into his mouth. He chewed energetically while looking at Gus who was beginning to feel invisible.

"You have a good time in LA?" Major Darling said.

"Not really, sir," Gus said.

"Not really. Well, that's better than 'Fuck no,' I guess."

"Yes, sir," Gus said.

"I didn't have a good time either," Major Darling said.

"Sorry to hear that, sir," Gus said.

"You don't have to kiss my ass, Reppo. San Antonio was a fucking disaster. Maybe you heard about it."

Admitting he knew how Major Darling destroyed his career in San Antonio was probably not a smart thing to do. "No sir," Gus said.

"I won't go into it. Let me just say there are some people with birds and stars on their shoulders who would like to take my nuts off with a butter knife."

Gus nodded carefully.

Major Darling chewed his peanuts.

After a long moment, Major Darling said, "You've heard of the OSI, Reppo?"

"No sir."

"OSI—Office of Special Investigations. Air force's version of the gestapo. They might pay us a little visit. They might want to ask you a few questions. I'd advise you to clean up your act before they do. On second thought, no. Go just as you are. Be yourself. Maybe they'll appreciate your honesty."

Gus felt the stubble on his chin. He squirmed in the hard, uncushioned chair. He nodded in agreement, as if he saw good sense in Major Darling's advice.

"My pension is at stake, Reppo," Major Darling said. "Maybe more than my pension. When those bastards want to string you up, they find ways to do it that would test your powers of invention."

Gus squirmed, nodded.

"You remember steering the C-47 from LA to Salt Lake?"

"Yes sir!" Gus said. Now that the terrifying experience was history, Gus recalled it fondly, even with some pride.

"No, Reppo, you do not. You don't remember a fucking thing about sitting in the copilot's seat and steering the C-47. In fact, you slept the whole way back to Malmstrom. Isn't that right, Reppo?"

"Sir?"

"You've heard the term 'flight pay,' right?"

"Yes sir," Gus said.

"Do you think you're eligible for flight pay, Reppo?"

"No sir. Definitely not, sir."

"That's good because you're not getting a red cent in flight pay. Only the pilot gets flight pay. You know that, don't you?"

"Yes sir. Only the pilot. Absolutely, sir."

"Some OSI jerkoff asks if an unqualified airman was alone in the cockpit of that C-47, what are you going to tell him?"

"Nothing, sir."

"Not *nothing*, Reppo! You're going to tell him that Major Clive Darling flew the old bucket of bolts all the way to Great Falls while you and your buddy sacked out. You woke up when we touched down. You with me on this?"

"Yes, sir," Gus mumbled.

"God*damn*it, Reppo, speak up! I'm in a fucking jam here!"

"Yes, sir!" Gus said.

Major Darling lit a cigar and put his feet up on the desk. "You ever see that movie about the bombing of Hiroshima? Called *Above and Beyond*? Just before Colonel Tibbets takes off in the Enola Gay his commanding general says, 'Tibbets, I can't give you any guarantees your plane will come back.' And Tibbets says, 'Sir, this uniform didn't come with guarantees.' Truer words were never spoken, Reppo."

"I believe it, sir," Gus said.

"It's not the money, you understand. My flight pay this year won't buy me a carton of cigarettes. That's not the fucking point, Reppo."

"Yes sir," Gus said.

"I'm talking about the discrepancy. I'm talking about false statements. Misrepresentations. You see? That little discrepancy is leverage, Reppo. I don't want to give them any goddamn leverage. You with me on this?"

"Yes sir," Gus said.

"Convince me, Reppo."

"I'm with you, sir!" Gus said.

"Say it again, with more conviction, airman."

"I am with you, *sir*!" Gus said.

"Leverage, Reppo. Leverage is everything. Your enemies want leverage. Don't give it to them. Remember that, you'll do well in this fucked-up world. You understand me?"

"I understand you, sir," Gus said.

"Let's have a little drink on it."

Major Darling opened the file cabinet side of his desk and took out a bottle of expensive scotch. He filled two paper cups and handed one to Gus.

"I flew sixty low-level B-26 missions with the 484th bomb group in Italy. Flattened the Montecassino monastery twice. Probably killed a dozen monks to every Kraut. Got a DFC for it. I flew C-54s full of supplies into Tempelhof during the Berlin Airlift. Now the bastards want to lynch me for getting my knackwurst nibbled by a general's wife. They can't nail me for that since it's too delicate a subject for them to make public—no leverage there—but now there's this flight pay shit and Christ knows what else. That strike you as fair, Reppo?"

"Not fair at all, sir," Gus said.

"Reppo, let me ask you something," Major Darling said after knocking back his cup of scotch.

"Sir?"

"Did you know it's against the law to be a member of the Communist Party?"

"No sir, I didn't."

"The Communist Party was outlawed by Ike and the Congress in 1954. That's what the HUAC hearings were all about. Party members, unless they renounce their affiliation and pledge allegiance to the USA via loyalty oaths, are going to find their Commie asses in a federal prison."

"I didn't know that, sir," Gus said.

"Sergeant Runkle tells me you have some pinko friends in town—those kids who tried to make trouble at the Hanford Works. Is that right?"

Gus felt blood rushing to his face and neck. He squirmed. He finally recognized what Major Darling was driving at. "They're just college kids, sir," he said.

"Lenin was just a college kid once, airman. Listen to me, Reppo. You don't want the OSI finding out you've been trafficking with Reds, am I clear on that?"

Gus stopped himself from squirming. He looked at Major Darling. Major Darling looked at Gus. Some unspoken deal was being offered.

"You understand what I'm saying here, Reppo?"

"I shouldn't see these people anymore—or else—?"

"No, Reppo. See them all you want. Fuck those little pinko twats cross-eyed. Pussy is pussy—pink, or red white and blue. I'm just telling you that you don't want OSI agents finding out who you're keeping company with."

"I see, sir," Gus said. "I think I understand, sir."

"You scratch my back, I'll scratch yours. You screw me, I'll throw you to the dogs. You get my drift?"

"I do, sir."

"Now: Who flew the C-47 all the way back to Great Falls, nonstop?"

"How did they find out you didn't, sir?"

"Christ knows. Some flight inconsistencies. Radio chatter, or the lack of it. Maybe your fat buddy let it slip. In any case, they're just guessing at this point." Gus drained the scotch out of his paper cup and Major Darling refilled it. "I recall that you lost your stripe a few months ago for hitting Sergeant Runkle, the AP."

"Yes sir."

"That's too bad. Personally, I don't think fighting is a good reason for demotions. Fighting shows spunk. Spunk is a good thing. Shows spirit. There are other punishments for fighting besides demotion. Like a month of KP. Or a month restriction to the base."

"Yes sir. I agree sir."

Major Darling relit his cigar. "Get yourself some corporal stripes, Reppo. Sew them on today. I don't care to see a highly trained technician with a naked sleeve."

"Thank you sir."

"I believe we understand each other. Am I right about that, Reppo?"

"Yes sir," Gus said.

Major Darling poured scotch into his cup. He looked at Gus as if still undecided about his loyalties. He tossed some peanuts into his mouth. He chewed thoughtfully. He sipped his scotch. Gus, feeling invisible again, squirmed in the hard wooden chair.

"You need some cash, Reppo? Is cash a problem?"

"No sir."

Major darling took out his wallet, slipped out a twenty-dollar bill. He held the money out to Gus. Gus hesitated.

"Take it, Reppo. I insist."

"Sir . . . ?"

"Take the money, goddamn it. Buy your commie girlfriend a Bible. You don't want her to go to hell for her dumb-ass political views, do you?"

Gus started to laugh, appreciating Major Darling's sense of humor, but the Major frowned and Gus managed to choke off the mistaken impulse, but not soon enough.

"You find that amusing?" Major Darling said. "There's nothing amusing about the goddamn Bible, Reppo. You find a joke in the Bible, I'll promote you to staff sergeant."

"Didn't mean to laugh, sir."

"Soldier gets a blow job from a general's wife in the Bible, they make him cut his own pecker off. That make you split a gut, Reppo?"

"No sir."

"Some things are not funny."

"Definitely not, sir."

Major Darling's eyes went distant again as he chewed his peanuts.

After a full minute, he said:

"You still here, Reppo? What is it? Twenty not enough? You want more?

"No sir. I didn't . . ."

"Glad to hear it, airman. Now get your blackmailing ass out of my office. Remember, two can play that game."

Gus stood, saluted, and almost ran out the door.

He met Lyle Dressen outside the administration building.

"How much did he give you?" Dressen said.

"Twenty bucks," Gus said, "and corporal stripes."

"He gave me ten and a boost to buck sergeant."

"I look at it as flight pay," Gus said.

"I think the major's flipped his wig," Dressen said.

"The Big Empty strikes again."

"I hear you, airman."

30

Lamar Harkey, failing to get his secondhand TV to produce pictures, asked Gus for advice. The TV was a black-and-white table model manufactured in the late 1940s. It had an ebony Bakelite cabinet and a circular five-inch screen. Harkey had attached rabbit ears to it but couldn't find a test pattern on any of the twelve channels.

"You need more than rabbit ears, Lamar," Gus told him. Once Harkey thought he heard a voice coming through the static. Gus said it was just background noise—universal static from cosmic space, not human speech. Harkey persisted. ("There's a talker out there, Reppo!") He spent half the day studying the tiny electrical snowstorm, determined to find a picture to match the imagined voice.

"I paid a feller sixteen *dollars* for this TV set," Harkey said, as if a sixteen-dollar TV should be able to bring in pictures from a distant station.

"You could've asked some questions before you bought it," Gus said.

Harkey stared hopefully into the pictureless five-inch screen. "It's a good-lookin little TV set, though, aint it, Reppo?"

"It's beautiful, Lamar, even without pictures."

It was too nice outside to sit around in the barracks. Gus walked the perimeter of the radar squadron twice. The snowdrifts were melting and water in little streams guttered along the pathways between buildings.

A pair of Scorpions flying low and slow passed over the radar domes. One of them waggled its wings. Gus saw the pilot's white helmet. The pilot waved and Gus waved back. The Scorpions, flying home after making practice intercepts on each other, turned a wide circle. Black smoke trailed from their muttering engines. They flew by again, even slower. Both pilots waved. Gus waved back.

Gus wondered if it was too late to change the terms of his enlistment. Could he still apply for OCS and flight school? How great would it be to fly a Scorpion! He imagined himself in the cockpit of the plane that waggled its wings, imagined himself waving to an airman on the ground below.

The pilots lit their afterburners and the Scorpions slanted upward into the steep sky, engines belching thunder until they were too small to follow.

Gus went back to the barracks.

"Gosh *dang* it!" Lamar Harkey said. He'd wrapped aluminum foil around the metal rods of the rabbit ears but still found nothing as he clicked the selector through the channels.

"We're a hundred forty miles from the nearest TV station, Harkey," Gus said. "You can't expect to pull in a picture from that far away with rabbit ears. Besides, a woman who should know once told me that TV was Satan's tool."

"Yeah, that's what my ma says," Harkey said, dejected.

"Then why'd you buy it?"

"I like to have a TV to watch, Reppo. I don't think the devil gives a cow pie one way or t'other about it. I like to watch it even if it's just snow."

"You got a serious mental problem, Harkey."

"I sure wish I could get just one TV show, like that one with the talking horse, without going to a whiskey bar in town."

"You need a real antenna, Lamar."

"You got any idea how to fix one up?" Harkey said. "I'll let you watch any program you want, you make this thing work."

"I'll think about it," Gus said.

31

Light snow dusted the alley. Gus looked at his wristwatch. It was too dark to read the dial but he felt that at least a half hour had passed. Gus thought: The greedy pig's paying five more cartwheels for a blow job.

Gus didn't know if he had the stomach to go through with it. He thought of Ray. What would Ray say? "Pull your head out of your ass," is what he'd say. "Don't fuck up your life. This is not the right thing, Gate."

You're the one to talk, Gus argued. Besides, it's not just about you. For me it's exactly the right thing. I can't look at the son of a bitch without getting sick to my stomach. I don't do this, I'll get an ulcer.

"This is the wrong right thing. Think about it. Use your goddamn head."

I have thought about it, Ray. I'm done thinking.

"That's what I'm afraid of, Gate."

The voices in his head stopped arguing: Mutt Runkle came out of the Moomaw whorehouse. He unzipped, spread his legs wide to avoid the spatter. He hummed a toneless tune.

Gus came out from behind the rack of garbage cans. His right hand ached from gripping the jack handle while he'd waited for Runkle to come out. His hand felt frozen to the steel bar. He didn't think he'd be able to open his fingers when it was over. The jack handle felt like it had become a permanent part of his anatomy.

He stepped up behind Runkle, jack handle held high. It was a good GM jack handle, an inch thick and almost two feet long. Gus swung it at Runkle's head. He put all he had behind the swing but it was a glancing blow, not the dead-on shot he'd meant it to be and, worse, the jack handle flew out of his suddenly weak hand and clattered down the dark alley.

Runkle didn't seem affected. He didn't turn around to see what had hit him. He broke stream, shook the drip, tucked his penis back into his pants, zipped up. He touched the back of his head and looked with some surprise at the blood on his fingers. He started to turn, arm raised defensively, but then his legs gave out. He dropped to his knees.

After a frantic search Gus retrieved the jack handle. He stood over Runkle, who was now on all fours mumbling curses, and swung again, a two-handed log-splitter's stroke that landed squarely. The blow jarred his bones all the way to his shoulder and Runkle flopped face down into the yellow puddle he'd made.

Gus walked back to the Buick, jack handle held down at his side. The car was parked on Main, in front of the Moomaw Dairy. He peeled the locked fingers of his right hand off the jack handle one by one, then tossed it into the trunk next to the spare. He looked up and down the empty street but saw no one. He got in the car and started the engine. Then turned it off.

"Shit," he said. He rested his forehead against the cold steering wheel. He'd forgotten an important detail.

He walked back to the alley. But now his legs were shaky, knees unlocking with every step. Runkle was still face down in yellow slush. Gus took Runkle's wallet and the few silver dollars he had in his pants. He took the bills—thirty dollars—then tossed the empty wallet next to Runkle. The cops would see it as a random mugging behind a whorehouse: These airmen should be more careful. Could happen to anyone.

Gus went back to the Buick, forcing himself to keep a casual gait though his legs were unreliable. He got in. The adrenaline surge had ebbed. He felt weak and disoriented and sick to his stomach. His mouth was dry and he wanted a drink.

He was shaking hard and couldn't get the key into the ignition. When he did, he raced the engine until the fan belt screamed. He slipped the gear lever into drive and the car fishtailed away from the curb and bolted west.

Half a mile down the road Gus pulled off the highway. He set the brake, opened the door, leaned out, and puked.

Then he drove off again, accelerating to eighty miles an hour. After a while at this speed he rolled down the window and tossed Runkle's thirty dollars into the wind. He tossed the silver cartwheels after them.

"Feel better?" Ray said.

Gus would have to think about that.

PART FIVE

32

Son of a bitch had it coming. Tell me about it. Is he dead? The only one who gives a shit is his partner Jeff Sparks. Tell you the truth, I don't think Sparks is all that broken up. I mean, did you ever see Mutt and Jeff eat together? Drink together? Play cards at the same table? Fuck no, Mutt was a psycho loner. Jeff just did what Mutt told him to do. Hell, Jeff Sparks, he's a good ole boy down deep. But Mutt, shit, no one really knew him or wanted to. How could you like a fuckhead like that? Is he dead? They kill him? Someone tried. Kicked his ass and took his cash. Town boys been getting more and more pissed at airmen sniffing around the local herd of heifers. Yeah, but that's just normal kid stuff. Why would they kill the guy, especially Mutt who only went to the whores for his poon? No, you're wrong there, shit-for-brains. Runkle had a thing with the town pump. Mutt the city slicker aka the kitty licker. The town boys wouldn't get worked up over that. Even so, they catch an airman alone they don't let the opportunity go by. Ever since the viaduct brawl they be looking to stomp flyboy ass. They went overboard on this one, don't you think? What I think don't mean jack. I advise you airman, do not get caught alone in Milk River. Travel in pairs. Carry a weapon, like a sock full of shot. You might of wished you had if you get caught in a blind alley, I shit you not. You better believe Mutt wished he had his .45 or a stick. But is he dead? Don't know, don't care. How about you Gogolak? Don't know, don't care. You Norton? Don't know, don't care. Perez? Don't know, don't care. If you guys could harmonize we'd have a quartet. We be goin to town, find us a town boy and shank his crank. Will that help Runkle? Who cares? Fuck Runkle. Runkle can eat shit. Okay, but answer me this: anyone know if the muthufuckah be dead? Is Mutt muthafucken Runkle dead?

Gus busied himself with other things. He couldn't sleep, so he stayed up at night working out the problem of the feeder line. He'd need two-hundred feet or more of coaxial cable. It had to be quality stuff, capable of being buried in a shallow trench without cracking or rotting away in a year or two. He'd leave that part of the job to Lamar Harkey.

"Harkey, here's what we're going to need," he said. "Two hundred feet of 75 Ohm Belden RG6 weatherproof coax. I don't think you'll be able to find that much in Milk River. Go to Great Falls, or, if you have to, Billings or Rapid City. Some electronic shop in one of those towns should have it. Hell, you might have to go to Minneapolis or Seattle. I don't especially care where you go. That's your part of the job, not mine. But we can't move ahead on this until we get that cable."

Harkey looked sorely troubled. "Geez, I don't know, Reppo. That's kind of hard to think about. I mean, Seattle? Minneapolis? You want me to go by myself? I don't care to fly. Would I have to fly in a airplane?"

"Why'd you join the air force if you're afraid of airplanes, Harkey?"

Harkey shrugged. "Recruiter said I could go to college on the GI Bill when I got out. All expenses paid."

"You want to go to college?"

"Shoot no! He just made it sound like a good deal and that I'd be dumb to pass it up. Heck, I never even went to high school. When I was ten my Pa . . ."

"Listen to me, Lamar. You want the talking horse? You want Saturday night wrestling? You want to slam your ham watching the Miss America contest? You'll do this."

Harkey's lips tightened into a grim line as he fought to master the terrifying idea of air travel. He nodded stoically, accepting the awful necessity of searching the Northwest for coaxial cable. "I'll do it, Reppo. I'll take some leave time and do it."

Gus told Harkey that he intended to fashion a forty-element "fishbone" antenna out of the supply of tubular aluminum that was kept for antenna repair. He'd channel-cut the elements precisely to the wavelength of channel 13, the one channel they had a chance of receiving with decent signal strength.

He gave Harkey the technical details:

Wavelength 1.388 meters. Half-wave elements would work just as well, and the smaller antenna would be less noticeable, less vulnerable to weather. He'd cut the elements to .70 meters. He'd make a stacked array, totaling forty elements, twenty on top of twenty. This would give the antenna maximum directional gain. Even a weak picture flying through the air at the speed of light should be caught and enhanced by the double-fishbone array.

"How come you call it a fishbone?" Harkey asked.

"Because that's what it looks like, gills to tail—the skeleton of a filleted bluegill."

"Oh," Harkey said.

"We'll need to have an antenna preamp," Gus said. "With a couple hundred feet of coax lead-in we'll lose about five decibels of signal strength. We'll get it back with a preamp."

Harkey looked at Gus with bovine wonder.

"Did you get all that, Harkey?"

"Say what?"

"I'll write it down."

Gus looked at Harkey and Harkey looked at Gus. There was no meeting of minds and no chance there ever could be.

Harkey sucked on a tooth, already dreaming of the talking horse. After a minute of tooth sucking, he said, "When they passed out body parts in Heaven, Reppo, they must of give you extry brains whilst I stood in line for double size feet."

The buzz went on for days:

The paper says the town boys probably did it, but no one's taking credit. Watch yourself. I mean it, airman. Hell, I'm going to buy a gun, Sarge. No you are not. You can't carry a concealed weapon in town. The heck you can't, this is Montana not Hoboken. You can strap a goddamn rocket launcher to your ass in Montana. You can fish with grenades and hunt with machine guns. Few years back when the base was new, this Captain, Theo Woodcock, armed twenty airmen with M-1s then went to town to break a pair of flyboys out of jail. Captain Woodcock himself carried a .45 caliber grease gun with a thirty-round magazine. The airmen had been beat up and rolled by cops and were being held on resisting arrest charges. Drunk? Sure they were drunk! That don't have shit to do with it. That be fucking irrelevant. So the bus rolls up to the police station and Woodcock and his twenty armed men went in. Deputy come near to fill his drawers. They took the keys to the cell the flyboys were in and got them out. Thomas Woodcock had crazy eyes. He could scare you without a grease gun. Tell you somethin, airman: They under-

stand guns in Milk River, I guarantee it. This still be the wild muthafuckin west. Me? I carry a nine-millimeter German Luger. Got it on sale in a Milk River gun shop, left over from the war. It's against air force regs. Fuck the regs! Fuck the REGS? Are you nuts? You keep talking crazy shit like that Major Darling's going to restrict everyone to the base permanently. Your dick won't see the inside of a twat the rest of your enlistment. Sure, like Major D. gives a shit. But what I want to know—Is Mutt Runkle dead? Flip of the coin. Roll of the dice.

Harkey bought a heavy roll of RG6 coax and a preamp guaranteed to boost far away signals by ten decibels. He found the stuff in Glasgow, Montana, a hundred sixty miles east of Milk River, where a big SAC base was located. He took the train there and back for less than thirty dollars.

There were over a thousand airmen stationed at Glasgow and downtown businesses thrived. The electronics store Harkey found was loaded with goodies, including cathode-ray tubes. Harkey bought one the same size as the one in his TV set, just in case.

Gus climbed the mast at night so he wouldn't attract anyone's curiosity. He didn't wear a safety harness—too cumbersome along with all the gear he was carrying. He didn't think he'd fall, but if he did—well, maybe he deserved it. Fear, though, was not a factor.

He aimed the array in the general direction of Great Falls, then clamped the 40-element antenna to the top of the mast with U-bolts. The other antennas that occupied the mast made a confusing geometry of aluminum rods that the double-fishbone could hide among. He attached the coax to the array then dropped the roll of cable to the ground.

The installation of the antenna reminded Gus of the antenna

he'd repaired for Marva Gunlocke, and for a moment he felt his strength draining away, thinking he might topple. You'd like that, Marva, he said to himself. You'd like to see me do a hundred foot topple, wouldn't you? "I dearly would," he heard her distant voice say. "You have earned it."

As he descended he used friction tape to bind the loose coax to the mast. On the ground, he laid the cable into the six-inch deep trench Harkey had dug the previous night using a meat cleaver for a pick and a steel serving spoon for a shovel. A week of Chinook winds had softened the ground enough to make the shallow trench possible. Gus buried the cable as he uncoiled it. When he reached the barracks he tapped on the window of their room. Harkey opened it and Gus handed him the cable. Harkey pressed the cable into the groove he'd made in the sill with a rat-tail file and closed the window on top of it. Inside, Gus attached the lead to the preamp, then connected the preamp to the little TV. Harkey turned it on.

A strong picture rolled into the screen. A man who looked like an animated corpse read the news. He told of floods, earthquakes, assassinations, and wars, with the same dead expression as when he reported festive seasonal activities, and the birth, in Iowa, of quadruplets. He gave the weather forecast as if it were an obituary for the greater world. Harkey, nonetheless, was thrilled. "Hot dog!" he said, "We got us our own TV set, Reppo!"

"Merry Christmas, Lamar," Gus said.

33

Gus approached Jeff Sparks. "Got any idea what happened to Runkle?" he said. He'd forced an innocence on his voice—which only made his question sound more like a confession than a casual inquiry.

"What's it to you?" Sparks said.

Sparks was the tallest man in the squadron, all elbows and knees on the basketball court. He had narrow shoulders but his chest was deep and muscular. He wasn't an intimidator, not intentionally at least, but no one tested him. He wore buck sergeant stripes even though he had three years time in grade. Which meant someone who counted didn't think much of him. Three years as a buck sergeant was a year too long. Sparks felt he'd been unjustly denied promotion to staff sergeant by men in his chain of command who outranked him—Mutt Runkle excepted. When in the vicinity of his superiors, Sparks carried himself with an insolent correctness.

"Just wondering, Sparks," Gus said.

"Wondering, huh? You have something to do with it, Reppo?"

"No."

"You and a couple of your asshole buddies take him down in that alley? Maybe it was those commies you hang out with?"

"It was a simple question, Sparks."

"Was that what it was? Tell me something, Reppo. You get off on other peoples' hurts? That why you asked about Runkle?"

"Forget it, Sparks. Sorry I bothered you."

"Runkle's in the hospital," Sparks said. "St. Bonaventure's in Milk River. You thinking to bring him flowers? Won't do any good. He's in a coma. Maybe he'll come out of it, maybe he won't. The shithooks are making odds in the NCO Club. Ten will get you twenty he doesn't make it. He's got a cracked skull. He bled into his brainpan. You want to put some money on him one way or the other, or do you want to help?"

"Help?"

"Major Darling's asking for volunteers. We need the full complement of APs, plus a few extras to check out the bars in town. He wants to increase the patrols."

"You mean you want me to pull AP duty?"

"No, I want you to sit in the AP shack and stroke your crank. What did you think I meant, Reppo?"

"I got too much to do. Besides, I wouldn't be a good cop."

"Yeah, I figured you'd find an excuse," Sparks said, yawning. "I don't get me some help the major will get it for me."

A pair of second lieutenants from OSI visited the radar squadron. Gus was called into their makeshift office in the Special Services building.

The lieutenants were seated at a folding table that served as a desk. The small windowless room was jammed with athletic equipment, along with outdoor sports gear. Hunting rifles—mostly World War I Springfields and Enfields—were kept locked on a wall rack, along with a half-dozen light shotguns. Fishing rods, nets, creels, bait boxes, were stacked in a corner. A wooden bin filled with basketballs and footballs occupied another corner.

"Take a chair, airman," one of the OSI men said. His name tag identified him as Lt. Darrel Woodbine. The other OSI man was Lt. Kevin Lockerbee. Both lieutenants had Styrofoam coffee cups in front of them along with a thermos. A packed accordion file sat between them on the table.

Gus opened a folding chair and sat down. The OSI men shuffled papers. After a minute, Lt. Lockerbee said, "When exactly were you dismissed from flight school, Airman Reppo? We don't seem to have a record of that."

"I wasn't dismissed. I was never there," Gus said.

Both men looked at Gus. "Excuse me, airman?" Lt. Woodbine said. "Are you telling us you *failed* to report to the Randolph Air Force Base flight school? That you never . . ."—he shuffled through some papers—". . . *soloed* in a PT-19?"

"No sir. I mean, yes sir. I didn't report because I didn't apply for it. I don't know anything about Randolph Air Force Base. I was never in a PT-19. I don't even know what a PT-19 is."

"You didn't apply, but you were accepted. You've never been in a PT-19 but you soloed successfully. How do you explain these seeming incongruities?"

"I wasn't accepted. I didn't apply. I didn't solo. It's impossible to explain what you never did."

"*Impossible*, airman?" Lt. Woodbine said. "Walking on water is impossible. Squaring the circle is impossible. I don't think we're asking for the *impossible*."

"There appears to be a rather serious gap in your records, Reppo," Lt. Lockerbee said. "Could it be you went AWOL for a week or two, after you soloed?"

"I've never been AWOL, sir, before soloing or after, even though I didn't solo."

"So you say, so you say," Lt. Lockerbee said. "Your commanding officer, however, says something less definitive, yet in some ways more instructive, regarding your, ah, reliability."

"I don't understand you, sir," Gus said.

"Poor hygiene. Poor military correctness, uniform-wise. Dangerous work habits. Disrespect. In wartime, a probable deserter. Poor attitude in general." Woodbine turned pages as he spoke.

"Dangerous work habits, sir?" Gus said.

"Climbing radio towers sans safety harness. 'Poor attitude' is obviously related to that charge."

The lieutenants from OSI studied the papers spread on the table before them. Lockerbee looked at Woodbine, Woodbine looked at Lockerbee. Lockerbee refilled his coffee cup, Woodbine refilled his.

"Says here you ran out on your car payments down in Biloxi," Woodbine said.

"I don't have a car, lieutenant."

"A convenient answer, airman."

"You are aware, are you not, that you have a compelling death wish?" Lockerbee asked.

"Sir?"

"That's what the headshrinker we consulted called it."

"I don't have any death wish, lieutenant."

"You don't have a death wish, you never soloed, and you never even *reported* to Randolph," Lt. Woodbine said. "Are we to take it that while you never *reported*, you nonetheless were accepted for training? Hardly seems possible, doesn't it?"

"No sir. I mean, yes sir. I didn't do any of that, sir."

"Are you familiar, airman, with the Uniform Code of Military Justice definition of prevarication?"

"No sir."

"Of desertion?"

"No sir."

"You should make it your business to be so."

"I'd never desert, sir."

"Never is a very long time, airman."

"It is sir."

"Are you saying there are no imaginable circumstances that would cause you to desert?"

Gus hesitated. "Yes sir. I think so, sir."

"Somewhat less certain, now, are you, airman?"

The OSI lieutenants looked at each other and grinned sagely. Both men wore horn-rims. Each wore the bright orange and pale yellow Good Conduct ribbon. They refilled their coffee cups.

They looked through their file for more papers. They were lawyers, recent graduates, and had never served on a military installation.

"On an unrelated subject, Airman Reppo," Lt. Lockerbee said. "A serious complaint has been filed against you by a Mrs. Orson Gunlocke of Chula Vista, California. Are you familiar with such a person?"

Gus thought: Fuck oh dear. He felt light-headed. Don't topple, he told himself.

"Sort of, sir," Gus said.

"Interesting response, airman. Sort of. By that you mean you have had some intercourse with the aforesaid Mrs. Gunlocke."

"Intercourse sir?"

"We mean in the socially acceptable sense. Intercourse in the conversational, afternoon tea party sense," Lt. Woodbine said.

"If you'd like, we could speak of it in the carnal sense, as well," Lt. Lockerbee said.

"What's this about?" Gus said.

"We told you. She's filed a complaint against you with the Judge Advocate General's office."

"Complaint? I should file a complaint against *her*."

"Is she the reason you went AWOL from Randolph, even though you soloed in the PT-19 and thus qualified for advanced instruction in the T-33 jet trainer? You fell in love with Mrs. Gunlocke—if it can be called love—and decided flying airplanes for your country just wasn't good enough for you. Does that about sum it up, airman? You placed your personal interests over your sworn duty?"

"Jesus Christ, sir! That's crazy!"

"Calm down, airman. Of course it's crazy, we're agreed on that point. There is much here that's not kosher, in the psychological sense. For one thing, Mrs. Gunlocke is over forty years old. Can you tell us what your present relationship is with Mrs. Gunlocke?"

"I don't have any present relationship with her. Marva Gunlocke was married to my father, Orson Gunlocke. He was killed in the war."

"She's your *mother*?" Lt. Woodbine said, rising out of his chair.

"No sir! She's not my mother! She was married to my father, that's all."

"That's *all*?"

"Is not one's mother married to one's father?" Lt. Lockerbee said. "Am I missing something here?"

"My mother lives here in town," Gus said.

"Keeping her close so you can continue your carnal relations with her?" Lt. Woodbine said. "This is a step or two beyond the pale, airman."

"It explains his death wish," Lockerbee confided to Woodbine.

"You've got it all wrong!" Gus said.

"You sit atop high radio towers without safety equipment, staring at the sky . . . contemplating—understandably *suicide*?"

"No, sir. I mean yes, I've climbed without gear, but . . ."

"He says no when he means yes, yes when he means no," Lockerbee observed. "He's not clear about so many things. Does he know what his position is now? Does he know who he is and what he wants? Does he know the depth and extent of his psychological disturbance? The depth and extent of his guilt?"

"I'm ready to recommend this airman for an immediate Section 8 discharge," Lt. Woodbine said. "The man is clearly mentally unfit, and, as such, a threat to squadron morale."

Lt. Woodbine warned, "Before you say anything else, airman, I suggest you hear the charges Mrs. Gunlocke has brought against you."

Gus felt his throat constrict. He needed more air but wasn't getting it.

Lt. Lockerbee said, "Mrs. Gunlocke—the woman you speak

of as your father's wife—in other words, your *mother*—claims you raped her, and that she is now carrying your child."

"If it's a boy," Lt. Woodbine said, "he's your son as well as your brother. If a girl, your daughter and your sister. You see? This is why we have laws against incest."

The room darkened, as when a swift cloud blocks the sun.

"I personally am filled with disgust," Lt. Woodbine said. "I've never encountered such unmitigated foulness. The devil himself in his filthy brimstone cave couldn't . . ."

"Take it easy, Woodbine," Lockerbee said. "The evidence speaks for itself. No need to wax poetic."

Gus slid out of his chair. He toppled.

He woke up in sick bay. "Nothing's wrong with you," the medic, Phil Ecks, said.

Toppled, Gus did not walk across the ocean floor. Did not see Orson. Saw no gutted *Fisk*. Heard no voices. Saw no fish nibbling the ragged remains of his father. For which he was thankful. He'd simply passed out. Fainted dead away. Two airmen who'd been shooting pool in the day room carried him to sick bay.

"I think I'm coming down with something," Gus told Phil Ecks, the medic.

"Probably goldbrick-itis. There's an epidemic going around," Ecks, said.

"I'm serious," Gus said.

Ecks gave Gus two small bottles of GI gin. Gus went to his barracks and drank the medicine. GI gin, a mixture of alcohol, decongestants, and opiates, was the standard medicine for colds and flu. It tasted like a blend of turpentine, vinegar, and corn syrup, but the effect was quick and strong. Gus drank the first bottle while watching TV with Lamar Harkey. Harkey was sitting on the floor, picking black lint from between his toes.

"You gonna give me a swoller of that?" Harkey said.

"No. I need it," Gus said. "I'm sick."

"I feel like I got something coming on," Harkey said.

"Then go to sick bay and get your own medicine."

They watched *What's My Line*. They didn't talk much except to scoff at the blindfolded panel of big-name stars who couldn't tell the famous wrestler, Gorgeous George, from a New York hairdresser. Gus got drowsy and didn't want to watch anymore. He climbed into his bunk. Harkey kept on guffawing at the dumb-ass stars as they grilled the next celebrity guest.

"You figure they're actin dumb on purpose, Reppo," Harkey said, "or they really can't figure out it's Mickey Mantle instead of Margaret Truman? Course, old Mick's talking high up like a girl just to fool them, but even so it shouldn't take them five dang minutes to figure it out. I mean, they ask the secret guest did she once play in a big house in Washington DC and ole Mick says in that fakey girly voice, 'Kinda biglike, but not exactly a house. Lots of grass for carpet but no roof and people everywhere packed in like sardines,' you'd think that might get them off the Margaret Truman idea, right? But no-oo. Betsy, the pretty blond-haired lady says, 'It's a pianer concert on the South Lawn?' cause she knew Margaret Truman played pianer real good, like her daddy the president did."

"Could you please shut up, Harkey?" Gus said. "I'm trying to sleep."

"Want me to turn it down, Reppo?" Harkey said.

"Just turn yourself down, Harkey. I don't mind listening to the TV while I drop off."

Harkey wasn't offended. He was happy with his TV and grateful to Gus for making it work so well. Gus could do no wrong as far as Harkey was concerned.

The GI gin was making Gus feel numb behind the eyes. His thoughts became slow and random. Time itself crawled by. It moved with the leisure of a flower closing in evening shade. The last thing Gus said to Harkey still echoed in his mind as if he'd just spoken, but he wasn't sure he'd actually said it out loud. "I don't mind listening to the TV while I drop off," he said again.

Harkey nodded and grinned. "Got the message, little buddy," he said.

Gus finished the second bottle of GI gin. He felt himself dissolve. "I don't mind listening to the TV while I drop off," he heard himself say.

"Got the message loud and clear," Harkey said.

A panelist said, "Hmmm. Kinda *like* a house but *not* in DC"

"That ole Mick, he's something aint he?" Harkey chortled.

"I don't mind . . ."

"Roger and out, pardner."

"I'm thinking sports," the panelist said. "Are you a famous sports star?"

"Hot dang! Cook my grits in baby piss! We got us a real breakthrough!" Harkey sneered.

"Could you be the great Babe Didrikson?" a panelist said and Harkey slapped his knee and scoffed.

"I believe Babe died last year," the secret celebrity said in a hoarse falsetto. The delighted audience laughed.

Gus felt his lips forming the same words again, but silently this time as he sank into a pool of shimmering green light. *I don't mind . . .*

"We got hit by a Jap torpedo this morning," Orson Gunlocke said. He was sitting on Ray Springer's bunk. He crackled as if the meager fat under his torn skin was burning. What hair he had was on fire. Half his head was gone. Brain matter slumped like pale mud onto what was left of his shoulder and chest. A vampire squid drifted through his blown-out rib cage.

"You died because of me," Gus said. "I killed you."

"Spread the blame, boy. You didn't make the goddamn rules."

"But people are responsible for what they do."

"A point comes in your life when you got to just say 'No sir, I've had enough of your shit.'"

"Say no to who?"

"That's the sixty-four dollar question, son."

"Hey, Reppo! Who you talking to?" Harkey said. He looked worried. Worried, then alarmed.

Gus rolled over and pulled his pillow over his head and made a noise that sounded to Harkey like the solemn voice of an owl.

34

Gus walked past First Sergeant Burnside's desk and went directly into Major Darling's office without knocking and before Burnside could stop him.

"What the goddamn hell . . . ?" Major Darling said. He had his feet up on his desk and was drinking scotch out of a coffee mug.

Gus sat down in the chair across from Major Darling's desk without asking permission. "They're recommending me for a Section 8, Major. How the fuck did that happen? What did you tell them?"

"You don't come in here asking questions and demanding answers, airman," Major Darling said. "Remember your place."

"Bullshit," Gus said. "I don't have a place. I'm getting kicked out of the air force. I don't give a shit about protocol or whatever the hell it's called."

"Calm down, Reppo. For Christ's sakes. Getting a Section 8 isn't the worst thing that could happen to you."

"'Mentally Unfit.' I'll have to wear that for the rest of my life. Discharged from the air force for being mentally unfit."

"Look, Reppo. I admit I sicced the OSI jerk offs on you. I wanted them off my ass. They were giving me shit about my girlfriend, Heidi Zechbruder. I sneaked her across from East Berlin and brought her with me to the States. Cost me two months' pay in bribes and forged papers. Heidi lacks credentials but she cooks, cleans, and fucks like a goddamn monkey. She also has some political baggage the OSI shits don't like. You have any idea what an East German citizen has to put up with under the Reds? The secret police are everywhere. No one messes with the Stasi. You play their game or they put you in a hole under a concrete lid. So she worked for them. Translations and cryptography. I had to get OSI off Heidi, so I kept them talking about you, which is what they were mostly interested in anyway."

"I'm totally fucked," Gus said.

"For a good cause, Reppo. I'll make it up to you."

"You can't make up for a Section 8 discharge."

"Look here, Reppo. With a few more words, I could have had you put away in Leavenworth for ten years. All I needed to do was link you with those punks who went to the plutonium works at Hanford. And oh, what's this about the lady who filed a rape and paternity complaint against you? The OSI paperpushers couldn't talk enough about that caper. What've you been up to, Reppo? I believe you *are* Section 8 material. You're a twisted little guy."

"I could have told them you ordered me to fly the C-47 from LA to Salt Lake."

Major Darling leaned back in his chair and lit a cigar. "Don't you get it, airman? That's why I paved the way for your Section 8 discharge. Who's going to believe the ravings of a goddamned mentally incompetent bubblehead like you? In any case, what I told them about you washing out of Randolph wasn't entirely false, was it? There's a speck of truth there, right?"

"Speck of fly shit maybe."

"You didn't get your eight weeks in a PT-19? You didn't solo?"

"I don't know where you get this crap from, Major."

"And I don't think you're in a frame of mind, airman, to know what is crap and what is not."

"I think I am."

"Then what were you doing behind the controls of my C-47? Answer me that."

"I don't have any idea."

"You see? You're obviously not thinking straight. Would I have trusted you with a C-47 if you didn't have basic knowledge? Only a lunatic would have done that. You read me, airman?"

"If I was able to read you Major, I'd fucking shoot myself."

"You're hurting your cause, Reppo, coming in here with this attitude. You're going to rot in a hell of your own making."

"I guess you'd be the expert on that, sir. But thanks for the heads up."

35

Gus thumbed through a stack of magazines in the waiting room. He pulled a full-color brochure from the stack. The handout described the shield-like emblem for the 29th Air Division. Gus read the description. It seemed to have been written in English, or a form of English, but Gus couldn't understand a word.

"Azure within a diminished bordure," it said, "issuant from a sinister base, a cloud formation proper, overall superimposed on the border and issuant, also, from the sinister base."

Gus read and reread the passage, failed to grasp the meaning, then went on to the next passage:

"A demisphere with axis bendwise, light blue surmounted by a lightning flash of the second, between the missile symbol gules and sable, emitting a vapor trail of the second, all-fimbriated argent."

Gus thought: Something's wrong with me or with the man who wrote this.

He read more: "A radar screen of the fifth detail, detailed of the sixth, and edged of the seventh, emitting a light beam of the like, all bendwise, in dexter chief an aircraft symbol of the last, voided of the fifth, and in sinister chief, the owl, the bird of prey, and four mullets—one, two, and one of the seventh."

He read it again and again understood nothing. He hated the man who wrote it, blamed himself for not understanding it. He thought: Is this my future? Would there come a time when he understood nothing? Would his inability to understand make him unfit for any kind of occupation, civilian or military? Would he one day see only unintelligible gibberish wherever he looked? And where would that lead him? Would the world he lived in become a madhouse of unsolvable cryptograms? A wave of terror rocked him. He dropped the pamphlet and stood up. He read a sign on the wall: PSYCHIATRIC WARD. LOUD CONVERSATIONS NOT PERMITTED.

"The doctor will see you now," a nurse whispered.

Gus went into a dim office. It had a window, but the blinds were drawn. The main illumination came from an antique floor lamp with a fringed shade. The floor lamp was next to the doctor's desk, also an antique. The doctor, Colonel Adrian Makepiece, was decorating a small Christmas tree. He fixed a glittery star to the blue spruce's leader then stepped back to admire it.

Doctor Makepiece made an offhand but affable gesture offering Gus a chair while he wound a string of lights through the branches of his tree. When he was satisfied the lights were distributed evenly, he attached silver and red balls to the outer branches. He stood back every so often to judge his progress. Gus sat down and watched the doctor work.

Though a meticulous tree trimmer, Doctor Makepiece was a man not comfortable in a uniform. His tie was loose. His shirt was unbuttoned under the tie. He wore colorful Scandinavian slippers. Their tasseled, turned-up toes made them look like toy buckskin canoes. "Would you like to help decorate, airman?" he said.

"No thank you, sir."

"Well, it's almost finished. I don't like this new tinsel they have now—silvered cellophane of some kind." He shook a handful of it at Gus. "You see how flimsy it is?" he said. "The old tinsel was made of lead foil and looked so much better. It had proper heft, don't you think? Icicles require heft."

The doctor stepped back to judge his work. Satisfied, he went to his desk and sat down.

"Now," he said, "who do I have the pleasure of interviewing?"

"Airman Gus Reppo," Gus said.

"And your MOS, Airman Reppo?"

"Radio tech," Gus said.

"And this is also your vocation?"

"Sir?"

"Vocation. The vision you have of yourself making a positive contribution to society. Do you understand me, airman?"

"I, uh, yes. I mean, I guess so, sir."

"I knew a man once," Dr. Makepiece said, "who had no vocation and wanted none. He was all essence as opposed to substance. He was widely loved and esteemed but he contributed nothing tangible to the well-being of society for the simple reason he had nothing to contribute. He was, as we say, *disconnected*. He had *person*hood, but was otherwise vacant. What do you make of the Disconnected Man, airman?"

Gus made nothing of it.

"You see, all men must find their vocation or rely solely on the power and conviction of their personalities. If it's the latter, then their only commodity is themselves. But should a man be proud of himself though he lacks common ability? Most politicians are such men, which casts a dark shadow upon the future. If I had my way, all politicians would be forced to learn a trade and apply that trade humbly five to ten years before entering the political arena. What is your reaction to that, airman?"

"Sounds like a good idea, sir," Gus said.

Dr. Makepiece studied Gus for a moment, then jotted something in a notepad. The whispering nurse entered with a packet of official documents for the doctor. Gus looked at her and their eyes met for half a second. Gus saw either sympathy or disdain in her eyes. He couldn't tell which. She left the room, whispering to herself.

Dr. Makepiece read quickly through the documents. "It says here you suffer from gross indifference. Can you explain that, airman?"

"No sir."

"I suppose it's my job to do that. Tell me, son. Why do you

want a Section 8 discharge? Surely you know that it will be an irradicable stigma that will follow you the rest of your life? Whatever vocation you choose will be compromised by it."

"I don't want a Section 8, sir."

"No? But your papers here indicate acquiescence to the Section 8 process."

"I want to stay in the air force, sir. I was hoping to apply for flight school. I'd like to fly a Scorpion."

The doctor looked momentarily bewildered, then said, "I knew a man who had an admirable vocation, yet he negated his good fortune by taking his own life. In the end, his accomplishments meant nothing to him. What do you make of such a man, son?"

"Crazy?"

"An over-used and under-comprehended word. The mind is a labyrinth. In its deepest recess lies a Minotaur."

"I don't understand, sir," Gus said.

"No one does," Dr. Makepiece said.

The doctor stood up and went to the room's single window. He opened the blinds and looked out at the gray day, then turned back to face Gus. He was now silhouetted against the window and appeared to Gus as a dark, featureless shape.

"Do you know why we celebrate Christmas, airman?" he said. He didn't wait for an answer. "We celebrate the birth of the man who understands us. The man who's gone into the labyrinth, faced the Minotaur, and come back alive. This is what is meant by resurrection. It could be anyone, not just some first century Jew. The problem is, he's in hiding. You see?"

"Not exactly, sir."

"My little tree is a token reminder that the man exists, or did exist, but will not make himself known to us in our time. Why do you suppose that is?"

"No idea, sir."

"We light our decorated trees to lure him out of the shadows.

We sing our carols to tempt his ear. But where is he? Does he scorn us, does he decry what we've become?"

"I see what you mean, sir."

"No, of course you don't. But no matter. I am going to upgrade your discharge from the air force to 'medical,' which is perfectly honorable and will not follow you through life like a black cloud." Dr. Makepiece returned to his desk and sat down. The cushioned chair expelled an almost human sigh.

"There's nothing wrong with me," Gus said.

"If only it were that simple."

"Sir?"

"Incest, overrated as a factor in delayed-onset psychosis, can be contributory, however, to an aberration of character. This condition, while serious, will nonetheless allow you to function as a productive member of society, though in a somewhat attenuated fashion. The prognosis falls short of being bleak provided you grasp and then accommodate your shortcomings. You will lack enthusiasm, a sense of purpose, loyalty, and companionability, but in all other respects you will be relatively normal."

Gus felt like crying. "There *was* no incest, sir."

"I understand why you need to believe that."

"No, really sir . . ."

"Listen to me, son. In certain limited areas, the attenuated personality can lead a rewarding life. Be of good cheer."

Dr. Makepiece leaned back in his chair and swiveled so that he faced the window. He looked out at the gray buildings of Malmstrom Air Force Base and hummed a carol. Gus recognized it. "O Little Town of Bethlehem."

Gus went to Ray Springer's ward. Ray's bed was behind a privacy screen. He could hear him chatting with Lt. Dorio. He opened a pack of cigarettes and lit up. Lt. Dorio came out from behind the screen. She had a sponge in one hand and a shallow pan in the other and an amused smile on her face.

"Go down one floor if you want to smoke, airman," she said. "This is a non-smoking area."

Gus ground the lit end of his cigarette against the sole of his brogan, pocketed the butt. "How's Ray doing?" he said.

"He feeds himself but likes me to bathe him. Men are babies, when it comes right down to it." She collapsed the privacy screen and rolled it against the wall.

"You mean that in a good way, right?" Gus said.

"I mean it in the only way. Men are simple animals. Basic pleasures are all they want out of life. Sex, food, shelter, security. The rest is mischief. Don't you agree, airman?"

It sounded right. It also sounded too easy. "I don't know," Gus said.

Lieutenant Dorio laughed. "Don't break a blood vessel thinking about it, airman. It's not nuclear physics." She leaned against the end of Springer's bed.

Ray Springer was sitting up in bed, eating an ice cream bar. His jaws were no longer wired together.

"How you doing, Gate?' he said. "You look a little fried."

"I'm okay," Gus said. He knew he didn't look good. He knew he looked pale and nervous and shifty eyed. He was glad to see Ray, but worried about what Ray might see in him.

"Glad to hear it," Springer said. "Have a seat."

"You look good, Ray," Gus said. It wasn't a lie. Springer's hair was clipped short on the sides, and there were circular indentations the size of dimes behind his ears where drains had been inserted, but his color was good and his eyes clear.

"I hear someone killed that AP hardleg. I hope it wasn't you, Gate."

Gus looked away. "They're saying town boys did it," he said. "But he's not dead. Not yet, anyway."

"Town boys, huh?" Springer said.

"Poetic justice," Gus said.

"There's no poetry in getting your head bashed in, Gate."

Gus looked at Springer's hands. "Where's your ring?" he said, glad for the chance to change the subject.

"Right here, airman," Lieutenant Dorio said. The self-devouring shrapnel snake was on the third finger of her left hand. "We're sort of engaged."

"No lie?" Gus said. "You're actually thinking about marrying this old dog?"

"Stranger things have happened, airman. I married my first husband in Reno on a bourbon-fueled bet. I don't recommend that approach."

"How'd you pull it off, Ray?" Gus said.

"I didn't yet. She's reckless and a little crazy. That works in my favor. But don't get too excited. We're just trying out the story, see how it plays out in our heads."

"Like it's a game?"

"Like that, with some serious smooching and hanky-panky thrown in. So far, so good. I think the old girl's ready to settle down."

"I like the heck out of this little bugger," Lieutenant Dorio said. "I think I could stand hanging out with him for a few years, maybe longer."

"My job is to prove she isn't wrong," Springer said. "She also thinks I'm cute as a bug's ear. I won't hold that against her."

"We're going out tonight for a trial celebration," Lieutenant Dorio said. "Nothing too fancy. The Officer's Club is serving filet mignon tonight. They'll let you in as my guest. Want to join us?"

"This is really a kind of game with you two?" Gus said.

"A game with a possible jackpot," Springer said.

"Excuse me for saying so, but I think you're both bullshitting me."

Lieutenant Dorio leaned down and kissed Springer on the mouth. It lasted long enough for Gus to walk to the end of the ward and back.

Later, in the Officer's Club, after stuffing himself with filet mignon, lobster tail, and several glasses of red wine, Gus said, "I'm getting kicked out of the air force."

"No shit?" Springer said. "What'd you do, piss on Major Darling's shoes?"

"Something like that, I guess. I don't know for sure."

"We're all getting out," Lt. Dorio said. "You can come live with us. You can be our number one son—on a trial basis. You can earn your keep by feeding the chickens and milking the cow. We're going to farm a few hundred acres outside of Big Sandy while land is still cheap. You find yourself a nice girl, then you and Ray can build a little cabin behind our house for you and your bride. How does that sound, flyboy?"

It sounded like a dream. And Gus knew that's exactly what it was.

36

FDR and Flora decided to go back to La Jolla. FDR paid the remaining five months of the lease then sold the furniture and appliances by placing ads in the Milk River newspaper. Flora packed up Gus's high school memorabilia in a cardboard box. Gus set the box out for the garbage truck to pick up—next to the Christmas tree Flora had bought but never decorated. The memorabilia, like the tree, meant nothing to Gus. He thought: It's part of the trumped-up past.

Flora looked at the naked tree and cardboard box and wept. She swallowed a Milltown and packed their clothes. FDR got the Buick washed, serviced, and gassed up. He also bought new tires for the long trip home.

Then they all said goodbye.

"Mommy can't take it anymore," FDR said. "To be honest with you, neither can I."

Gus knew FDR meant more than the emptiness of the Great Plains. Gus also knew the thing they were running from would follow them to La Jolla, like an abandoned dog with a keen homing instinct. Lock it out, it would scratch at the door and howl at the sills.

I'm sorry, Gus wanted to say, realizing at the same time the fault did not lie in him, or them, or anyone else. Fault was part of the scenery. It was hidden in the grab bag you started with. Surprise!

By pulling out and leaving him behind, FDR and Flora were

banishing Gus from his former position as beloved son and heir. FDR and Flora seemed to realize this; neither had the nerve to give it voice.

Gus had become a dark mystery masked in a familiar face. He was sorry about that, too, but had no reason to apologize for the changes. He was what he was and what he'd always be—a mistake, a blood and bone symbol of betrayal, a by-product of vagrant lust: Gus Gunlocke.

He thought: I should have been stillborn, kept in a brine-filled jar in a whore's crib, an emblem of everyone's mistakes.

Flora looked at him sidelong, as if sneaking peeks at an unsavory stranger whose eyes were too terrifying to meet straight on.

You're not one of us, Gus.

There were no hugs or kisses. Only nervous murmurs and verbal twitches.

We won't make a fuss, Gus.

FDR shook Gus's hand and wished him well. FDR's good wishes were stiff and formal.

Flora, as she got into the car, burst into tears. She got back out and gave Gus a quivering forceless hug.

"Now that you're going to be free of the air force you'll come see us?" she said.

Gus noted that this was not an invitation to move back in. He could come home as a guest, for a limited stay. Which was fine.

"I will, Mommy," he said. "This isn't the end of the world."

But it was the end of *their* world, and they all knew it.

Flora got back into the car.

The Buick idled away from the house.

Gus waved at it.

37

While Gus waited for his discharge orders to be cut and teletyped to the squadron, he continued to work his shifts. No one had much to say to him. He felt avoided, as if his bad luck was contagious. Reppo, the squadron leper. He began to feel invisible.

Invisible was good. He did not want to be seen. His separation from the air force was unjust. Even so, he felt shame. A medical discharge was nowhere near as bad as a Section 8, but Gus felt stigmatized just the same. He was content to be shunned. The only people on base who didn't shun him were Lamar Harkey, Lyle Dressen, and Jeff Sparks. Sparks looked at him with suspicion and contempt.

Gus hadn't been relieved of his duties but he didn't spend much time in the radio shack. Now that the air force had turned its back on him, he performed maintenance checks in a perfunctory way. In the end it was a pointless exercise. What did it matter if a vacuum tube lost its glow or if a sealed electrolytic capacitor leaked oil? What did it matter if the American Scorpions couldn't defend the country against the Russian Bears? Life would go on, one way or the other.

Better Red than dead? he asked himself more than once. It was a perplexing question. He didn't like it. There seemed to be only one acceptable answer: Absolutely not. Sometimes this softened to Probably not. On other occasions he thought: What is Red, anyway?

Dead, he knew. Dead was dead was dead—a final unchange-able state—the country a radioactive ember, a memory. No more chances to set things straight. White picket fences, children playing in the yard, Dad mowing the lawn, Mom packing the car with picnic goodies, grampa dozing in his rocker—all of it gone. And look, here comes the Good Humor man! Mister! Mist . . . *Poof.* Gone in a flash. Did any of it ever exist? No one left now to prove that it did. The intricate and fabulous dream of the unknown dreamer, evaporated. *Splat.*

These thoughts didn't depress him. They made him, as his evaluation papers said, indifferent.

He'd become indifferent to his job. Why? Was he just a spiteful self-centered reject? Had he lost his sense of patriotic duty? Is this what his medical discharge was all about? Is this what Colonel Makepiece meant? Was *indifference* the outward sign of a warped and defeated character? Could you *fake* enthu-siasm, a sense of purpose, and loyalty? Could you really lead a productive life without the gift of companionability?

He climbed the VHF mast to check on the double-fishbone antenna he'd made for Harkey, but he also climbed for the sense of isolation and peace he found one hundred and twenty feet above the radar squadron's complex of buildings and all-weather domes.

On clear nights he stood on top of the mast without safety harness or lanyard and studied the star-printed sky. The stars were fixed in permanent clusters, from horizon to zenith—extravagant decorations on an infinite tree. The immense gravity of the glowing astral mass urged Gus out of himself, as if his pos-itive physical weight had flip-flopped into negative physical weight. He felt an upward tug.

When this happened the giddy impulse to leap free of the mast and sail away in an anti-Newtonian upward fall made him tremble and he knew this was not the time or place to entertain *that* level of insanity.

"Whatcha aim to do when you get out?" Lamar Harkey asked.

"Don't know," Gus said.

"My cousin Maynard? He's a pipe fitter in Mobile. That's a real good job, and they always need a extry man. You want me to get a hold of him and recommend you?"

"I'm thinking of joining the marines under another name."

"They let you do that?"

"Why not? A name's just a name."

"What name you thinking of?"

"August Gunlocke."

"That sounds like a marine name, all right. Where'd you come up with a moniker like that, Reppo?"

"Didn't come up with it. It's who I really am."

"You give the air force a fake name when you signed up? That why they kicking you out?"

"I didn't lie. My name was a lie."

"You're giving me a headache, Reppo. Or am I supposed to call you Gunlocke now?"

"Take your pick, Lamar."

38

Gus took the shuttle to town. He walked from the Milk River Hotel to St. Bonaventure's, about a mile an a half away. He was nervous. Every so often he wanted to turn and walk the other way. His stomach was jumpy. He didn't want to do this, didn't know why he was doing it, but felt it needed doing just the same. Arctic weather had returned and it was below zero again. By the time he got to the hospital his face was burning from the freezing air.

He found Mutt Runkle on the fourth floor. Runkle had just been moved out of Intensive Care. A nurse in starched whites showed him the way to Runkle's room. Her whites made electric crackling sounds as she walked briskly down the hall. "The poor man doesn't get very many visitors," she said. "He'll be glad to see you."

"He's awake?" Gus said.

"Came out of the coma three or four days ago. Did I say he doesn't get very many visitors? What I should have said is you're the second since he was admitted."

"Is he going to be all right?" Gus asked. His voice wobbled. He fought to get it under control.

"Depends on what you mean by all right," the nurse said. "There's a subdural hematoma in the occipital region of his brain along with possible tissue damage. He can't see color. He sees things in shades of gray, with considerable blurring. They're sending him to Seattle for neurological tests and maybe surgery."

"You think they can they fix him?" Gus said.

"Can't tell yet," she said. "You a friend of his?"

"Not exactly," Gus said.

She left the room. Gus pulled a chair up to Runkle's bed. "How you doing, Sergeant Runkle?" Gus said.

Runkle, who had been staring at the ceiling, turned his head toward Gus. His eyes looked past Gus to the left, then to the right. He seemed unable to single out Gus from other objects in the room. His forehead creased as he tried to separate one thing from another. "Can't see jackshit," he said.

"It'll get better, Sarge," Gus said.

"Maybe. Maybe not. Who the hell are you, anyway?"

"Gus Reppo."

"Hey! Reppo the muff diver! How you doing, Reppo?"

"How am *I* doing?"

"A natural fuckup like you is bound to step on his own dick sooner or later. No offense."

"They're kicking me out of the air force," Gus said.

"Sorry to hear it, Reppo."

Gus had expected Runkle to take the opportunity to agree with the wisdom of the air force, but instead he seemed genuinely sympathetic. Gus was uncomfortable with Runkle's sympathy.

"The air force is a good career," Runkle said. "Put twenty years in and they give you a decent pension. Thirty years, you get a better pension. Looks like I won't make either one. The fact that I got thumped outside a whorehouse probably means I won't get disability pay when they turn me loose. Non-service connected injury, they'll call it."

"That's the shits, Runkle."

"It is, kid, it is. You see me begging on a street corner, drop a nickel in my tin cup."

The notion amused Runkle. Gus was amazed that Runkle could smile at a prospect that wasn't all that implausible.

"I'm really sorry, Loftus," Gus said.

He put too much sincerity in the sentiment. Runkle stared

curiously in Gus's direction as though sifting through a triptych of shadows. Then he relaxed back into his pillows.

"Them's the breaks, kid," Runkle said. "Not your fault. Thanks for coming by to see me, though. You and Sparks were the only ones. Most everyone else thinks I'm a son of a bitch who deserves what he got."

"That's not true," Gus said, his voice faltering again.

"No? You don't think I'm a son of a bitch?"

"I don't think so," Gus said.

"After I worked you over, you think I'm a sweetheart? I'm a son of a bitch, Reppo. That's my job description. It's right there in my MOS file. If you don't know that nobody does. Why're you bullshitting me like this, anyway? Why'd you come here?"

Gus got up to leave.

Runkle detected movement. A gray shape sliding away from other gray shapes. "Wait a minute, Reppo," he said. "You willing to do me a favor?"

"Sure, anything."

"Write a letter to my ma. Tell her I got hurt falling off a horse or something. Just make up some shit. I don't want her to know I'd been visiting the whores when I got rolled. She thinks I'm as religious as she is. At least that's what she hopes." He fumbled around in his nightstand drawer. He pulled out a letter. "Her address is on this envelope. Be convincing, okay? I don't want her to get upset by anything that piss-poor excuse for a major might tell her. She'll be going to Mass six nights a week, she finds out I been paying for pussy."

"I'll tell her it was a hit and run accident," Gus said.

"Just make it convincing. Tell her you saw some drunk cocksucker run me down, but don't say cocksucker in the letter, she can't tolerate cuss words."

Gus, improvising quickly, said: "The guy was drunk. He ran a red light. You were crossing Main Street at Third Avenue. He hit the brakes too late and the car skidded on the ice. You went under the wheels. The guy took off and the cops never found out who he was. A witness identified the car as a 1957 red and white Plymouth Belvedere with out-of-state plates, possibly from Wyoming or maybe Alberta. The driver was a white male, around twenty years old, and back home safe by now in Boise, Laramie, Medicine Hat, or Calgary."

Runkle chuckled. "You got a real knack for bullshit, kid. I could almost believe it myself since I can't remember dick about what happened. You sure it wasn't you that ran me over with that Plymouth? Don't tell me you wouldn't of wanted to, right? You had plenty of reasons."

Gus paled. Runkle laughed. Then Gus laughed. Runkle's laugh was genuine. Gus's laugh was thin and lasted too long.

"How about a game of checkers?" Runkle said.

"Checkers?" Gus said. "How are you going to play checkers if you can't see?"

"I'll trust you to move my men. You tell me where you move, then I'll tell you where I want to move and when to king me. Okay? I see good enough to catch you cheating. That goddamn Sparks wouldn't play me one game. The board and checkers are in the bottom drawer of the nightstand."

They played three games. The effort exhausted Runkle. He sank back into his pillows. "Thanks, Reppo," he said.

Gus got up and stretched. His back ached from leaning over the checkerboard. Each game took almost an hour. He made sure Runkle won all three.

Runkle dozed off. He began to snore. Gus wanted to leave but something held him back. He hadn't said what he came to say, even though he knew now that when the opportunity to say it came he would have weaseled out.

Gus confessed to the sleeping man:

"I didn't think I could do it, Runkle. I'm sorry I did."

Bullshit. You knew all along you could do it. Don't lie to yourself. You can be a vicious little bastard, like the rest.

"I'm not like that," Gus said.

You're exactly like that. Most people are exactly like that. You're no different than me, except you tend to weasel out, like you're doing now. You claim the righteous high ground even though you didn't earn a square inch of it.

"Shut the fuck up," Gus said to himself.

39

Gus went to the VFW club and had a shot of Lemon Hart and three beers. Then he went to the Milk River Hotel and sat at one of the writing desks in the lobby. The desks were provided by the hotel for the paying clientele. Gus looked at the desk clerk to see if he objected. He didn't seem to care, one way or the other. Gus opened the desk and took out a sheet of high-quality water-marked writing paper. Pens were also provided. He lit a cigarette to help him concentrate, then wrote:

Dear Mrs. Runkle,

I am ashamed to write to you because I am the one who ran over your son with my 1957 Plymouth Belvedere causing him brain damage so bad that he is almost blind. I hope you can believe it was an accident. I admit I'd been drinking and, yes, I didn't much like your son, but I didn't plan on hurting anybody. Some will say it was no accident and that I did it for revenge since your son beat up a friend of mine. Come to think of it he once beat the stuffing out of me, too, only because I objected to the way he spoke of my girlfriend—foulmouthed. So I guess I had a good reason to run over him on purpose but it wasn't on purpose. My friend was drunk and a little out of his head but that's no reason to work him over with nightstick and boots so that he's got to leave the service before he can collect his pension, right? Now your son, thanks to me, is in the same fix, and about to get a medical discharge short of <u>his</u> pension. Maybe they'll be able to fix him and he can stay in the air force, I don't know. Personally I hope so. I really do. The air force is a good career. I myself chose it over dentistry and would again. I guess you could say I love the air force and would like to be a jet pilot some day. Those Scorpions are something, aren't they? But I don't think I could qualify after all that's happened. However, the air force and its many benefits is not what I'm writing about.

I have come to feel a lot of regret for having run over your son Sergeant Runkle even though it was an accident. It was snowing and my windshield was iced up and I admit I have a lead foot besides being unfortunately drunk at the time. I must have been loco driving like that in that weather. I think I probably <u>am</u> a little loco since I see and talk to my dead father every so often and every time I do I see him more clearly as if he was actually there, still alive under a mile of ocean, which is kind of scary. Loco or not, I sure wish I hadn't hurt your son. I hope you can believe this in your heart. I believe it in mine.

I also wanted to say that your son is a better man than I am. You're probably laughing bitter tears at that because, of <u>course</u>, he's better than the reckless drunken moron who ran him down. That's a given. What I mean is, Sergeant Runkle is taking it like it was something minor, like a broken toe or a bad tooth, even though he's probably eighty percent blind or even worse.

Here's another thing that shames me but also makes me feel good at the same time. I hope you can follow my thinking here. Your son used to be a mean-hearted SOB, excuse my French, but now he seems goodhearted, even friendly and considerate. We played checkers for over two hours! How do you explain that? He ordinarily wouldn't pass you by without making some remark about your abnormal sexual tendencies or your mongrel family background, and so forth. Here's what I think—I don't know what he was like back home in Pennsylvania, but I bet you and Mister Runkle were glad to see him go off and join the air force. Someone told me about his dog Rascal who killed neighborhood cats and how proud he was of Rascal coming home with dead cats dripping from his jaws, their guts ripped-out, and so on. Anyone, even his Mom and Dad, would be glad to see someone like that join the air force. Maybe <u>especially</u> his mom and dad. He must have been a disappointment to you in a number of other ways, too. It only stands to reason.

Here's what I'm trying to say: I think you're going to find him to be a much better person now. I don't mean to claim that my running him over did him some good, but it kind of looks that way. My friend, the sergeant who your son put in the hospital with that unjustified beating I mentioned a minute ago, calls it the shithouse rule. (Pardon the French again, but there are no other words to describe it, none that I can think of anyway.) Every accomplishment or disaster has an upside and a downside. It goes something like that. Think of yourself in an outhouse, having great success doing your business but someone before you has used up all the toilet paper. That takes some of the satisfaction from your success, right? Or the other way around, there's ten rolls of high-quality toilet paper available but all you can do is beg the unmovable stones locked in your bowels for mercy.

I hope you are well and that your son improves a lot in the Seattle hospital where they are sending him. I'm sure he will. I am sorry for having nearly put his lights out permanently.

Sincerely Yours,
Gus Reppo (A/2C, USAF—Almost Retired Myself!)

Gus folded the letter and put it into an envelope. He sealed the envelope and addressed it. He went to the front desk and bought a seven-cent airmail stamp. He licked the stamp and stuck it to the envelope.

He went back to the writing desk and sat down. He thought hard for a minute or two then tore the letter in half and dropped it into the wastepaper basket next to the desk.

40

Gus and Tracy went to the Orpheum. *Forbidden Planet* was the main feature. Gus liked it, Tracy did and didn't.

"The special effects were very good," she said. "But the message was a bit much, don't you think?"

"Here we go again," Gus said, affecting a weariness he did not feel.

"You didn't see it? It was practically spoon-fed to the audience."

"You mean, 'You never know what you're going to find on alien planets.' That message?"

"Superficially. But the real message, the bogus one they want you to believe, goes a bit deeper than that."

They were in the Winshaw house, curled up on the sofa in front of the fireplace drinking hot buttered rum. Dr. and Mrs. Winshaw were on an overnight trip to Pocatello, Idaho, visiting Mrs. Winshaw's sister.

"Bogus?" Gus said.

"The id thing at the end."

"The invisible monster that burned its way through solid steel doors?"

"It killed off the Kel, the super-advanced people who lived on the planet a million years before the American space travelers arrived. The Kel engineers dealt with everything except the id."

"What's bogus about that? I thought it was pretty neat when that thing burned through those fifty-ton doors."

Gus put another log on the fire. It was dry and full of pitch. It exploded into flame. He closed the fireplace screen but not before some big sparks flew out. He stepped on them, ground them into the carpet. The blond carpet was covered with little black burn marks. Gus figured a few more shouldn't upset the Winshaws.

"Freudian gibberish," Tracy said. "They want us to believe that no matter how advanced a civilization becomes, it will crumble before the subterranean forces of the id, the primitive animal inside all of us."

"They. It's always 'they' with you."

Tracy ignored him. "Why try to create a classless proletarian society if there's a self-gratifying destroyer roaring around in the unconscious of every human being?"

"More bourgeois bullshit?" Gus said.

"Of course. Freud got his theories by treating middle-class patients, mostly women. Queens of the bourgeoisie."

Gus stood up and stretched, then collapsed into the sofa. He was not quite drunk. He was holding onto a first-rate buzz. It was a good place to be. He reached for his buttered rum and allowed himself a calculated sip.

"The ego serves the needs of the id," Tracy said. "The ego is a fake, a servile tool of the id. In other words, nothing with a human face on it is genuine. The civilized mask hides the monster in charge. It's a degenerate, reactionary idea. And totally bogus."

"The movie had a happy ending," Gus pointed out.

"A phony tacked-on happy ending. If the id exists, then the space travelers are taking it back home with them. They think they're escaping, but—if you allow the premise—they can't escape. No one can. All civilizations are doomed."

"Hold on, professor," Gus said. "If the Kel have been dead a million years, how come this id beast is still stomping around the planet, tearing the hell out of things?"

"It isn't the id of the Kel. It's Dr. Morbius's personal id."

Gus thought about that. "Gotcha!" he said. "That's where

your argument doesn't hold water, Miss Winshaw. Dr. Morbius and his daughter Alta had been living peacefully on the planet with no id in sight years before the space men came along. How do you explain that?"

Tracy sipped her rum. "Incest," she said.

"Incest?"

"The space men flirt with Alta. One of them kisses her and she immediately gets hot. This arouses Dr. Morbius's jealousy, and his anger releases the power of the id from his unconscious mind. His incestuous relationship with his daughter is so obvious. The movie practically rubs your nose in it. The scene where the tiger attacks the space man? That tiger is a symbol of Dr. Morbius's jealous rage. And his name, Morbius? It's from the Latin *morbis,* meaning disease! God! How transparent can it be?"

"Let me get this straight. You're saying that Dr. Morbius was screwing his own daughter?"

"But not because of some underground demon called the id. He's screwing her because he's a filthy old pervert."

"And that's it? That's what the movie is about? A dirty old man shipwrecked on a planet with his daughter?"

"Why do you think they called the movie *The* Forbidden *Planet,* unless they meant to suggest a taboo?"

"Well, I guess poor old Dr. Morbius will still be able to lead a productive life even though he'll lack enthusiasm and a sense of purpose."

"What in the world are you talking about?"

"Loyalty and companionability are out the window, too."

"I'm serious, Gus. There are no demons. Science has gotten rid of all that mythological baloney."

Gus thought about that. He thought about his life to date. "I respectfully disagree, Professor," he said.

"Ignorance can't disagree with knowledge," she said.

They watched the fire and sipped their hot buttered rums. The log Gus had thrown in was almost burned down to charcoal. Gus tossed in another. Sparks flew out like tracers. Gus stepped on them. Little curls of smoke rose up out of the carpet.

"Explain this," Gus said. "Walt Disney made the movie. How could Walt *Disney* make a movie about a filthy old pervert messing around with his own daughter?"

"Did you ever notice that Donald Duck has no pants hiding his feathered glory?" Tracy said.

"His *what*?"

"Feathered glory. It's from "Leda and the Swan," a poem by W. B. Yeats, another dirty-minded reactionary."

Gus pulled Tracy close and kissed her. He put his hand on her small breast.

"Not so rough, you beast," she said.

"I'm all id, tonight," he said.

They kissed again.

"Let's go to bed, honey," she said. "Bring your feathered glory with you."

Gus was stunned. *Honey.* She'd called him honey! That old bourgeois term of endearment! He couldn't have been more thrilled if she had torn his pants off with her teeth.

"Come on, let's go to bed," she said.

"Can we take off our clothes this time?"

"No."

"But . . ."

"Not negotiable, honey."

41

Gus was the only customer in the Athenian. Milk River High hadn't let out yet. He was going to meet Tracy, but he was an hour early. When Tracy found out he was getting kicked out of the air force she was thrilled. Gus became a hero. She wanted to talk to Gus about enrolling in college. "You're basically bright and perceptive," she said. "I think you'd make a wonderful student."

Gus daydreamed about student life over his cup of coffee. He was imagining himself attending classes with Tracy and her bright and perceptive friends, talking philosophy and politics and saying smart things in French, when the front door of the Athenian swung open with a bang and Jeff Sparks came in with a Milk River police officer.

Sparks grabbed Gus by the collar and yanked him out of his booth with enough force to send him airborne. He picked Gus up and threw him down hard, slamming the air out of his lungs. Gus couldn't breathe.

Sparks turned him over and put a knee in his back. Gus's mouth was open but he couldn't draw air. He felt like a beached fish. Which made him think of Beryl Lenahan. Then it was more than a thought: He saw her dig the eyes out of a rainbow trout, watched her slip a knife into its rectum, slit its white belly open all the way to the gills, pull out the guts in one sure gesture. Yum, she said. Gus smelled fish frying in the aromatic bacon grease.

"What's going on?" Gus whispered. Kneeled on and handcuffed, he tried to organize his thoughts. Sparks pulled him to his feet.

"He's all yours," Sparks said to the police officer. The officer took Gus by the arm. Gus sucked in air with some difficulty. The officer and Sparks walked him to the jailhouse.

"What're you booking this boy for?" the desk sergeant said. The desk sergeant was a three hundred-pound man with a pink head round as a basketball. What little hair he had was combed forward into oily black bangs. He had a jovially sinister smile that seemed a permanent feature of his face. One of his front incisors was rimmed in gold.

"Attempted murder, assault, hit and run, resisting arrest," the officer said. "And anything else we can find that needs cleaning up. These flyboys are handy for that."

"Add treason to that list," Sparks said. "He runs with the local Better-Red-Than-Dead crowd."

"We got some of those here?" the desk sergeant said. "I thought those pussycats were all in England."

"I guess you don't read your own newspaper," Sparks said. "You got your share of Red professors and college kids right here in Milk River. The OSI—that's the air force criminal investigation unit—keeps tabs on all subversive activity anywhere near a radar base. If war comes the Reds will try to put the radar bases out of commission first. Radar is the eyes of our defense."

"Well put," the desk sergeant said. "You have a flair for the poetic."

"Sparks here says this little guy's the one bashed in the brains of that fat-ass AP," the arresting officer said.

"Finally caught the raving maniac, did we?" the desk sergeant chuckled. "He's kind of a mild-looking prospect to be running around bashing people's heads in."

"I've been keeping my eye on him, and now I got his confession," Sparks said. He showed the desk sergeant the letter he'd retrieved from the wastepaper basket in the lobby of the Milk

River hotel. Sparks had used Scotch tape to mend the torn pages. "Says he ran down Runkle with a Plymouth Belvedere, but I believe he used a baseball bat and snuck up behind him."

"Either weapon gives the smaller man a considerable advantage," the desk sergeant observed.

"That's how a yellow bastard like him works," Sparks said.

The desk sergeant yawned. "I believe you have a few more such miscreants out at that radar station," he said. "Like the sexually disturbed deviant who waved his engorged member at some ladies in the parking lot of the Northside Club last week, suggesting they kneel before him and pay oral homage to it. The ladies' escorts, stout farm boys from Box Elder, kicked most of his teeth out. The bulk of these deviants are from the big cities where behavior is less guarded. You should keep them confined to the radar base. They don't seem to fit in with small town life."

Sparks, who was from Cleveland, took offense. "I differ with you on that point, sergeant. This boy here is *from* a small town on the California coast."

Spark's sensitivity to the subject made the desk sergeant's constant grin grow wider. "Sure, and you've got a bunch of Benedictine monks out there at the radar station reading the Bible to each other and singing Gregorian chants."

Overmatched, Sparks said nothing.

Gus had a cellmate. He recognized the man. Solomon Coe. "Mr. Coe," he said.

Solomon Coe looked as if he'd fallen out of a rolling cattle car. He reeked of whiskey and his wrinkled suit was speckled with mud and partially digested food. He was sitting on a hard bunk trying to roll a cigarette. Tobacco spilled out of both ends. The thing he lit was mostly paper. Gus sat on the bunk opposite Coe's and watched the pathetic cigarette flame with each puff.

Coe looked at Gus without recognition. "And who might you be, son?" he said. Coe's voice startled Gus. The basso and alto modes, working simultaneously, produced an eerie harmony. Gus thought Coe might have been kicked in the throat.

"I met you in the Milk River Hotel bar a while back," Gus said.

"I meet a lot of people in bars. Why are you here?"

"Attempted murder," Gus said.

"Did you confess?"

"No."

"Good. Don't. They'll want you to confess to all unsolved crimes committed in Antelope County since the attack on Pearl Harbor, but I advise you to hold your tongue. I'll defend you, if you wish, whether you did the crime or not. If you did, I'm sure you were justified."

Coe got up and vomited into the cell's lone toilet. He cleared his throat but the basso/alto harmony persisted. "I think I have a form of food poisoning," he explained. He went back to his cot. He stretched out on it. "We can't change the wind, son, but we can adjust our sails."

"I'd write that down if I had a pen," Gus said.

"Ah, now I remember you," Solomon Coe said. "You're the insolent boy with the girlfriend problems."

"I don't have a girlfriend," Gus said.

"Easy to see why," Coe said. "Tell me, young man. Have you wised-up yet or are you still beating your head against the wall?"

"I don't follow you, Mr. Coe."

"Then you haven't wised-up. You go ahead and beat your head against that wall, son. Eventually you'll break through to the other side. What do you think you'll find when you do?"

Gus shrugged.

"More wall, son. You have my personal guarantee."

Coe rolled over, turning his back to Gus. He released a trumpeting fart. A minute later he began to snore. His breathing was labored. Now and then he stopped breathing altogether. At one point Gus thought Coe had died. Then his body shuddered and a dry rattling noise issued from his chest, and his wheezy lungs began to labor again.

The rotund desk sergeant and a chinless deputy brought trays of food into the cell. The deputy affected a brutal seen-it-all look that was undermined by his weak chin, shifty eyes, and large velvety ears. The lunch trays were meager: Fried baloney, toast, fried potatoes burnt black at the edges, and a small cup of what looked like applesauce.

"Lunch," the deputy said.

"What's going on?" Gus asked. "How long do I have to be here?"

"*Have* to be here?" The desk sergeant exchanged winks with his deputy. "You don't have to be here at *all*. The Assistant County Attorney is still laughing at your so-called confession. We checked up on you, son. You don't even have a car, much less a new Plymouth Belvedere. Why did you write such a foolish letter?"

"Runkle asked me to," Gus said. "He didn't want his mother to find out he was rolled behind a whorehouse."

"Very decent of you, but you could have bought yourself a world of trouble. The attempted murder, assault, and resisting arrest charges have been dropped—besides, a jury would never believe a mild-looking blue-eyed boy such as yourself could do such grisly work. Anyone can see your mama raised you right. Stay for lunch. We feel we owe that much for inconveniencing you."

"I'm really free to go?"

"If you were in that alley we have no evidence that puts you there—no witnesses, no weapon, nothing. We should have had footprints, but the snow melted away before the scene was examined."

Gus was grateful that the jack handle he'd hit Runkle with was on its way to La Jolla.

"The victim had a fracture of the left side of the occiput," the desk sergeant said, "with bruising of the left occipital lobe of the brain. In short, he was hit with a blunt instrument while *kneeling*. It was an odd place to pray, outside a whorehouse, but perhaps the victim had a religious experience inside. Who can say? Whatever the case, anyone could have done it—an abused whore, a juvenile delinquent—or you."

"Why did you lock me up in the first place?" Gus said.

"Sparks seemed a sincere enough fellow, though not overburdened with intelligence. We try to cooperate with your air police as much as possible. It's just good policy."

The desk sergeant was sweating even though it was cold in the jailhouse. His shirt was ringed at the armpits, his rolls of neck fat glistened. He leaned close to Gus, close enough that Gus could smell his sour sweat.

"Tell me, son," the desk sergeant said. "Did you do it? Just between you and me. It will go no further than this cell."

Gus froze.

"Ah. You *did* do it then. I'm sure you had a good reason."

Solomon Coe rose up from his cot as if propelled. "Say nothing, lad!" he said, his voice a clarion of mixed tones. "You're dealing with a clever man who lays a thoughtful trap."

The desk sergeant's constant smile faded. "Solomon exaggerates as usual," he said.

42

Gus went back to the Athenian. Tracy wasn't there. It was hours past the time they were supposed to meet. The ice cream parlor was now packed with high school students. A few boys identified Gus as an airman and began to make hostile remarks. Gus left.

He went to the Stockmans Bar and Café, ordered a beer and a hamburger. He sat in an empty booth. Stockmans catered mainly to farmers and ranchers, the jukebox loaded with country tunes and polkas. Airmen usually avoided it. A few ranch hands sat at the bar drinking dime-glasses of tap beer. No one paid any attention to Gus.

Norrie, from the whorehouse behind the Moomaw Dairy, came in carrying a large brocaded traveling bag. She took off her heavy wool coat and hung it on the coatrack near the door. In street clothes she almost looked respectable. She wore a red jumper over a white, long-sleeved blouse. She seemed less saggy, less used up. With her dime store pearl necklace, hoop earrings, fur-trimmed boots, she reminded Gus of Flora on a good day. Gus figured she was wearing a girdle and an uplift bra to shore up her figure. She spotted Gus and came over to his booth.

"Hey, if it aint Little Britches," she said. She set her bag down, slid into the booth opposite Gus.

Gus looked around to see if anyone was looking their way.

"You afraid someone's gonna see you with me, Sunshine?"

"Heck no," Gus said, looking around the room again.

"Don't worry. Nobody in this dump's gonna tell your mama."

There was something different about Norrie. Her face seemed sunk in on itself a little. Her cheeks were hollow. Her thin lips were sucked inward as if there was nothing behind them to keep them firm. She had too much hair. It coiled on her head like a bright red helix. No steel barrettes. Gus realized then that she was wearing a wig.

"You look real good, Norrie," Gus said.

"Yeah? You think so? How about you buy this pretty lady a cup of coffee. Cream, no sugar, a shot of Four Roses."

Gus went to the bar and came back with a steaming mug.

"You're wondering why I'm out on the street instead of working out of my crib," she said. She kept her lips almost closed as she talked, and she was lisping.

"What happened, Norrie?" Gus said.

"I got let go," she said. "'Over-the-hill,' Syndicate people said. They give me fifty bucks severance then cut me loose. So I work on my own hook now. Trickin for street trade like any two-bit punch. I might get cribbed-up again with a house in Wallace, Idaho. The silver miners over there aint too particular. Meantime, I got a five-dollar a week room at the Y Bar U roadhouse."

"I'm sorry," Gus said.

"I don't need you to feel sorry for me, young'n. I got into the profession twenty-plus years ago of my own free will. My Pa sold me to an old beet farmer. Ma was dead by then. The rank sod-buster was so ugly he had to buy himself a wife. Gave Pa a hundred bucks. The farmer was fifty-eight years old. I was twelve goin on thirteen but my tits were in full bloom. I hated gettin hitched to that old hardleg son of a bitch, him expectin me wash his clothes, cook his meals, and suck his cock seven days a week for no pay. I was so innocent I believed him when he said cock suckin was part of what wives pledged to do at the altar. Ask any reverend, he said, which I wasn't about to do. So I ran off to Kansas City when I was fourteen, still mainly a virgin since the beet farmer wanted it one way only. In KC I hooked up with an honest pimp name of Jeremiah Jukes. JJ, we called him. Had me some good years working for JJ. Then the syndicate that owned us farmed me out to Milk River. Now it's come down to this. Don't care much for backseats and alleys, but over-the-hill is over-the-hill. I turn forty tomorrow. Once in a while some kindly gent will take me out on the west highway to a nice road house and next mornin order breakfast in bed. It don't get much better than that for a workin girl my age."

As she went on her lisp became more pronounced.

"What happened to your teeth, Norrie?" Gus said.

Norrie compressed her lips. It made her mouth look like a coin slot. "Dadburn teeth went bad," she said. "So I got 'em pulled. Dentist wanted forty bucks up front to do the work."

"A dentist here in Milk River?" Gus said.

"This cheap sack of crap—Warsaw, Whiplash, Wickdick."

"Winshaw?"

"Yeah, that's the jackass." She sipped her coffee, made a slurping sound. She eyed the cowboys at the bar. A telephone lineman came in and she gave him the eye, too. Trolling. The fish ignored the bait.

"Wickdick, he asked me what I did for a livin," she said. "Nosy bastard. I told him I ship and receive. 'Ship and receive?' he says. 'What's that involve?' I told him it involved *ship*ping and *receiv*ing—like I was talking to a simple child—and that I did it in Seattle and I was here to visit my sister, Chloe. I guess if I'd a told him I was workin my moneymaker on the street for two cartwheels a trick he'd a refused to put his clean fingers in my mouth. As it was he put his paw up my dress. I told him, 'Give me back the forty, doc, and you can have all you want of that.' But all the cheap hump wanted was a free feel."

The thought of Tracy's father slipping his hand up Norrie's skirt made Gus smile. He finished his coffee, put out his cigarette. He got up.

Norrie tugged his sleeve. "Wait a minute, Little Britches. I don't get to talk to many folks these days. Sit with me a while."

Gus got another cup of coffee and came back to the booth. He found himself admiring her, her toughness, her ability to adjust to hard new circumstances. She was able to take anything the world threw at her and not break. No teeth, no crib, her youth and good looks gone, but her spirit had not withered. She seemed more alive than anyone he knew. Her spirit would eventually crumble in the onslaught but wouldn't everyone's, eventually?

She leaned close to Gus and whispered, "I saw you knock that peckerwood cuckoo, Sunshine."

Gus's admiration switched to fear. "What?" he said.

"He needed it."

"I guess I'm not sure what you mean, Norrie."

"Hell if you're not, kid. I was in the doorway about to come out and blow holes in the son of a bitch myself. Then there you were, layin his head open with a lead pipe."

Gus scalded his throat with hot coffee. "Not me," he said, hoarse with burn. "Somebody maybe looked like me."

"Listen, I'm glad you did it, Little Britches! He wrecked my new teeth. Now I got to save up for another set. I gave Wickdick a handjob for ten percent off of what he wanted but it still's gonna run me a hundred-twenty."

"Why did he wreck your teeth?"

"I never liked to see them come in drunk like that. Crazy and mean. He wanted head for openers but didn't like my new teeth. Called them 'choppers.' Said they scared him. He yanked them out of my mouth and stomped them, busted them all up. Said he wanted me to gum him. Me along with the other girls threw the drunk asshole out. That's when you come up on him with your lead pipe."

"Jack handle," Gus said.

"You give it to him good, Little Britches!"

"You going to turn me in?"

"Aint you been listenin? I was gonna do it myself with the sawed-off twelve-gauge shotgun I kept in my crib. You saved me from a stretch in the state prison. I owe you, kid."

"You don't owe me anything, Norrie," Gus said.

"If I had extra money I'd give you some of it. All I got is a few dollars and what's in my bag." She reached down, set the brocaded bag on the table.

"Is the shotgun in there?" Gus asked.

"All I own is in here," she said. She opened the bag, pulled out the short-barreled shotgun, set it on the table.

Gus had to ask but didn't want to know: "You got *Wayne* in there, too?"

She took the jar with the pickled baby out of her bag, set it on the table next to the shotgun. The baby turned in the disturbed brine, the vacant eyes coming to rest on Gus.

"Wayne and my chopped scattergun go where I go," she said. "One's for protection, the other for reminders. Got nothin else in the bag but some clothes. I'd like to give you a present for what you did, but aside from the shotgun and my trick baby, all I got is girlie stuff. I expect you get all a young feller needs, so I don't figure you'll be wantin any jelly roll from old Norrie, but I'd like to do somethin for ya anyways."

"You could do something," Gus said.

"Name it, Sunshine."

"Put Wayne back in the bag."

"Sure, kid." She returned the jar to the bag, carefully, as if the trick baby in it was asleep.

Gus said, "Norrie, the guy who broke your teeth is Staff Sergeant Loftus Runkle. He's in St. Bonaventure's. Go see him. Tell him you need a new set. Remind him what he did. I think he'll spring for it. He's not the skunk he was."

"Skunks don't lose their stripe, Little Britches. I see him I might work my twelve gauge up his ass and ventilate him some."

"I think Runkle's changed, Norrie."

"How does me going to see him do anything for you?"

Gus thought about it for a minute.

"I'm not sure," he said.

43

After his sixth bourbon ditch Gus decided he was a nihilist. Life is a waste of time and effort, Lyle Dressen's father had said. Or something like that. It was the underlying rule of the game no one tells you before you suit up. Nothing mattered, nothing meant anything. There were no winners, no losers. Everything was exactly and only what it appeared to be. The future was a dice roll and the past was a graveyard. Opinions were exercises in educated bullshit. Nil and Null ruled the fucked-up world. Why pretend otherwise? Blah blah blah and then you die. "It's all shit," Gus concluded aloud.

Solomon Coe, two stools away, overheard him. "You're partly right," he said. Coe slid off his stool, moved next to Gus.

Gus, depressed at being kicked out of the air force, said, "I'm going to be a nihilist, Mr. Coe. That's what I was meant to be. I'm signing the enlistment papers tomorrow."

"I doubt that very much, son," Coe said. "The minimum age for nihilism is thirty-five. At your age all you are allowed to do is hope for the best."

"Doubt all you want, sir. It's all fresh dung piled on old manure. Put a scoop of ice cream on top, it's still steaming green shit underneath. What they knew for sure a hundred years ago looks like nuthouse babble today. What people think today is gonna look just as lame a hundred years from now. And so on and so forth until it all blows up and we go back to square one. You got proof otherwise, Mr. Coe? The whole world is the shithouse. That's what Ray meant. And Ray Springer is a very wise man."

"Define 'shit,' define 'wise,' define 'square one,'" Coe said. "And while you're at it, my young philosophizing buckeroo, define 'Ray Springer.' Take ten years to dismantle and define your headstrong metaphors. When you understand them, you can then decide if it's all a waste rather than a highly refined mystery with no solution."

Gus regarded Solomon Coe. The old lawyer's voice sounded, to Gus, like two flutes piping a very old tune. Gus laughed, but not in a mean-spirited way. "You are very severely drunk on your very severely drunk ass, Mr. Coe, your honor," he said.

"I've had a few," Coe admitted.

"Define a few, your honor," Gus said.

"More than two, less than twelve."

"What do you call over twelve?"

"The beginning—or the end—of a career."

"I think I'm there," Gus said.

"The end? The beginning?"

"Both maybe."

"Good luck to you, my boy," Coe said.

"Barkeep!" Gus said. "Two more Jim Beam ditches here!"

"I need a ride," Gus said to Tracy. He'd found her at the Athenian sitting with Josh. "I am very drunk."

"Failed another existential test, did you?" Josh said.

"If getting your ass kicked out of the air force is a flunked test," Gus said.

"An antiestablishment hero!" Josh said. "I mean that sincerely, *mon ami*."

"I'll drive you to the base," Tracy said. "Give me your keys, Josh."

"Do *not* let him behind the wheel, Trace," Josh said.

In Josh's car, Gus said, "I can't go back to the base but you can drive me to Great Falls. They'll let me stay in the TDY barracks a couple of weeks while I process out. But I don't think they'll let you stay in the barracks with me."

"Don't worry about me," she said.

"Come to think of it, maybe you shouldn't drive me. You don't want them to see a Communist driving a nihilist to an American air force base."

"You're not a nihilist. You're a victim of the system."

"Is that why you won't fuck me? You don't want to pity fuck a victim of the system?"

"That's not it."

"Then it's because I'm a nihilist."

"A nihilist is someone who doesn't believe in anything. I don't think that describes you. Besides, you haven't read enough to call yourself a nihilist. It's about as dumb as calling yourself an existentialist or a subjectivist or a Buddhist, without having studied any of those things."

"I am a shithouse rule-ist," Gus said. "I need ten years in the shithouse to define my headstrong metaphors."

"Is that one of your jokes?"

"It's a very funny joke. The world is a big stinking shithouse, see. Nothing works out like you figured. Sometimes that's good, sometimes that's bad. Either way the joke's gonna be on you. You're a good example, Tracy—you'll go to bed with me but only if you've got three layers of clothes on. That's pretty funny, don't you think?"

"And that's what you believe in? A philosophy of low expectations?"

"That sounds about right."

"It's stupid."

"So far it's the only thing that makes sense."

"What about love? You believe in love, don't you?"

"Define love," Gus said.

"You want the bourgeois definition, or the no-nonsense dialectical one."

"Either one since both are bullshit."

"According to you everything is bullshit."

"Definitions are bullshit."

"Is there anything at all in the universe that is not bullshit?"

"Bodies. Your body. My body. What our bodies would like to do to each other. Also good food and good drink and a warm bed—those things are not bullshit. A good ole nurse told me that once. A nurse should know, right?"

"Then you're a hedonist, not a nihilist," she said.

"Is that bad?"

"Not if you believe the capitalist notion that the world is the rich man's playpen."

"The world is a shithouse."

"Yes, that's why we have revolutions."

"Whatfuckingever," Gus said.

Gus retrieved his pint of brandy, unscrewed the cap, guided the bottle to his lips. He swallowed in gulps as Josh's old DeSosto lurched down the road on its tired springs.

They stopped at a roadhouse in Black Eagle, just short of the city. Gus flopped on the bed.

Tracy, without prologue or hesitation, undressed. Naked, she looked just as he'd imagined she would. Round pink-tipped teacup breasts, too lightweight to be affected by gravity. Ribs visible. Bony hips, lovely slender legs, long narrow feet. The dark delta. The sight made his head swim. Brandy crawled up his throat and he choked. Then she was stepping toward him, shy and bold, modest but determined, shivering in the chilly room. A slight tremble in her lower lip. Gus was awestruck, drunk as he was.

"You made a decision," Gus said, his voice hoarse.

"I have," she said.

"You're going to fuck your antiestablishment hero."

"I am," she said.

She straddled him. Unbuckled his belt. Unzipped his pants. Reached in. Found nothing useful.

Gus moaned shamefully.

"Looks like you're too damn drunk, Mr. Nihilist," she said.

"The shithouse rule strikes again," Gus said.

44

Gus reported to building T572 at 0730, January 18, to process out of the air force. He was given a medical exam and two hundred dollars in separation pay. He shook hands with the old gray sergeant who gave him the two hundred dollars out of a cash box. "Better luck next time, kid," the sergeant said.

"What do you mean, 'next time'?" Gus said.

"You fucked up this time." He pointed to his clipboard. "Says so right here on your separation papers. Maybe next time around you won't."

"What's it say?"

"Says 'medical' but 'medical' doesn't have to mean physical, like you got a bad liver or something. You look pretty healthy to me. The exam you just had proves it. So I figure it's got to be *mental*. You went mental on them—like you choked your chicken in a public place, a pervert thing like that. So they showed you the door. Happens more often than you think. Lucky you didn't get a Section 8."

Gus went back to the TDY barracks, packed his B-4 bag, put on his parka, and walked to the front gate.

There was a woman in the AP shack arguing with the AP. Gus recognized her. He recognized the car blocking the gate. His heart thumped, then accelerated. She saw him. She came out of the AP shack taking long determined strides in his direction. The AP tried to hold her back.

"This is restricted air force property, lady," the AP said. "Get in your car and back out."

The woman broke free of the AP.

"Orson!" she said. "We're going to have us a child!" She seemed both elated and frightened. "It's a miracle, Orson! God blessed us with it! You have to honor it!"

"You know this woman, buddy?" the AP said.

"Never saw her before," Gus mumbled.

"Why is she calling you by name?"

"I don't know what she's talking about, sarge. My name is Gus Reppo."

"The child and I come for you, Orson!"

Gus flinched at her voice. It was as if lying about knowing Marva had legitimized her claim on him.

Gus took out his DD-217, his certificate of service. The card identified him as Gus Reppo and that his discharge was medical, and thus honorable. He showed it to the AP.

The AP gave the card back to Gus.

"She's been coming here every day for nearly a week," the AP said. "She parks her old wreck down the street, then runs up to cars coming in and going out and asking people if they'd seen some guy named Orson. She described him to me—little guy with a hungry look—and you kinda fit the description, so you can understand her mistake. I'd figured her for a nutcase but today she went too far. She drove her wreck through the gate behind General Balderra's car. Just plowed right in after the general's Lincoln. I'd a been in my rights to shoot her." He turned to Marva. "All right, lady. You leave or I'll have your car towed."

"I'll go but he's got to come with me!" she said, pointing at Gus.

"No he doesn't," the AP said.

"You deny me, Orson?" she said.

"I'm not Orson," Gus said.

"Who's this Orson?" the AP said.

"Who knows, Sarge?" Gus said. "She's nuts."

"Come along, Orson. We're going home now," she said.

Marva was wearing a thin coat, threadbare at the cuffs and collar, and a chintz housedress printed with forget-me-nots under the coat. She wore high-top tennis shoes with no socks. Her legs were blue with cold. Wind gusts billowed open her buttonless coat. She was dressed for Chula Vista, not Great Falls.

"You're going to freeze to death, lady," the AP said. "Why don't you get in your car and warm up?"

"Listen to me, Orson," she said. "You need to come home with me and the child or I am liable to do something God will not forgive you for."

Gus wanted to ask her how she found out he was mustering out of the air force at Malmstrom. Maybe she went to La Jolla and made FDR and Flora tell her where he was under the threat of violence. Maybe by making claims against him to the air force bureaucracy she'd culled out the place and date of his discharge. He remembered telling her his ID number. Maybe that was all she needed to find him.

The OSI investigators knew about her. She'd contacted the Judge Advocate General's office. But that meant she'd used his real name in her complaint. Maybe she told them "Gus Reppo" was an alias and that, because of the rape, she was carrying his baby and that he was on the run to avoid his responsibility in the matter. If she was shrewd enough to do that, she was shrewd enough to track him down. In any case, she was here, calling him Orson, not Gus, for which he was thankful. She'd driven her rattletrap Ford all the way from Chula Vista at tweny miles an hour in second gear, stopping only to fill the gas tank, which in itself was a kind of miracle of determination and endurance.

The AP looked to Gus for help.

Gus shrugged.

The AP said, "For the last time, lady, get you and your car out of here or I call the local cops."

Marva screamed.

Gus and the AP jumped. Gus felt the hairs on the back of his neck stiffen.

It was a throat-tearing scream rising from the black hollows of her madness. She drew her eight-inch kitchen knife from her coat pocket.

"Jesus Christ!" the AP said, unsnapping his holster.

"No!" Gus yelled, his voice strong now. "Don't do it, Marva!"

Marva's eyes were wide. Gus had seen that look of single-minded determination in Chula Vista.

"Don't!" he begged.

Marva threw her coat open. With both hands on the wooden haft she drove the knife into her torso under the rib cage. She grunted, withdrew the knife, then plunged it in again. The eight-inch blade made a ripping sound as if cutting into wet fabric as she forced it into gristle and flesh. She growled—teeth clenched so that the growl would not deteriorate into a scream of pain and regret. She worked hard to widen and deepen the wound. Gus would not forget either sound: the unwavering clenched-jaw growl; the fabric of her body accepting the knife.

A wash of blood spread down her dress. The first wound sent out a fine red mist from a nicked artery. Marva tried to remove the knife from the second wound but her strength was gone. She sat down on the ice-encrusted macadam, then slumped over.

"Get an ambulance!" Gus yelled at the AP, who was leaning on Marva's car, immobile, pale, his gun drawn.

Gus knelt down next to Marva and held her head off the cold surface. He put his hand against her belly through running blood. Please God no baby.

"Orson," she said.

"Marva," Gus said.

"Topple with me, husband," she whispered.

She closed her eyes and let out a long shuddering breath that she would not be able to replace.

Gus, his moans failing to become clear speech, toppled.

He sank into familiar green light, the underwater scene dark now at the edges like an old photo in a dusty album. The *Fisk* was still sending up bubbles of trapped air. It was 1944 again. It always would be. Just like today would always be 1958. Every day, though it made no sense to Gus, had its own permanence. Things committed were always committed, without erasures. It spooled out one way and one way only. The days of 2008, fifty years from now, were already installed, like carvings in granite. Gus would always believe this though he would never be able to explain it to himself, much less to others. Nor would he want to. It wasn't a comforting notion. It was not a sane way to think. Maybe the air force was right to get rid of him, even though their reasons were wrong.

Orson Gunlocke was tilted backward in repose as if restful sleep was a possibility. Small lantern fish emitting delicate light worried their way through the confusion of bones like miners lost in a collapsed drift.

"What have you learned from all this, son?" Orson said.

"Nothing," Gus said.

The ghost yawned. "Maybe there's nothing *to* learn."

"That would be a lot to learn right there."

"Yes it would, son. That would be a *hell* of a lot to learn."

The medics checked him out, gave him a whiff of smelling salts. They gave the AP something for his stomach, which he'd emptied next to Marva's car.

A crowd had gathered. An AP captain and a second lieutenant arrived in a jeep. They questioned witnesses:

Yes sir she came unglued, saw it in her spooky eyes.
The boy she yelled at looked about to fill his drawers.
You see her try to gut herself? She didn't fucking TRY,
she flat GUTTED herself. I saw that gray intestine
worm out of her like a toy balloon! He is cursed with
ignorance, she said through red teeth. I didn't see it like

that, Captain, no sir. He saw more than what was there. The whole thing's getting blown up into something more than it actually was. Things happen, you don't need to make them seem special as if nothing like it never happened before. She was crazy I grant you that, the way she was yelling at this airman, stuff you couldn't figure, stuff about her baby, gonna name it Warson or Herson and the airman stroking her bloody belly like he believed a thing was in there that shouldn't be, like the baby was his and he would not admit it, him moaning like he'd been gutshot himself, who knows? He's a stranger to himself, she said, her teeth red.

Shit happens to a lot of these airmen. They don't tarp their load—you know what I'm saying? Is that what you think, Sarge? What's your take on it? Weird shit in the boonies, sir, end of story. You think maybe he knocked her up even though she's twice his age and maybe then some? How would I know, Lieutenant? Five stripes don't make me Alfred fucking Einstein. Go easy Lieutenant, the sergeant's had a hard day. It's said she'd filed a grievance with JAG and the boy was trying to assay the width and depth of his moral responsibility, vis-à-vis her condition, physical and mental. Throttle back, college boy. Sorry, Captain, maybe that's taking it too far, making a tragedy out of a backcountry soap opera. Back in Comp Lit 301 . . .

Stifle yourself, lieutenant! Right, sir. Consider me stifled, sir. So, how do you airmen see the incident? Don't have the first clue. Some rank shit transpired. He don't know what he is, she said, red teeth gritted against a scream. He aint able to wake hisself up. Who SAID that? Step up if you know more than we do! Sergeant Cochran? What do you think? Lieutenant, sir, they don't pay me half-enough to fucking think.

The AP captain pulled Gus aside. "My gate sergeant believes you called the woman by name."

"How could that be, sir? I've never seen her before."

"You deny you called her by name?"

"Yes sir, Captain, I do."

"My sergeant here thinks what you said sounded something like mother, or mumbled, as in muvver, right before you passed out. Is that right? Is the deceased woman your muvver, I mean mother?"

"My mother drives a new Buick," Gus said.

"Well la-dee-da," said the captain.

The captain looked at the decaying lopsided Ford. The sight of the old car seemed to draw him into a morose reverie. His lingering regard of the car made Gus think the captain came from people who lived in squalor, drove lopsided wrecks, and who said la-dee-da when Buicks passed by.

"She's not your mother then," the captain said, "though you might have called her something that sounded like that?"

"I might've said mother as in motherfucker, sir," Gus said, remembering that he'd called out her name, Marva, several times, the source of confusion. "I was kind of rattled after what she did, Captain, and careless with my language."

"Is that what you heard, Sergeant?"

"Couldn't swear to it, sir. He might have said mother as in motherfucker. That's possible. I just heard the mother part for sure, or maybe it was muvver, like you said, Captain. I'm not positive about the fucker part. Though he could have said muvvermucker all mumbly like that so it wouldn't sound so bad like sometimes you say 'fricken' instead of 'fucken' for the same reason and then there's 'mammyjammer' which also takes the edge off but I couldn't swear to it in his case since I don't know him personally. Sometimes you will hear the word shortened to 'mu'fuckah,' especially among Negro airmen when talking jive, or even 'mu'fuh,' but I'm pretty sure he didn't say anything like that, him not being a Negro . . ."

"Drop it, Sergeant," the captain said.

Gus said, "If she was my mother, don't you think I would say so?"

"Maybe yes, maybe no," the captain said. "I'm not sure what to think. I've seen some nutty goddamn things on my watch."

"There's nothing to think about, sir. She's not my mother. Period. End of story."

The captain didn't care for Gus's tone—thought he heard disrespect, perhaps insubordination. "Report to your barracks, airman," he said. "I might want you to clear some things up later, since you were a witness."

"No can do, Captain," Gus said.

The captain, a small man, drew himself up. "What the hell do you mean, 'No can do,' airman?"

"I'm a civilian as of an hour ago."

Gus showed the captain his DD-217 and walked off the base.

"Stop!" the captain said.

Gus kept walking.

"Stop, goddamnit!" the captain yelled.

Gus broke into a trot, the captain's shouts dying behind him.

45

He trotted, then ran, all the way to downtown Great Falls. He stopped at a used car lot on Tenth Avenue South and ducked down among the sedans, coups, and pickups. He squatted between vehicles, listening, sucking air into his aching lungs. Strings of colorful pennants strung on ropes between light poles flapped in the rising wind. After another minute he stood up and looked around. He realized then that he needed a car.

He found a 1947 Pontiac Torpedo, a two-door sedan with massive straight-eight power. It had dented doors and rusted bumpers but the doors opened and closed and the bumpers didn't matter. He got the key from a pudgy, gnomish salesman. The salesman was sitting next to a kerosene heater in his shed-like office reading the *Great Falls Tribune*. The room smelled of hot wet wool.

"Haven't cranked her up for over a week," the salesman said. "Been so darn cold the battery might be low."

The car started without complaint. The eight-cylinder motor had an urgent throb to it. The radio buzzed with spark plug noise but it brought in all the local stations. Gus tried the gears and the car moved forward and backward without clutch slippage or grab. He put the transmission into neutral, reset the parking brake, and got out. He walked around to the back of the car and put his hand over the exhaust pipe then checked to see if his palm had blackened with burnt oil. It had not. He looked at the tires. They were recaps but had reasonable tread. He got back into the car and turned the wipers on. They worked. He turned off the engine and sat in the driver's seat for another minute listening to the cooling engine tick. He tried the horn. Even that worked.

It had begun to snow. Heavy wet flakes in the driving wind soon turned the car lot and the avenue it fronted white. The salesman came out of his office. He wore unlaced mukluks, a heavy wool coat, mittens, and a fur-lined cap with the earflaps down. A drop of clear mucous glistened on the tip of his bulbous nose. He looked up at the bleak sky. "Whiteout coming," he said.

Gus felt under the dashboard for loose wires. Looked under the rubber floor mats for burn holes in the carpeting. He found a frozen mouse in the glove compartment, found the gap that let the mouse in.

"Great touring car in her day," the salesman said. He caressed the Pontiac's rear fender in a familiar way. "This honey'll flat take you down the road, you betcha. Good traction, specially in this type of snow. She's got a good cold-weather thermostat to boot. You'll get heat before you drive off the lot."

Gus examined the tires again, looking for cuts and bulges and signs of loosening tread. The salesman wiped snow off the hood ornament and polished it with his mitten. The hood ornament was a pitted chrome image of Chief Pontiac.

"She's yours for a mere hundred," he said.

"I can give you seventy-five," Gus said.

"That straight eight's got enough low-end torque, you could make a living pulling up stumps."

"I'm not going to pull up stumps," Gus said.

"Hold on a minute," the salesman said. "Is that blood?"

Gus looked at his hands. They were rusty with Marva's blood. The front of his parka had large dark stains.

"You're an airman, right?" the salesman said.

"Was," Gus said.

"You weren't involved in that brawl last night at the Ozark Club by any chance? They say the razors came out."

"No."

"You a hunter? You the one poached that cow elk in the High-woods yesterday?"

"No sir, I did not."

"Ninety dollars and my lips are sealed."

"Eighty," Gus said.

"Cops or the APs come around asking questions, I never saw you. It's none of my business what you did, right? Why should I involve myself in something that's none of my business? How about eighty-five?"

"Okay," Gus said.

"Why don't you come into my office and wash off that blood while I type up the registration papers."

Gus gave the salesman his driver's license, then went into the tiny washroom and cleaned up. When he came out he gave the salesman four twenties and a ten. The salesman gave him five in change along with his license and registration papers. The salesman taped a temporary permit inside the rear window of the Pontiac that proved it had been paid for and registered.

He gave Gus a handful of candy mints. "'Preciate your business, son. You take it easy now, all right? My advice? Lay off the rough stuff. That gets you nowheres. Get yourself a good job. Finish growing up, then find yourself a good woman who will tolerate you. Raise a nice little family. The world don't need another hell-bent roustabout."

"I'll do my best," Gus said.

"Lay low. Show the people that count that you're dependable. Keep a clear head and a ready hand, things will come your way sooner or later. Take it from one who knows, bad luck don't last forever."

"Does that guarantee come with the car?" Gus said.

The salesman laughed. "You got my word on it."

The salesman looked at the sky. "I wouldn't try to drive the highway today," he said. "Whiteout like this, you'll be lucky to see past the hood."

Gus got in the car and started the engine. He turned the heater on and took off his bloodstained parka and threw it into the backseat. The vacuum powered wipers were strong enough to clear the windshield of snow.

He drove the car off the lot. The snow, coming down in horizontal sheets, had turned the world white. The glare was painful. He reached up to pull down the sun visor and discovered the driver's-side visor had been removed. In another minute he couldn't make out street signs or identify intersections. His eyes felt scorched by sub-zero light. He stared into hard blue halos. He was sure that if he exposed his eyes to them much longer he'd become snow blind. He kept driving.

Ray Springer's "It" was out there—under the snow, past the snow, and was the snow itself. He saw this and it made sense for a split second. Then it broke apart like an overturned jigsaw puzzle and made no sense at all. And yet a powerful current of unsought joy had flashed through him in that split second. Gus tried to recall it but failed.

He turned the radio on. "My Baby Loves Western Movies" was playing. He turned the volume up and eased down Tenth Avenue until he came to a junction of highways on the north end of the city. Highway 87 would take him back to Milk River. Highway 200, the old Lewis and Clark Trail, would take him west to Missoula and beyond. Canada was an option. Or he could turn around and drive south to Boise, Salt Lake, or Denver. All options looked the same in the white landscape. There was a maze of options. All of them right, all of them wrong.

RICK DEMARINIS is the author of eight novels, including *The Year of the Zinc Penny*, a *New York Times* Notable Book, and six short story collections, including *Apocalypse Then* and *Borrowed Hearts*. In 1990, he received an Academy Award for Literature from the American Academy of Arts and Letters. Each year, *Cutthroat: A Journal of the Arts* awards a short story prize in his name.